PAPER NAMES

A Novel

SUSIE LUO

HANOVER
SQUARE
PRESS

**HANOVER
SQUARE
PRESS™**

Recycling programs
for this product may
not exist in your area.

ISBN-13: 978-1-335-01240-1

Paper Names

First published in 2023. This edition published in 2024.

Hanover Square Press
22 Adelaide St. West, 41st Floor
Toronto, Ontario M5H 4E3, Canada
HanoverSqPress.com
BookClubbish.com

Printed in U.S.A.

For my sister, Linda,
my greatest champion, my light in the dark. You are pure gold.

And for my parents.
Your journeys are more inspiring than you'll ever know.

CONTENTS

ONE

Tony

1997

There were bruises on his daughter. Tony counted three. One from when she fell off her bike. Another from a game of tag on the playground. The last one was fresh. Barely noticeable, a dash of pink on her cheek. It could even be mistaken for blush.

Tony scooped Frosted Flakes by the handful, straight from box to mouth. It tasted like sugary cardboard. His daughter was seated at the table with a rigid posture. Her straight back, a silent fuck you.

"Your cereal is getting soggy," he said.

Tammy didn't move, eyes glued to the floor, ignoring both her father and the bowl of golden specks in front of her. At fifty inches and sixty-two pounds, she hit the exact numbers for an average nine-year-old girl, but Tony knew that she was anything but. She had a ferocious curiosity beyond her years. And a stubborn will that impressed him as much as it ignited his temper.

He said, in a singsong voice this time, "Do you want something else for breakfast?"

Again, the little girl didn't reply, and as she tugged on her dress, two sizes too big, Tony's entire body tensed. For a moment, he thought the mark on her cheek had darkened, but it was only a flicker of shadow. He whispered his adopted American phrase of relief: *thank God*. Not that he believed in God. He could only count on himself.

If she'd let him, Tony would wrap his arms around his daughter and hold her until she softened. He would braid her hair the way that she liked, tell her how sorry he was for raising his hand to her the night before. But he knew that she wouldn't let him off the hook that easily.

His wife, Kim, swept into the kitchen in a bakery uniform. She took one look at Tammy and the untouched bowl of cereal, rummaged through the cabinets, and stuck two Pop-Tarts in the toaster oven. As the scent of cinnamon filled the air, Tammy's lips turned up. Tony clenched his jaw so forcefully that he felt the muscles in his neck twitch.

Kim could always sneak a smile out of Tammy.

"Can I eat in my room?" said Tammy.

Of course not. She knew the rules. Food stayed in the kitchen. Tony waited for Kim to say no, but instead, she brushed her hand against Tammy's back, kissed her on the top of her head, and said, "Just this once." Without another word, Tammy disappeared.

"What's the point of having rules if you keep letting her break them?" he said.

"She's still not talking to you?"

Tony shook his head, defeated.

"You have to control your temper," said Kim, tsk-tsking.

"My temper? If I had talked to my father that way—"

"Tammy isn't you," said Kim. "She's stronger."

Too strong, especially for a girl. He knew he'd lost control last night, but his daughter had provoked him. He had to parent her. Children needed discipline and boundaries. He was grateful that his father took the wild out of him. Tony handled Tammy with much more care. Unlike his father, he knew the difference between an open palm and a closed fist.

"She mocked me. My English," said Tony.

Kim sneered. *"Ni diu mian zi le?"*

Did you lose face? A phrase that he'd grown up with. Defended against. His father used to spit it at him at every opportunity. That one time he missed top honors in the third grade. Or when, from the stern of a small fishing boat, he struggled to drag up the net, a three-meter-long cylindrical mesh contraption that was too unwieldy for a twelve-year-old boy. Or on his sixteenth birthday, when his father read out loud a newspaper's rejection letter of his short story. Afterward, he tore up the paper. "You wrote about a talking calculator? You just made me lose *my* face."

Tony hadn't heard that phrase since he'd left the village for college. By then, he had made himself unobjectionable. Not only was Tony brilliant—the top engineering student at the Dalian University of Technology—but he also played basketball. A rare meld of brawn and brains in China. Girls hung around the court after his games, hoping for some attention. They all knew he was going places. Everyone—from his professors to his roommates—knew he was special.

Every department needs a student like him, they would say.

Golden boy.

His parents must be so proud.

Ta men dou gei ta mian zi. Everyone gave him face.

Now, his wife and daughter, his new country, his new life kept clawing it away. He wasn't sure how or when he'd earn it back.

"I'm ready." Tammy had returned to the kitchen with her backpack, her hair swept back in a braid. The top section was uneven, and she had clearly missed a step in the 1-2-3 pattern near the tail. In recent months, she had insisted on styling her long locks herself.

"Do you want me to redo your hair?" asked Tony.

"What's wrong with my hair?" she said, cutting him down with her gaze.

Kim gave him a look that said, *See? Stronger.*

He saw. His little girl could spar. She had confidence at her core, a quiet flame that neither he nor Kim possessed.

"Don't wait for me for dinner. My shift ends at ten," said Tony.

Kim nodded. "Buy something hot to eat."

"Let's go," said Tammy, pacing around her mother.

Tony held the door open as the two most important people in his life walked out.

Alone, he fetched a pair of scissors from a sticky drawer that took a few tries to open. The drawer was like most things in the cramped kitchen: partially broken. Snipping the blades of the scissors anxiously, he wandered through the basement apartment and paused at Tammy's room. Her stuffed Dalmatian sat in the middle of her queen-size bed, as if guarding it for her return. A diary lay on the nightstand, closed shut with a silver lock. Tammy always seemed to be writing in it.

There were days when Tony wondered what her tiny hand was scribbling. Other days, he knew.

Tony carried on to the room he shared with Kim. The only things that fit in there were a frameless mattress and a dresser. Even though it was smaller than Tammy's room, he never complained. She needed a desk for her homework.

Tony opened the small closet and picked out one of his three dress pants. He had steamed them last night but was checking for any stains he might have missed. With machine precision, he cut off the stitching that had started to fray. The material was so stiff that he had to wriggle his legs into it. He put on his button-down shirt, top hat, white gloves, and long-tailed overcoat. When he'd finished, he looked like a cartoon character, a bellhop from another century. The uniform, particular right down to the black socks and oxfords, signaled his status. *I'm at your service*, it said.

In China, he had been the lead mechanical engineer on a project for autonomous elevators that could calculate and adjust their own speeds—something that no university engineer had ever solved. It could've changed the way large buildings operated in the city of Dalian, in all of China. But he abandoned that path six years ago, in 1991, when he moved to New York. Not Manhattan, but Flushing, Queens. None of his degrees or awards had followed him across the Atlantic.

For the first two years, he renovated and repaired elevators, mechanically, with his hands, on his knees. His clothes were regularly stained with oil and smudged yellow and black. The company didn't give him personal injury insurance, and he knew he had no bargaining chip to ask for it. After nearly losing a finger on a finicky cable wire, Kim demanded that he find a desk job, even if it meant less money for the family.

He became the on-call handyman at an Upper West Side co-op building called The Rosewood. Maintaining the building called for electrical, HVAC, and basic construction skills, but the most popular request he received from the residents was to fix their toilets. Those with delicate snowy skin refused to plunge their own hard turds down the pipes. He did battle with over a hundred overstuffed porcelain bowls before working his way up to the title of doorman.

At night, he took computer science classes at Queens College. Software didn't hold a light to his old career in hardware, but at least they were two halves of a whole. Now he was only a year away from graduation and daydreamed about offers from the likes of Netscape and AOL. What his former colleagues in Dalian would think about him then.

The American-born were puzzled when he spoke of trading his successful life in China for this immigrant struggle. Sometimes, he questioned it too. His parents had taught him to *chi ku*—eat bitterness—but they hadn't prepared him to eat shit.

Back in the kitchen, Tony squeezed three sandwiches into his backpack. Kim had made them the night before. Jif peanut butter in between slices of Wonder bread. His usual, save for the weeks when ham and cheese were on sale at the grocery store.

His green JanSport was heavy, already carrying three large textbooks and his personal bible: the compact edition of the Oxford-English dictionary. One perk of the doorman job was the dependable lulls in the day for studying. Before he left the apartment, he made sure to check the stove. He pointed his finger at each knob and mouthed *off, off, off, off* as he went down the line.

On the crowded subway, Tony itched his sweaty neckline and unbuttoned his cuff links. The polyester wool blend suit grew tighter on him by the minute. Suddenly, the train jolted to a halt, wheels shrieking. The conductor garbled over the speakers about a signal malfunction—the first words of English that he'd heard that day. The other passengers checked their watches in a panic, muttering curses. Tony didn't worry. He always gave himself extra time to arrive anywhere—thirty minutes for work and school, an hour for Tammy's piano recitals, and three hours for any international flight. Being on time was simple—just plan ahead. He was always planning ahead.

Above him, colorful subway advertisements ran along the walls. A narrow-necked bottle of sparkling water "designed for the bold since 1981." A flower delivery service "guaranteed to make your wife fall in love with you all over again." And an antidepressant that declared "a new dawn." None of those ads appealed to Tony. Tap water served him just fine, Kim would kill him if he wasted money on roses, and he didn't have time to be depressed. Another banner, with faded black lettering, warned that skipping fares on the subway could result in an arrest or fine. That one made Tony pull his jacket snug on his shoulders.

Above ground again, Tony checked his pant pocket for his wallet and felt a hard object lodged underneath it. A glass containing a dark coarse powder and labeled *cat's claw— immunity booster*. Kim had purchased it on her weekly visit to the traditional medicine man on Kissena Boulevard. "Sprinkle some in your coffee," she'd told him as she unloaded the rest of her purchases onto their mattress. Valerian root and passion flower for sleeplessness. Gingko and pennywort for brain boosters. "Natural remedies are the secret to a long and healthy life," she said as she gazed at her collection of tiny corked bottles. Her nonsense powders. It was her way of staying close to her occupation in China: a medical doctor whose practice had been solely grounded in science.

During the early nineties, a wave of Chinese immigrants turned their backs on their old careers and descended upon the States as an army of software engineers. Anyone could quickly learn to speak in 1's and 0's and single-word functions and semicolons. Tony still didn't understand why Americans themselves didn't want such high-paying jobs. Kim guessed that it was too much work for too low of a profile. Regardless, they saw the opportunity and crawled through that hole to America. Neither of them regretted their decision, but it didn't mean it was easy to live with either.

In China, they had had everything, but by way of a trusted grapevine, they learned that everything they had was better in America. In America, middle-class people could afford to live in single-family houses instead of cramped apartments. They didn't only have a washing machine for laundry, but a dryer *and* a dishwasher. Indoor heat was theirs to adjust—not controlled by a building's stingy landlord. The streets were cleaned by a small truck with a mechanical sweeper and vacuum instead of a man with a wooden broom. While only 5 percent of students could test into college in China, most American children who wanted to go to college could. Some even went to Ivy League schools. Still, the most memorable comparison they had heard was that in China, they could only spring for cake with cream once a year, but in America, they could eat it every week.

A block away from The Rosewood, an older gentleman in a three-piece suit cursed into his cell phone. The man growled,

"I don't care if it's before 6:00 a.m. in Los Angeles. He works on my time." A woman with puffy eyes wiped her nose on the sleeve of an oversized sweatshirt. Her face—sallow, carved with a desperate loneliness. Tony shrank as he passed her.

What a strange land he'd discovered. He had witnessed children screeching profanities at their nannies. Protesters marching with signs to arrest the nation's president. Americans had no shame, no commitment to public decorum. He admired them. They were fearless; they were real.

The sun glared against the glass entrance of The Rosewood. Tony's shoes made ugly slapping sounds against the grand marble floor as he passed through the revolving door into the lobby. Magic, one of the other doormen, was at the front desk, already packing up to leave. He was a Polish immigrant, tall and wide as a giant, and a ceaselessly buoyant gossip hound. His name tag said "Maciej," but everyone called him Magic.

"You can't let Daphne into apartment 615 anymore," said Magic.

"Mr. Waldron's girl?" said Tony.

Magic nodded. "His lawyer is getting the paperwork together for the restraining order. Think she threatened to tell his wife about them."

Daphne would soon be number seventy-four on the blackballed list, which mostly consisted of media outlets, stalkers, and ex-wives. The residents of The Rosewood were prone to filing restraining orders—drawing an invisible legal shield around their lives. The doormen were their first line of defense. Twice, Tony had to use the bat he stored under the desk to chase off a man whose life goal was to sleep in Bruce Willis's bed. Still, Tony preferred to work here over other, less dramatic apartment buildings. The residents of The Rosewood were particularly generous over the holiday season. Last year, he'd cobbled together fifteen thousand in cash bonuses—more than half his annual salary.

"I haven't seen Mrs. Waldron in days. Do you think she found out about Daphne?" said Magic, stroking his chin.

"You're the detective," said Tony. "Any theories?"

Magic lit up. "Maybe Mrs. Waldron's visiting her brother. I overheard her on the phone last month. He's in a rehab facility upstate," he mused. "Or, she could be recovering from her third face-lift. The doctor's office sent a new bill." Tony hated to admit it, but this was probably going to be the highlight of his day.

Tony used to despise gossip, but once he became a doorman, he began to understand its entertainment value. His twelve hours at the desk were filled with frivolous small talk, passing out the mail, and responding to convenience requests from the residents. Unit 204 needed a thirty-five-pound pail of cat litter carried to its front door. Ring the Carlsons on the fourteenth floor when a man in a dinosaur costume arrived. If it weren't for Magic's snooping, the job would be unbearably boring.

"Did you hear?" said Magic. "The Liddles are moving out. Sold their apartment for over three million."

Tony gave a long whistle. The Rosewood address alone must've doubled the price of that unit. He'd been inside a few times to repair the air conditioner and shower drain. It was a modern and sleek three bedroom, with an exceptionally elegant pass-through kitchen, but three million was absurd. He was developing a good eye for the cost of things.

On the first Saturday of each month, his little family would visit six or seven open houses. Sometimes, they stayed within the perimeter of the city, mostly looking at apartments and brownstones. Other times, they took a road trip to see the mansions out in the suburbs—Bronxville, Scarsdale, Pelham. Everything was comically out of their price range, but that was the fun of it.

The real estate agents hosting the open houses ranged from civil to outwardly annoyed, even though the Zhangs made it a point to be polite ghosts. One place, he remembered, had a plate of cookies on the kitchen counter. Golden-edged with generous chunks of chocolate. When Tammy went to take one, he tugged her arm away. "We don't do that," he said. The real estate agent gave him a weird look. She was fine, thought Tony. He had barely touched her.

The Zhangs toured each house together—through the airy hallways, round the living room, up the stairs. "I would've placed the coffee table at the other end of the sofa," Kim would often opine. In a sun-filled room with a slanted ceiling, Tammy planted herself in a corner and said, "My bed could go here." Sometimes, they would look out the window at the houses next door. Wondering if the neighbors were as kooky as Steve Urkel in *Family Matters* or as rowdy as the Bundys from *Married with Children*—sitcoms they had watched to learn English.

In each house, Tony fantasized about the same imaginary routine. Kissing his wife on the cheek as he came in the door. Checking his daughter's homework. Complaining about the furnace and then calling someone else to come fix it. Having a yard with a rosebush and a flag billowing in the wind. A house that they bought, a place they could call their own, that could never be taken away.

On his way out of the building, Magic said, "I finished sorting the mail already."

"Cool," said Tony. He studied Magic's reaction. There was none, which meant that he had probably used the word in the right context. Tammy had been throwing around the word lately, but he wasn't sure where it belonged and where it didn't. He just knew from the way she said it that he had to sound casual. Quick and relaxed. He wouldn't have dared to experiment with it on one of the residents.

Alone for the second time that day, Tony tidied up the desk. He neatly piled the paper clips next to stacked pads of Post-it notes. Gathered all of the pens into the mesh metal cup. Wiped down the desk with antibacterial spray. Then, finally, he opened his dictionary to the dog-eared page.

He underlined a word near the top: *net*. He thought that he could skip over it, having used it many times already. A volleyball net. Catching fish in a net. He had even known that it was an abbreviation for the internet. That should have been more than enough for one word. He had no idea that it was also an adjective. "Free from all charges, deductions, or debt," the dictionary gods had written. Net earnings, net worth.

His brain rolled over, overstuffed with the strange rules and allowances of the English language. Mandarin was simple. One sound for one word. A character might have the same pinyin, but accents set each apart. The four tones dictated whether *"ma"* meant *mother, hemp, horse,* or *scold.* No exceptions.

Tony had already studied six pages of the dictionary and was in the middle of reading the definition of *noteworthy* when he heard the elevator doors open.

A woman glided past the front desk. She was wrapped in a brilliant emerald scarf. It draped around her tiny shoulders and beneath her bony little elbows, finally ending in a tied ribbon in front of a well-fed belly.

Tony stood up and with a slight bow said, "Good morning, Miss Abadi."

"Oh, you? You're still here?" she said. "Remind me to fire that assassin I hired!" She paused to hear Tony's laugh before making her way out the door. Clara did this every morning— recited a line from one of her old films. Magic had told him during his first week on the job that Clara Abadi had been a movie star, famous in the fifties and sixties for a string of blockbusters and an even longer string of torrid affairs. Her Rolodex of lovers included all the obvious A-listers, publishing heirs, Saudi oil kings, even female Olympic athletes. The woman was blind to age, gender, geography, and marital status. "A tabloid sweetheart," Magic had called her, whatever that meant.

Over the years, Tony had sent crates of European wine, exotic birds that looked at him funny, and jewelers accompanied by their bodyguards up to her apartment. She also had deliveries that didn't fit in the elevator. That month alone, Tony had to carry a painting wrapped in Mylar that kept threatening to slip off his back, and drag something heavy in a body bag, up the twenty-three flights of stairs.

Clara's was the one unit in the entire building that Tony had never entered. Whenever she went on vacation, he dreamed of sneaking in with the extra key at the front desk. He imagined her apartment awash in gold—golden tables, chairs, beds, floors. Plush velvet covering every surface. Chandeliers, chilled champagne, and fresh fruit in every room. He was fascinated by Clara. She didn't just live life. She luxuriated in it.

Clara was on the street now, but he could still see her

through the glass doors. A bundle of bracelets laced her fore-arm. A Chanel purse, the color of a strawberry milkshake, in her hand. He was squinting at her shoes, trying to remember the term for a sandal with a high heel, when Oliver, the law-yer in unit 505, approached her on the street. From behind the desk, Tony observed the young man's profile. Gelled brown hair, high-bridged nose, a strong chin. Even in a striped cot-ton shirt, Oliver looked more like a professional than Tony did in his suit.

Tony hoped that Tammy could carry herself with the same charm and easy confidence when she grew up. He did some mental math to see how quickly Tammy could graduate col-lege, then law school, join a firm, save up and live in a place like The Rosewood. Maybe when she turned forty. But Oli-ver wasn't even close to that age. Lawyers must make even more money than he had assumed.

Then Oliver strode into the building and greeted Tony. At least a hand over six feet, he towered over him. "How's your family? How's your daughter, Tammy, doing?" Oliver asked.

Some residents did this—engage a few inches in the shal-low end with the doormen. It was a nice gesture, but Tony hated it. He called it *pity attention*. The residents paid him to be there. They didn't have to pretend to be friends or equals.

"Tammy got all As on her report card again," said Tony. "Her math teacher says she's the smartest fourth grader she's ever seen. She doesn't need a pencil or paper for her multipli-cation problems. She does it all in her head! I can't even do—"

But Oliver was already on his way to the elevator bank.

Tony bit his tongue. He should've just given a generic an-swer, a simple "Tammy's good, thanks for asking," but when it came to talking about his daughter, he found it hard to stay quiet. He was still berating himself, hearing Kim's reprimand—*people don't like to hear about your successes*—when it happened.

He had heard it first.

A howl. It cut through the city noise and echoed through the lobby.

He scurried out from behind the front desk and sprinted outside.

The first thing he saw was blood. Clara's blood, running down her face. She was lying on the ground.

A man grabbed her pink purse and began to run away.

Now Tony was running too. On instinct, on sheer nerve, that flame—alight in Tammy—now flickered in him.

He reached out and caught the hood. The man fell back. A strangled yell. They were on the ground together. The man on top of him. Tony took a blow to the chest, and the pain reverberated through his rib cage. A windmill of arms and wrestling. Knuckles crashed against his cheekbone. A rasp of tearing cloth.

The man hooked him with a fist to the side of his head, filtering his world red for a few seconds. His lungs hurt when he breathed, but he suddenly felt present in his body, pinned to the moment in a way he hadn't been for years. He pushed off the ground and leapt at the assailant, grabbing him by the shoulders. The two of them scrambled upright—like two horses on their hind legs—before the man crumpled underneath him. Tony punched down, slamming the man's skull against the concrete.

A small voice told him to stop fighting. But he was overwhelmed by how natural the movements felt. Each strike felt like a glimpse into the logic of the universe: his hands were made to curl into fists, to fight. Between punches, he met the eyes of the man. Frightened eyes, pleading. Like Tammy's the night before.

The high-pitched scream of sirens.

Tony's hands dropped to his sides. He was shaking and sweaty. Had he done something bad? Whatever it was, it was too late to take it back.

A metallic taste rose in his throat. The blood stained the sidewalk brown, already mixing with the city's filth. Red blotches and ripped holes in his doorman suit—that would come out of his paycheck.

Now Clara pointed at him. She looked mad, her nose still spouting blood. She was ready to blame someone. It would be him. It was all his fault.

"That China man," she cried, as a paramedic and two police officers surrounded her.

Finger still outstretched toward Tony's face, she shouted, "That China man saved me."

TWO

Oliver

Oliver was eating a chocolate croissant at La Belle Étoile, Kip's go-to breakfast place for clients. Waiters in crisp vests wove by him, delivering trays of Colombian coffee with ceramic creamers. Shunning pancakes and bagels, the menu offered crepes, tartines, and twelve-dollar pots of organic loose-leaf tea.

He wore a pair of black-rimmed glasses that pinched his nose. No contacts today. No three-piece suit or loafers. This client called for a different kind of costume: a slim-fit T-shirt and jeans. Evan was practically a boy, a college dropout. He was only a few years younger than Oliver, but he'd already launched a digital music start-up with millions in venture capital backing.

"Your company is the future," Oliver heard himself say. It came out flat. The exaggeration was supposed to express his admiration, even sound inspirational, but he still couldn't sell what he didn't believe.

But Kip could. "This technology is going to change billions of lives," he said.

Evan, whose long hair swept over his eyes, smirked. "Our version of the MP3 player is good. It's amazing if you consider the extra storage space for songs," he said, "but it's not going to change lives."

"You kidding me?" said Kip, cutting into his rib eye and eggs. "Songs give people courage. They give them a personal soundtrack, a boost to make them achieve something they would never otherwise believe they could. And the bigger the soundtrack? The more dreams you just green-lighted."

"If you put it that way," Evan said, as he lifted his chin in agreement. He took a forkful of his crepe. The sides of his mouth were lined with traces of powdered sugar. Kip knew how to stroke an ego—even a reluctant one.

That was why Kip Appleton was managing partner and had his name on the letterhead of one of the most prestigious white-shoe law firms in Manhattan: Steinway & Appleton. Kip had never even used an MP3 player. "It's vinyl or it's shit," he said when he saw Oliver's CD player in the office. Oliver brought the electronics back to his apartment that night.

Still, he couldn't complain about the old man. A mere second-year associate, Oliver wasn't even supposed to be at this meeting. Client events were normally reserved for senior associates and partners. But Kip—who had been his grandfather's protégé and best friend—always propped Oliver up, ever since he was little. Never wavering, even after the scandal broke. Unlike everyone else he knew.

Oliver didn't even notice that the waitress had refilled his

cup until it was suddenly brimming with coffee again. "Thank
you, Danielle," said Oliver. She smiled back. How unique and
thoughtful, she must be thinking, that a patron would bother
to learn her name. Kip definitely didn't know it, even though
he had been coming here for years. But it was fine. Kip probably tipped her well.

"So, you been hitting the clubs?" said Kip.

Evan gave a small shrug. "Actually, I've—"

"Oh, no, you're cooler than the morons who hang out at
the clubs. You're a music guy. Bet you went straight to CBGBs
from the airport to check out the talent," said Kip.

"What's CBGBs?" said Evan.

"Don't worry about it," said Kip. "Whatever you're into,
Oliver can take you around, show you all the best places."
He shot Oliver a look that said *pay close attention.* Kip believed
that to win business, a lawyer needed to be more than a client's confidant. He needed to be their best friend. Their genie.
Their wish was his command. That included making their
problems—from DUIs to sexual harassment—disappear. It also
meant serving up fun. Kip had box seats at Yankee Stadium,
a standing Saturday night table with bottle service at a mem-
bers-only club, and privileges for backstage meet and greets
with musical superstars at Madison Square Garden.

"I like reading," said Evan.

Kip frowned a little. Not in his repertoire. He nodded toward Oliver.

"Reading. That's cool," said Oliver. "What kind of books?"

"Fantasy," said Evan.

"Like *Lord of the Rings*?"

Evan perked up. "Yeah, have you read it? I read all the books
twice when I was a kid and again last year. I heard they're

being made into movies. It's going to be so sick." He said it all in one breath. Suddenly, the kid had come to life.

"I love them. What an epic story," said Oliver, even though he had never read one word of *The Lord of the Rings*.

"Sounds like you two have a date for a comic book convention," said Kip, leaning back in his chair.

"Can we get VIP passes?" asked Evan, almost knocking over his Sprite.

"Done," said Oliver. He would rather stick his nose hair trimmer up his butt than hang out with cosplayers, but Kip was letting him handle a client alone. Already. He hadn't realized that Kip believed in him this much.

After the client left, Kip ordered a Bloody Mary to go. "Good job, Big O," he said. "Want to ride to the office together? The chauffeur's waiting at Columbus Circle."

"I have to go pick up some files from home," said Oliver. "The Rosewood isn't too far. I'll just walk."

"Don't work too hard," said Kip. As if that meant something. As if they both didn't know that the firm required their associates to bill three thousand hours a year.

No one made eye contact with Oliver as he strolled up Central Park West. Not the trio of mothers, pushing their identical prams. Or the professional dog walker wrangling a pack of goldendoodles. Not even the teenager in a private school uniform, sprinting toward the subway station.

The only exception was the guy selling flowers on the sidewalk. "Flowers? Flowers? A guy like you definitely has got a girlfriend."

"Sorry, no, thanks," said Oliver. He did have a girlfriend, but bringing her flowers would be sending the wrong message.

"Three dollars off," said the flower vendor, with a hint of desperation. The man blinked back rivulets of sweat. It wasn't even noon yet, but he must have already been standing in the glaring sunlight for hours. Oliver knew how it worked. The man was parked here until all his flowers were sold. It almost made Oliver want to buy a bouquet just to help him out, but he continued walking.

He had met his girlfriend, Janna, last year at the Tenth Annual Blood Saves gala. Kip had bought a $5,000 table for the law firm, and after Oliver choked down his plate of over-cooked chicken and limp asparagus, he went over to the blood donation station. A pretty nurse with a contagious smile asked him to roll up his sleeve. He could tell that she liked him by the way she avoided eye contact and fumbled with the tourniquet.

"First time?" he said.

"I usually draw blood from children," she said. "At Memorial Sloan Kettering," she added, looking him square in the eye.

"I'm just a big kid. I get a little squeamish."

"Don't worry. This won't hurt a bit," she said.

Needle still in his arm, he asked for her number. They went out to dinner the very next night, and Oliver brought her back to his apartment the night after that.

At the beginning, she had been easy in the best ways. She was independent. Busy with her own twelve-hour shifts at the hospital and volunteer activities on days off, she barely noticed his long stints at the office. And she was endlessly patient and optimistic. One day, while they were waiting at an intersection, someone sneezed right on her bagel. She shrugged as she dropped it into the nearby trash can. "That Good Samaritan just saved me a gym session." At late-night dinners, she even had the sixth sense not to pry about his family when he clammed up. She didn't seem to want anything from him other than to be with him. If there was a person he should fall in love with, it would be her.

But after a year of dating, she had been dropping hints that she wanted more. Pausing to examine his reaction after saying that she had never been to Paris. Mentioning that her parents were coming to town in September. Dropping by The Rosewood unannounced with a basket of Levain cookies when he said he had to spend the whole weekend working.

This was about the stage he'd ended it with his past girlfriends. Still, in the middle of the night, he'd wondered if it could be different with Janna, if he could tell her the truth. She was kinder than most, more open-minded. She took care of children who had terminal cancer, for God's sake. Maybe she could draw the poison out of him as painlessly as she'd taken his blood at the gala. But time had a way of outing true intentions. She might be understanding in the first year, even flattered that he had confided in her. But in five years, when they had children, or ten years, or twenty, she'd grow to resent him. Worst yet—she might pity him.

His throat tightened. Relax, he told himself, there were more pressing matters to address. Like work. He refocused on the plan—home, files, office—and picked up the pace.

A few blocks later, The Rosewood appeared. The crown jewel of the Upper West Side. The building—with its gable dormers, terra-cotta spandrels, and pale red bricks—was home to two Nobel Prize recipients, a Beatle, a bevy of Oscar winners, and a C-suite member from each bulge bracket bank. The only thing more impressive than The Rosewood's list of residents was the list of people it rejected: rock stars like Axl Rose and Mick Jagger, America's sweetheart Julia Roberts, and even former president Jimmy Carter. There didn't seem to be any rhyme or reason to the application process. Oliver only lived there by the grace of Kip. Oliver didn't know what the old man had said to the board members to convince them to hand over the keys, but as usual, it worked.

A figure waved at him from under the building's awning. As he got closer, he realized it was Clara. Her eyes, crinkly yet childlike, made him feel as though she had been waiting for him all along.

"Could I interest you in a nooner?" she said.

Zero inhibition—the classic affliction of aging coupled with Hollywood bravado. New Yorkers had the thinnest of filters, but Clara was pure thought. She looked expectantly at his face, but Oliver could only gape like a fish.

"You're no fun," she said with a smirk.

Oliver laughed. "Well, no one's as fun as you are."

"True. There's only one Clara Abadi."

"Where are you off to today?" he asked.

"Lunch with the girls. They're going to choke on their mimosas when they see my new purse," she said, giddily clutching at her pink Chanel. The string of pearls across the front made little clacking sounds.

"Very fashionable," he said, despite thinking that it looked like a cheap plastic bag that a child would carry to a tea party with her toy bunnies. The compliment was compulsory. She was famous, sort of his neighbor, and most importantly, a woman. Part of his job as a good-looking man was to make women of all ages feel pretty.

Inside the lobby, he passed the marble desk, where Tony,

the doorman, was already standing. Oliver noticed the open dictionary. He couldn't remember the last time he'd seen Tony without it. It was admirable that his doorman was trying to assimilate into American society, though it might already be too late for him. No matter how much he studied, he would always sound foreign, never capturing the tempo or the accent quite right. It was like a silver spoon—you were either born with it in your mouth or you weren't.

"Good morning, Tony. How's your family?" said Oliver. "How's your daughter, Tammy, doing?" He looked around quickly to see if anyone else heard. Not only did he know his doorman's name, but he also knew the name of his daughter. Impressive.

"Very good. Tammy got all As on her report card," said Tony.

"Right on," said Oliver, walking to the elevator bank.

While waiting for the elevator, he caught his reflection in its brass doors. He brushed his fingers through his thick brown hair and turned his head this way and that. A sophisticated widow's peak. A chiseled jaw and a pair of sapphires for eyes. Such a handsome face. He wondered if ugly people thought the same about their own. If it were a biological imperative for people to think of themselves as beautiful. Sometimes, he wished that he were more plain-looking. As it was, his sharp features were a constant reminder that he was jinxed. If genetic material were a deck of cards, he got dealt the same hand as his grandfather.

Suddenly, a scream echoed through the lobby. It sounded like it was coming from outside. Then a scurrying of footsteps. He turned toward the entrance just in time to see Tony rush outside.

Oliver crossed the lobby to the front door, and that was
when he saw it: Clara was being attacked on the street by a
man in a gray hoodie. For a moment, it looked like they were
dancing. But no, they were tugging apart her pink purse. "Get
off!" she yelled, holding her ground.

Just as Oliver thought about running out to help, the hooded
man punched Clara, breaking her nose. Blood poured down
her face. Oliver backed away from the glass door, nauseous,
wiping his own nose as though it was bleeding too.

The man began to run away, leaving a breadcrumb trail of
pearls that had fallen off Clara's purse, but Tony was chasing
outside now, and grabbed him by the hood.

It all happened so fast. A flurry of limbs, sounds of ribs
cracking. Tony took two hits to the chest. As he staggered
backward, the mugger used that momentum to push him to
the ground. Oliver winced as the man threw a punch across
Tony's jaw.

The mugger was twice the size of the doorman. It wasn't
a fair fight. Oliver pushed against the glass door, but froze in
place when Tony spit out blood.

Then his phone buzzed. Kip was calling. Maybe he could
pretend that he had been busy on the phone and hadn't seen
anything. There were two other men nearby. They could in-
tervene if Tony really needed it.

Clara was still on the ground, clutching her nose. He should
go to her, but hadn't he read something in the paper about
how muggers acted in twos? One for backup. That guy could
have a knife. A gun. Things could get even worse if Oliver
stepped in.

Moments later, it was clear that Tony didn't need him. He
had pounced on the mugger, tackling him to the ground.

There was a thudding of flesh and bone against pavement. The man stopped resisting, his fists falling open on the sidewalk.

Oliver heard the sirens and crept closer to the entrance to get a better look at the scene.

Tony, with his fists hanging limply at his sides, straddled the attacker, who barely moved underneath him. Clara lying on the sidewalk, her face covered with blood and tears. Her pink purse lay in front of the revolving doors, the doors that Oliver still stood safely behind. His hand pressed against the glass. He was even more afraid to come out now.

THREE

Tony

"Who are you?" asked the doctor.

Tony understood what the question implied. An Asian man in a torn bellhop uniform and an elderly white woman with a head wound walked into a hospital. It sounded like the beginning of a bad joke.

"I'm Miss Abadi's doorman," said Tony. "Is she okay?"

"She's doing fine. Nothing's broken, but we're not ruling out a concussion yet." The doctor spoke slowly, enunciating each word as though he were speaking to a toddler. Tony was used to this kind of stilted English. He'd heard it before from the residents in his building, Tammy's teachers, recruiters from technology companies. Some did it as a polite gesture or out of self-ordained compassion. Many couldn't hide their impatience. A few were brazenly condescending. They all did it because they assumed that it was necessary. They weren't completely wrong. Tony was grateful for the decrease in their speech speed. It was their tone that could kill a man.

He returned to his seat in the waiting room where, the doctor had said, a police officer would meet him to take a statement. *The police.* Before this, his mind had been racing with thoughts of suspension or losing his job completely. The cost of a replacement uniform, the dry-cleaning bill to remove the bloodstains from his white shirt, whether Kim could apply makeup on his face to hide the bruises. The police had slipped his mind. Now it was all he could think about. They could arrest him, drag him to court, throw him in prison. His teeth clenched at a new thought: they could revoke his visa.

He had seen an episode of *Judge Judy* about a brawl between two men. The unassuming defendant said that he'd struck the other man with a chair to protect his girlfriend. How had Judge Judy ruled? He could almost hear her smoker's voice now, see the glasses perched low on her nose. He scratched at the sides of his pants and snapped off a loose thread. The defendant with the face of a cherub—hadn't she found him guilty?

Then he thought of someone who scared him more than the police and the courts: his wife. Regardless of how they sorted him, Kim was the final arbiter. With her he didn't have high hopes for a fair trial. She had told him to walk away from trouble. And what had he done? Chased trouble down and punched it in the face.

"Eighty-two, eighty-three, eighty-four." The bald man next to him was counting ceiling tiles. Tony looked up, squinting at the fluorescent light. He hated hospitals. This one smelled like old socks and bleach. The hallways wouldn't shut up. Clogs squeaking on the floor, metal carts clattering. The incessant beeping of monitors. Announcements over the speaker system paging doctors to the ICU. The sounds bounced off the sterile hard surfaces, amplifying his anxiety.

Back in China, Tony had only visited the hospital a handful of times. He remembered the day his father dislocated his shoulder for skipping school. *I fell*, he told the nurses.

"Tony!"

Someone was calling his name.

"Tony!"

He turned around and saw Oliver Wright from apartment 505. The young man looked less imposing outside The Rosewood. His voice—thin and uneven. Strands of loose hair dangled across his forehead.

"Why are you here?" said Tony.

"To help you," said Oliver.

"Help me?" Tony was used to being the help, not the other way around.

Oliver reached his hand out toward Tony as if to hug him, but then hesitated. "I'm so sorry," he said. "Your face."

Tony had caught brief reflections of himself in the ambulance window and the nurse's metal instruments, but he hadn't really taken stock of his injuries. He didn't need a mirror to know that it was bad. He cradled his face in his hands, slowly touching all the lumps and bumps: the taped gauze on his cheek, stitches on his lips, thick bandage on his nose. Every jolt of pain jerked his memory. He had hit someone, but he was a victim too.

Oliver said, "What you did was really brave."

"You saw?" Tony was hoping that Oliver could help him piece together what had happened and persuade the police that none of it was his fault.

Oliver's words tripped over each other as he explained,

"Yes, well, no, not all of it. I was on my phone. Client call. Inside the lobby. Can't always see clearly through the revolving doors. I know they're glass but sometimes the sunlight—it hits them in a weird way."

"I hope I'm not in trouble," said Tony.

"With who?"

"The police."

"It's just a formality," Oliver said, eyes narrowing with confusion, before leaving to get him something to drink.

Of course Oliver didn't get it, thought Tony. Why would he? Oliver was a US citizen, a lawyer. Tony was a thirty-four-year-old foreigner with an ugly accent and no green card. He didn't have money or influential friends to vouch for him like he did in China. No job at a prominent university that would afford him somebody's benefit of the doubt. The police could lock him up, or worse, deport him. It was a crime to be violent, and Tony had committed it in public.

He thought about Tammy. Kim would insist that they follow him if he were forced out of the country. He vowed to himself that he would make them stay in America without him. He would send money from China for rent and food and for all of Tammy's lessons—piano, Kumon, swimming, dancing. Whatever it took, however long they had to be apart. He would make Kim promise to keep Tammy in line with her studies. That was most important.

"I think you drink this, right?" said Oliver, setting a Styrofoam cup on the table. "It's green tea."

"I'm afraid," said Tony.

"It'll be okay."

"I can't talk to the police."

"Why?" said Oliver.

Tony stayed silent, taking in the creases in Oliver's face. His worry lines, Tony noticed, were etched with sadness. He met the young man's eyes, holding on until they softened, went watery at the edges. He sensed that Oliver was seeing him for the first time too.

"Let me help you," said Oliver.

"How?"

"I'm a lawyer. This is what I do."

"I can't afford it."

Oliver sipped his tea and shook his head. "I don't let friends pay."

Friends, thought Tony, with a happy lurch in his gut. He nodded slowly, keeping his head down so that Oliver wouldn't notice how emotional he was getting.

He heard Kim's voice in his head: *He doesn't mean it. Don't be a fool.* His wife didn't have faith in people. *There's always something in it for them.* Tony used to agree with her theory, but Oliver seemed different. He had come all the way from The Rosewood to the hospital. He was taking off from work. He didn't have to do any of this for his doorman, but he was offering to help. *You're too trusting*, Kim might say. But Oliver was a good man.

"So what happened here?" The police officer arrived in denim jeans and sneakers. The yellow notepad in his hand was the only indication of his authority. He had already talked to Clara, he said, and just had a few follow-up questions.

"He hit me and I protect her," said Tony, words tumbling out before his brain could correct them. That should have been past tense. His English regressed when he got nervous. "The man kept hitting me. I only hit back because he hit me." Tony pointed to his own bruised face as evidence. "I'm a doorman. It's my job."

Oliver nodded. "This is all true."

"I have a work visa," said Tony. "In my house. I can show you. Please. I have a daughter."

"Whoa, man, calm down. You're all over the place. Start from the top," said the officer, as if rehearsing a line that he had heard on a TV cop show.

"The top?" said Tony, shrinking into himself.

Oliver put a hand on Tony's shoulder and said, "Around noon today, a man assaulted Clara and stole her purse. He tried to run away, but Tony stopped him."

The officer and Oliver kept talking, but Tony was barely listening anymore. He could tell from the officer's stance—his casual slouch, the way he nodded along placidly, barely taking any notes—that he wasn't going to be in any trouble. He was safe.

"That's all I need," said the officer. He turned to Tony and said, "You did a remarkable thing today. Really banged up that guy. We have a criminal off the streets because of you."

The officer shook his hand, accidentally pulling at the stitches of his ripped flesh, but Tony was too relieved to care.

He had only talked to one police officer before today and had learned from that encounter to avoid them. On a rainy night in Flushing during his first year in America, a mob of teenagers had robbed him on his way back from the public library. He'd been there late, checking out grammar books after work. They took thirty-three dollars from him and left him on the wet ground. When the police officer arrived, he appeared irritated.

"Are you drunk?" the cop had asked. "What are you doing

out this late at night?" Without waiting for answers, he said, accusingly, "Only someone up to no good would be roaming these streets right now." He rattled off more questions that Tony couldn't understand at the time. What he did understand was that the cop was not on his side. The cop was more dangerous than the muggers. The muggers just took his lunch money, but the cop could ruin his future.

Since that night, Tony was robbed three more times. He surrendered forty-four dollars to a masked man who put a gun to his back, twenty-eight dollars to two boys circling him on bikes, and an even thirty to a man in an empty subway car who said, "Empty your pockets, chink." He wasn't scared anymore. Those people were predictable. Easy to satisfy. They just wanted money, and Kim always made sure that Tony had a wad of cash on him. *Mug money*, she called it. It was her way of protecting him. *Just give them the cash*, she would insist. *Don't fight back*.

Oliver nudged Tony as the doctor approached them. "You two are with Clara Abadi? Follow me," he said.

They strolled down a long corridor. A nurse passed them, holding a bedpan. Tony peeked into an open room. A slack-faced man wearing an oxygen mask stared blankly ahead. His TV flickered silently. Across the hall, a little boy was sleeping. The series of plastic tubes going in and out of his limp body looked like thick strands spun by a spider. Hospitals had a way of making people look sicker than they really were.

In the next room sat Clara, propped up by a legion of pillows. She sported a pair of black eyes and a splint on her nose, but she was humming a show tune as she furiously scooped Jell-O into her mouth. Clara didn't look weak. She looked battle-tested. When she saw Tony and Oliver at her door, she waved at them as if they were long-lost friends.

"How are you feeling?" said Tony.

Clara raised her spoon in the air. "Nothing like a punch to the face to start your day!"

His legs faltered at the joke. Even with a foam neck brace, bandages on her jaw, and a purpling bruise on her arm, she still managed to reach for humor.

"I know what you did for me," said Clara. She grabbed his arm and pulled him close. Splinted-nose to splinted-nose. Tony couldn't breathe. His lungs were too polite, too stunned. Without any of her usual bravado, she whispered, "You're my hero."

He didn't know what to say. This was the same woman who haughtily walked past him every day. The same woman who treated him like a servant. Who he was pretty sure didn't know his name. But here she was, in a hospital gown, no lipstick, scooping Jell-O, calling him a hero.

As he held Clara's gaze, a part of him he kept wound up and tucked away began to unspool. Just then, he did something that he'd never done since he had arrived in America. It was only now, an inch away from the lips of a movie star, that Tony let himself cry.

FOUR

Tammy

My father hit me last night. Though my cheek barely showed
it. I supposed that the skin had toughened up over the years.

But Yumi still noticed, despite sitting two desks away in
our fourth-grade science class.

She slid a note over. "What happened to your face?"

"I was stupid and tripped," I wrote back.

This was the second secret that I kept from Yumi. The first
was that I didn't go to church.

When I was six, my parents had sat me down and said, "One
day, you will die. Do you know what that means?"

I shook my head. I honestly didn't know, but I hoped that
I would be reincarnated as a cheetah.

"You go straight into the ground. The worms will feed on
you," said my mom.

"It's the natural order of things," said my dad.

I asked them about Heaven.

My mom said, "We can't believe in things just to make ourselves feel better."

I had more questions—how come everyone said *bless you?* Could I still eat those chocolate eggs on Easter if I didn't go to church? But my parents ignored them.

"The only thing you need to know is that when you die, you die. That's it," they said.

Even now, as a nine-year-old, I still couldn't get to the bottom of whether or not God existed. I couldn't bring up the topic with my parents again, and I absolutely couldn't talk about it with a friend. Everyone I knew at school went to church. They couldn't know that I didn't. So I made up a fake church that we went to out of state: St. Christ's Church. That sounded right.

The final bell of the school day rang. Yumi and I linked pinkies as we walked down the hallway. We swerved as one around the cheerleaders selling lollipops and boys trading Pokémon cards. A girl in a highlighter-yellow pinnie sprinted toward the gym. Without a word, we side-shuffled to the left, just out of her path.

When we got outside the building, I pulled my hand away from hers. My mother might be watching.

"I bet that's Sanjay's mother," said Yumi, pointing at a squat brown lady with a red dot on her forehead.

"Or it could be Nabeel's," I said.

"You're probably right. Nabeel's got bug eyes."

This was a game that we started playing last month. *Pair the mom with the kid.* Most of the time, the pairs made sense. Both Christie and her mother had shiny blond hair that curled inward at the ends. The horse logo on Soo-hyun's shirt matched that on his mother's. But Alfie's mom didn't have his Chia

Pet hair. Hers was glossy and black. And Lydia had monolids, but the woman who picked her up was Hispanic. Something strange was going on, but Yumi and I hadn't quite figured it out yet.

"Want to hang out this weekend?" said Yumi.

"Sure."

"My house or yours?"

"Yours," I said, "if that's okay."

"Of course."

Before we got to see which kid belonged to the Indian woman, I saw my mother on the sidewalk in front of the school. I said a quick goodbye to Yumi and ran down the lawn. My mother already had a small scowl on her face. I knew why, but all she said was, "We have errands to run."

We walked eight blocks and gave a nickel to the man who played violin at the gates of the cemetery. Then five blocks east to drop off checks at the bank. Past the men outside the library, chewing on cigarettes as they maneuvered mahjong tiles. After a few more side streets, we reached the Broadway of Flushing: the big, the wide, the filthy, Kissena Boulevard. Inside the post office, we paid for stamps, stepping around the wads of gum stuck to the floor. Pig heads hung from hooks in the window of the butcher shop. Their mouths open in shock. The butcher wrapped some roasted duck wings in paper and handed them to my mother.

Our next stop was the corner stand. It was run by a man with planet-sized nostrils. He had an obnoxious sign that read, Buy Your Sesame Balls from Sesame Joe. I heard the crunch of the golden seeds as my teeth sank into the gooey dough. It wasn't until my third bite that I hit the sweet red bean center. I finished it off in the toilet paper aisle of the dim phar-

macy as my mother scanned the tubes of toothpaste, looking
for the cheapest one.

Before we left downtown Flushing, my mother pulled a
quarter out of her purse.

"Only a quarter?" I whined.

"A quarter is a lot," she said.

"I got a hundred on my math test today," I said, negotiating.

"Fine," said my mother, placing an additional quarter in
my palm.

Just enough for a medium-sized taro bubble tea.

This was what it meant to be a grown-up. Having money.
Making money. Then using it to do whatever you wanted.
Buy a car without a roof. Streak your hair pink. Hire a magi-
cian with a live rabbit for a party. I couldn't wait to grow up.

"You're splashing," my mother hissed as my boba tea soaked
my left hand. In my right, I clutched a six-pack of single-ply
toilet paper. The plastic slipped from my grip with each step.

My mother hated anything clumsy. "Clumsy means care-
less, which is even worse than stupid," she liked to say.

A drop of purple milk landed on my sneaker. My mother
cleared her throat. I thought that she was going to scold me
again, but she brought up something else instead. Something
that I knew was coming from the moment I saw her face after
school.

"How's Yumi?" she said.

"Good."

"You're still friends?"

"Yes."

"What about Christie?"

Christie was white. That perfect kind of white, with her
nails polished a new color every week and pearls in her ear-

lobes. She had the latest Lisa Frank folders and never forgot to feed her Tamagotchi pet. Everyone liked Christie. She looked like she could be Princess Diana's daughter.

"She's my friend," I said.

"But not your best friend," my mom said.

"Why don't you like Yumi?" I said, but I knew the reason. My mother wanted me to play with kids whose families cooked mashed potatoes. Yumi's family ate kimchi.

"I like her just fine. Do you want to invite her over to our—"

I cut her off. "We don't have a Nintendo or a big couch."

"Your father is graduating this year," she said. "He'll earn a lot more money."

"So?"

"We'll move to the suburbs. To a nice big house in a white school district. Then you can invite your American friends over."

A man behind us spit on the street.

My mother pushed me ahead of her. "We're almost done being poor," she said.

Poor. We were poor, but our poor wasn't the stealing bread kind. It was the kind where, if we ordered the Chicken McNuggets, we couldn't add a side of fries.

In China, my parents hadn't been poor. They lived in the nicest neighborhood in Dalian, in a two-bedroom apartment with a view of the water. They had jobs that didn't have uniforms. They ate at restaurants whenever they wanted and went to the movies every weekend.

They never liked it when I asked them why they came to America. Acted like it was a trick question. "Why wouldn't we have?" they retorted. When water leaked through our bathroom ceiling, they whispered to each other, "It was the only choice." After a satisfying box of fried chicken, they said, sighing, "Hope for a better future." I tried to imagine that future they spoke of. One in which we'd have a personal pastry chef who was French and called us *Sir*, *Madam*, and *Mademoiselle*.

Our apartment building was gray. A woman in a wheelchair was in the front yard, rolling tire tracks into the patch of straw grass. My mother clutched her purse as two Black boys my age ran by, kicking a soccer ball. Their family lived on the third floor. We lived in the basement.

Before my mother put her key in the entrance, she turned to me, squatted so that we were eye level, and said, "Your father is very upset. I hope you say you're sorry when you see him."

I touched my cheek. "What do I have to be sorry about?"

"What you said last night," said my mother.

This was what happened last night: the phone rang. It was just after dinner and I was in the bathroom.

"Pick it up!" yelled my dad. It was always my responsibility to pick up the phone, just like it was my job to pay at the register when we went to the mall or ask strangers for directions. When we splurged on a taxi, I was the one who talked to the driver. I was the one who confirmed with the mailman that my mother had enough stamps in order to send her letter. The one who haggled over the price of our refurbished refrigerator from Sears.

"Hurry up!" said my dad on the third ring.

I barely wiped myself dry when I heard the answering machine pick up the call. I tumbled out of the bathroom. My dad, mom, and I stared at the little black machine.

I cringed as I heard my own voice on the recording. "Hello! You've reached the Zhangs. We're not home right now, but please leave your name and number and we will call you back as soon as possible."

Click.

Nothing.

The caller didn't leave a message.

"That could've been a company calling me about a job interview," said my dad. He didn't raise his voice, but I heard the violence in it.

"They would've left a message," said my mom. My dad looked at her so hard that his face pulsed. She sat down on the couch and held a pillow against her stomach.

"Why didn't you pick up the phone?" my dad said, towering over me.

Usually when he did this, I shrank. Instinctively hunched my shoulders, hung my head, looked at the space between my feet. My position of repentance. But this time, I surprised even myself—I laughed. It wasn't a normal laugh. It was a heaving, angry announcement, an animal sound that said *I'm not afraid.* Even if I was, my rage drowned it.

There was an upward shrug at the base of my dad's neck. I had become an expert at body language by now. His fury was coming. It was too late to escape. For the first time, that excited me.

"Why didn't *you* pick up the phone?" I said, each word escalating into a blurry scream. My heart pounded in my ears. I felt like a still lake, awakened under the assault of a torrential rain.

My dad's face dropped. His porcupine hair stiffened.

"I know why," I said. I couldn't stop. Someone new inside me had emerged and taken over. "Your dumb accent."

My left cheekbone took the brunt of the smack. I staggered backward but didn't fall down. I saw a flash of horror on my dad's face. The same look that he made every time he hit me too hard.

I didn't cry. I didn't even blink. I stared him down until he took a step backward.

It was only after I went inside my room that I let myself cry. I crawled under the blanket and pulled it over my head. I held my Barbie doll against my chest. I combed her hair with my fingers. Then I yanked on it. That was more comforting.

I hated my dad. I wished that he were dead. I thought about flinging him off a bridge with a construction crane, his body dropping into the ocean. Cutting him into tiny pieces and hiding them in different garbage cans in the neighborhood. Filling his coffee with a whole bottle of laxatives. Death on the toilet. That would be fitting. The more that I thought about those scenarios, the less I cried. The less I cried, the closer I was to dreaming. As my lids grew heavier, I thought of this: I was dangerous too.

Outside the building, my mother repeated her request. "So, you'll apologize for what happened last night?"

I didn't say anything. Instead, I pressed two fingers against my cheek. I liked to do this. The moments of pressure were painful, but it felt so good when I stopped.

Our apartment smelled of damp. A butter knife covered with peanut butter lay in the sink. A kettle that didn't sing anymore sat on the stove top. Mismatched chairs rounded our kitchen table.

My bedroom had no window. To ward off bad spirits, I had climbed a big ladder and stuck glow-in-the-dark stars on the ceiling. The *Boy Meets World* poster went up next, fol-

lowed by the Spice Girls one. Still, the bunny-eared clock on
my nightstand was my favorite protector. Its eyes moved back
and forth, as if on watch.

In my room I was safe. Nothing bad happened to me in
here. My parents knocked on the door, but never came in
without permission. Everyone had lines they wouldn't cross.

I was halfway through my history homework when I heard
the front door open and my father's feet clomping toward my
room. My pulse quickened. I double-checked that my door
was locked.

But when my father's voice finally came, it was soft.

"Tammy," he said. "Let me in."

I glanced at the scissors in my pen holder but grabbed the
wooden ruler instead.

I heard his body slide down the door, landing on the floor
with a thud.

He wasn't trying to break in.

A breathless, urgent: "I need to speak with you."

I inhaled sharply and held the ruler behind my back.

"Just for a minute," he said.

I opened the door a crack.

He was sitting on the floor, eyes looking up at me.

His doorman uniform was ripped. A big hole near his
left shoulder. Shredding all down the front like he had been
mauled by a jungle cat. Only two buttons were left dangling
on the jacket. His white shirt, smeared with brown blood. His
face was red and round, like a lumpy tomato, except for the
bandages on his nose and lips.

I dropped the ruler and touched the gash on his cheek. It
left blood on my fingertips. The liquid had soaked through

the taped gauze. He flinched but then covered my hand with his. He closed his eyes.

He looked like he was sleeping.

He looked like a little boy.

FIVE

Tammy

Today on *Their Burning Hearts*, Carter woke up from a coma. Last week, he had thrown himself in front of a bullet that his evil twin brother had fired at Angelique.

"I thought that I had lost you," said Angelique.

"I'll always come back," he said.

She twisted her fingers through his chest hair. He stroked her curly blond hair. The tips of my ears grew hot. They were having sex. I turned my head, but kept watching out of the corner of my eye.

I liked watching Carter and Angelique kiss. Their lips moved with hunger, like they were trying to swallow each other. The kind of passion that only came with forbidden love. A tryst between bodyguard and protectee.

My parents didn't kiss each other like that. They couldn't. My mom's lips were plump with a subtle dip in the middle, but my dad's were like two wooden boards lying on top of each other—thin, flat, and hard. My parents kissed with closed mouths. A quick, mechanical compression.

I heard footsteps closing in on the living room.

I clicked the Previous button on my remote control, which I always held tightly whenever I watched the soap opera for precisely this scenario. In a blink, a talking cartoon animal appeared on the screen.

"Did you practice the piano?" said my dad.

"Yes," I said.

He lifted his chin. "Show me."

I walked over to the piano. A third-timer, a twice handed-down upright that we bought at a garage sale. The music rack needed monthly applications of hot glue to stop it from falling over, and three of its keys didn't work.

My dad taught me the piano. He had learned to play the keyboard in China.

"Press this key, then this key," he would say.

"Like this." He would show me, his index finger stiff as a plank.

Every time I missed a note, he said, "No, again."

Repetition. That was my father's philosophy on learning. It applied not only to the piano, but my studies too. Before every test, he made me write out every single word from the textbook chapter, twice. "When you write with your hand, you carve the knowledge into your brain," he had lectured me. It was tedious and made my fingers cramp, but I couldn't deny the results.

After I played Beethoven's Ecossaise without any mistakes, my father said, "Good enough. Do you have a hair tie?"

Still sitting on the piano bench, I handed him the scrunchie on my wrist and turned around to face the keys again. My father stood right behind me.

He unknotted my hair with his fingers and sectioned it into three chunks. Then the crisscrossing began. Right over center. Left over center. Over and over, pulling together more hair each time. A million tingles ran across my scalp. A million happy nerve endings. My eyes closed as my father's fingers combed through my hair—soothing my mind into emptying itself of worry.

I couldn't remember when exactly we started this tradition. My mother used to French braid my hair when I was younger, but she didn't do it very well. She would leave random bumps here, loose strands there. Sometimes the whole braid was asymmetrical. I had complained. Loudly.

One day, my dad said, "Let me try."

Both my mom and I gave him the side-eye.

"It must be easier than stringing together electrical wires," he said.

I expected his hair styling to be harsh and tight. I sat there with my eyes squeezed shut, ready to wince in pain. But the only thing that came was the feeling of little birds fluttering through my hair.

After he wove my hair into a tidy braid, with volume on top, just the way I liked it, my mother said, "How did you do that?"

"With patience," he said.

From that day on, my dad was on hair duty.

As my father tied the ends of the braid together, he said, "There. You're ready."

We were going to a party for my dad. He was famous now. "Doorman hero," the lady on TV had called him. "What it means to be a real New Yorker," said another. They flashed a picture of my father from his driver's license on the screen. Most of the newspapers didn't even bother with that. They only showed a picture of the celebrity that my father helped— Clara something. She was beautiful like Angelique, but older. Grandmother-level older. "'Immigrants are the heart and soul of this city,'" they quoted her saying.

My mother had cut clippings from the newspapers—always without Clara's face—and stuck them on our refrigerator. She went around the neighborhood picking up extra copies and sent them back to China. "Our family and friends should know," she said.

"Where's the party?" I asked my dad.

"In Clara's home," he said.

"What's Clara's house like?"

"It's not a house."

"Apartment?"

"Kind of. It's the apartment on the top floor of The Rosewood. It's a penthouse."

"Penthouse? Why do they call it that if it's not a house?"

"Enough with the questions," he finally snapped.

My mother came into the living room, holding my wool dress.

"Can I wear something—"

"No," she said. "This party is important for your dad."

I shimmied into the dress in my room. The frills itched my neck and the tight armholes cut into my skin. I swiped on my *Marked 4 Luv* lip gloss. It was the only item of makeup that my mother let me buy. I smiled in the mirror. Once with teeth showing, but it looked better with my lips closed.

My parents were wearing their nicest clothes. My father in a new shiny silver suit. My mother in a long red dress. Her hair was out of its usual bun. It flowed in waves past her shoulders. She had on red lipstick and gold earrings. She looked like a queen, except for the plate of fried dumplings in her hands.

People stared at us on the F train. Mostly men sneaking glances at my mother. That made me proud, but my father didn't notice. He was focused on clutching my arm every time someone new boarded the train.

"There's The Rosewood," my dad said, pointing across the street. My eyes followed the line of his finger, and I gasped out loud. The Rosewood was gigantic, like three hotels put together. Its ruby-red bricks bore huge glass lanterns. White curtains billowed in its windows, and ivy covered each balcony. As we entered one by one through the revolving doors, I thought, *My dad worked in a fairy-tale castle.*

The man at the lobby desk wore the same work uniform as my father. He waved to us in his Mickey Mouse gloves.

"This is my wife, Kim, and daughter, Tammy," said my dad.

"Beautiful, beautiful," said the man. He had an accent, but rougher and deeper than my father's, like he was part of the Mafia.

"We're heading up to Clara's," said my dad.

"You deserve it," said the doorman.

The elevator doors were golden. I saw a taller version of my father in its reflection.

I counted the number of floors up to the penthouse. Twenty-three, but really twenty-two. Floor thirteen was missing.

The top floor only had one door, with a gold knocker shaped like a tiger's face.

My father rang the bell.

No one came but we heard a lot of talking on the other side. "Should we just go in?" I said.

My parents looked at each other with raised eyebrows. They had no clue.

I shrugged, twisted the knob, and pushed the door open.

Out spilled the scent of shrimp and perfume. Jazz played in the background. The apartment was filled with people dressed as though we were at an outdoor barbecue: polos, shorts, summer dresses. We stood out like mutant Gobstoppers in a bag of otherwise perfect Skittles. My parents never knew the proper dress code for white people events.

A butler came over to stop us from taking off our shoes.

"For the party," my mother said, holding out the plate of Saran-wrapped dumplings.

The butler looked confused.

"I made them this morning," my mother continued. "Cut the chives from my neighbor's garden."

The butler nodded and left with the plate.

An old woman in a gold-sequined dress danced over to us. "That's Clara," my dad whispered. *That was the movie star?* In real life, she looked like an elegant clown. Her face was caked with makeup—blue eye shadow and overlined lips—and her red hair was pulled back in a slick ponytail. Her earrings— long blue feathers—flapped around her neck as she moved.

"Tony!" said Clara, throwing her arms around my dad and kissing him on the cheek. My mother's neck snapped back at her boldness until Clara did the same to her.

"This is Tammy," my dad said, pushing me forward. I curtsied. I was used to making this kind of presentation for my parents.

Clara leaned over and said, "Why, aren't you precious!"

Someone else called for her. "Make yourselves at home," she said, disappearing into the crowd.

Another butler came up to us, totaling five in the living room. They balanced plates filled with tiny hamburgers, tiny hot dogs, even tiny waves of bacon on tiny sticks.

As we walked through the apartment, my parents conferred with each other in hushed tones. To them, this was just another open house.

"That fireplace mantel looks like it was imported from Europe."

"How high do you think this ceiling is? Eleven feet?"

"Can't believe she still has carpeting though."

My eyes weren't drawn to the architecture of the house or the expensive furniture. I couldn't stop staring at the paintings. One was a Dalmatian in a hat. Another was a bunch of squiggly lines. Next to it hung a white canvas with the word *haha* written all over it in different colors, sizes, and fonts. It made me want to giggle along with it. The biggest picture was a portrait of Clara, or rather, a younger version of her. She was naked but had a fur animal wrapped around her. I squinted. I couldn't tell if the brown spot was the tip of the fox's nose or her nipple.

In the kitchen, there was a steel refrigerator, quadruple the size of our plastic white one. A butler pressed a cup against it and ice came out—*holy shit*. Next to the fridge was an overflowing garbage can. I saw my mother's dumplings balancing on top of the disposable plates and forks.

When I went to go pick them out, someone tapped me on the arm. "You're not supposed to be in here," said the butler.

I ran into the living room and finally spotted another kid. He had cute freckles. I got excited when he walked toward me, but he blew past without a glance. It wasn't me he wanted to talk to. It was the girl in the butterfly-studded T-shirt with dice hanging from her ears. *Whatever she had, I didn't.* I wanted to sink into the floor.

I was about to go find my mother when the ivory grand piano in the corner of the room caught my eye. I admired its taut golden treble and bass strings—a gleaming harp at rest on its back. Instinctively I slid onto the leather-topped seat. The party faded away.

I fiddled with the end of my braid, hesitating. This piano didn't belong to me. Wasn't mine to touch. We shouldn't even be occupying the same room. But just as I was about to turn away, I thought, this might be my only chance. Not playing it would be tragic. I spread my fingers wide and played the first measures of the Beethoven piece from this morning.

The keys felt like butter. Crisp and responsive to every touch. My fingers glided across them. I felt the exhilaration of discovery—like the first time I rode a bike without training wheels. I hadn't realized that I had access to such speed, such agility. My tempo accelerated. My fingers craved more.

"Tammy!" said my father, gritting my name through his teeth.

I buried my hands in my lap.

"Get off of there," he said.

But I didn't. I could feel my hold over the room. Everyone had their heads turned toward me. Everyone had been captivated by my playing. My father wasn't in charge of this room. I was.

Clara ran over. Instead of scolding me, she said, "No, please continue. No one's touched this thing since I swore off dating musicians!"

"You don't play?" I asked.

She cackled, "Of course not, darling. It's beautiful to look at, but I imagine it'd be a headache to learn."

Then Clara turned to my dad, grabbed his arm, and said, "We need some alone time anyways. I got an interesting call from an editor at the *New York Post*."

As she led my dad away from the piano, she looked back at me and winked.

I flexed my hands before playing the rest of the Ecossaise. My fingers galloped across the keys. Stretched effortlessly for the chords that used to feel too hard to reach. I finished the piece without a single mistake. I turned around to see if my dad saw. He and Clara were talking intensely in the corner. Even though he wasn't looking at me, I stuck my tongue out at him anyways. *Take that, buttface.*

I heard a chuckle from behind the piano's lifted lid. A tall man—basketball player tall—with a smile that made his blue eyes sparkle, came closer until he stood right at the edge of the keyboard. He reminded me of Carter from *Their Burning Hearts*. "You must be Tammy. I'm a friend of your father's. Oliver," he said.

I nodded. My mouth, too dry to speak. Suddenly, I smelled the stink of the Gouda cheese and syrup on the figs from a passing tray. The hairs on the back of my neck stood up as the server's brisk walk generated a slight breeze.

"I used to play the piano. Still do when I can," he said.

"That must be nice for you," I said, remembering a line that Angelique said to Carter when they first met.

Oliver looked confused. "What?" he said, resting his hand on the piano. His fingers were long and elegant. They could easily cover an octave and a half.

My dad came over. He looked mad again, but relaxed when he saw Oliver.

"This is the man who helped me with the cops," my father said.

"What a talented daughter you have," said Oliver.

"She is top at her classes," said my dad. "Even English," he said with emphasis, before carrying on about how I won an award at the school's invention convention and was first in my dance class to do a split. His voice got all sugary when he showed me off as his trophy. "I am very proud," he said.

Liar, I wanted to say. That wasn't how he felt about me when we were alone.

"She's excellent at the piano as well," said Oliver.

"Piano is her weakness," said my dad. "I try, but she needs a teacher to get better."

"Really? You're looking for a teacher?" said Oliver.

My dad and Oliver kept talking, which gave me time to sneak looks at Oliver's face. His skin was creamy smooth, except for two small pimples on his chin. His lips were bubble-gum pink. Only his left cheek had a dimple. The holes of his nostrils faced down, out of sight, not like my dad's, which arched upward, just asking for two chopsticks to be pushed in.

I could feel Oliver's eyes fall on me sometimes, but I was quick enough to pretend to still be looking at the piano. As if that were the thing in the room that mesmerized me.

On the subway ride home, my mom wanted me to sit on her lap. I said no. I wanted to surf. My hands were off the pole, but my mom made me put them back on.

I was reading an ad for a face wash that "banished blemishes," trying to figure out what "blemishes" were, when I heard Oliver's name.

"He offered to teach her piano."

"For free?" my mother asked.

"Yes, free."

"Why would he do that?" she asked.

"He saw something special in Tammy."

My mother sat back, pleased.

My parents kept talking in code. A little in English and the rest using Chinese words that I didn't understand.

I hopped on my mother's lap. "What's going on?" I said.

"We'll tell you later," said my mom. "You were a good girl today."

I put my head on her shoulder and closed my eyes for the rest of the ride.

SIX

Oliver

Oliver was sick to his stomach. It wasn't from the bumper-to-bumper traffic that he'd sat through on Route 27, the main road in and out of the Hamptons. Soon he'd be arriving at his parents' home to celebrate his birthday, and the sour dread was inescapable. He had planned on staying just for lunch. That was about as much as he could endure.

Pulling up to the driveway, he passed a mailbox with THE WRIGHT FAMILY stamped in gold leaf. He had to give it a second glance to make sure he wasn't at the wrong house. Even after living with that surname for the last five years, it still looked foreign to him, especially here, at a home where he had once been an Agos.

The house was a shadow of its former self. The outside had mostly stayed the same, but the interior was gutted. The two Van Goghs that used to hang in the hallway were switched out with generic oil paintings of the ocean. Pottery Barn and

Ikea replaced the Noguchi coffee tables and Eames lounge chairs. The study still had a full bookshelf, but gone were the first editions of Charles Dickens and James Joyce. His parents had replaced everything that the Feds had stripped out and then some, but the house still felt hollow.

Along with a protected trust, this Hamptons property was the only other asset that the judge had let his family keep. It had only been their summerhouse at the time, but he understood why his parents had fought to retain this place over the Los Angeles home he grew up in. They'd thought that they could shake off their past by swapping coasts. An easy, swift move, like changing their last names.

Oliver was about to ring the bell when a long-limbed woman carrying a tennis bag opened the door on her way out. He recalled seeing her flame out at Wimbledon a few years ago. She put a hand on her hip and took a good look at him. "I'm Bianca," she said, tipping the top of her cap. "You must be Oliver. Maybe I'll see you on the court with your dad next time."

It used to be flattering, if not expected, when women came on to him. But now it felt false. Irritating even. They didn't know him—his past, the truth about his family. If they did, they wouldn't even be making eye contact. He gave Bianca a smile and said, "Have a good one."

As he entered the foyer, he heard a shuffling of footsteps and a familiar voice.

"Ollie!"

A warmth spread across his chest. Only one person got this excited to see him. Their live-in nanny-turned-housekeeper, Daisy. Filipino, barely five feet tall. She rose on her tiptoes to give him a hug.

"My boy is twenty-six! All grow up now," she said. The earnest lilt of her voice always comforted him. "I still remember your number one birthday. My big bald baby." As Oliver gazed into her soft eyes, his lips quivered. He had forgotten how much he loved her.

Daisy hadn't just raised him as if he were her own. She was the best person Oliver knew. Even after sending most of her salary back to her family in the Philippines, she still donated to an orphanage, volunteered at the church's soup kitchen, and spearheaded the annual Christmas toy drive. She tried to teach him that giving was a joy in itself. "Even your time is a gift," she would say. Daisy didn't have a bad bone in her body, which was exactly why his mother had hired her and also why she sometimes resented her.

"Come, come," Daisy said, holding on to his arm as they walked into the kitchen. He'd caught her in the middle of a meal prep. Bubbling pans sprayed thick oil droplets onto the stove top. Whipping bowls and spatulas and food processors crowded the counter. A few finished dishes sat on the kitchen island. Oliver eyed a plate that contained spongy-looking cubes in brown marinade. Strange. His mother preferred to eat "clean" foods, meaning steamed, no dressing, sauce on the side.

"What are you making, Daisy?" he said.

"It—" she began, but stopped short when his mother arrived in the kitchen.

"I told her to make you something special," said Marlene, giving him a kiss on the cheek. Daisy shrank a little as his mother inspected the dishes on the counter. Her nose twitched as she hovered over them, making Oliver want to apologize for her.

"How long before it's ready, Daisy?" she asked.

"Soon, Miss Marlene."

"Let's go get your dad, then, Oliver. He's outside."

"No, I'd rather stay here—"

"It's okay," said Daisy, not meeting his eyes. "It's okay."

"Phillip!" said Marlene from the patio. "Oliver's here!"

On the tennis court across the pool, Oliver's dad yelled, "One sec! I'm stretching!"

"I would show you the hive," said his mother, pointing at a fenced-off area in the corner of the yard, "but the bees are going through an adjustment period."

"Is everything okay?" said Oliver. Backyard beekeeping was his mother's latest obsession. Before that, it had been pottery throwing, breadmaking, and watercolor painting. Now there was a neglected kiln in the basement, a bread machine at the back of a bottom cabinet, and paint streaks on the natural stone tiles of the patio.

His mother hadn't always been this way. In Los Angeles, she used to constantly be out of the house, rubbing shoulders with the wives of the city's elite. She had a calendar packed with dinners in Beverly Hills. She hosted monthly book clubs and sipped champagne at trunk shows. But when his grandfather's scandal came to light, she retreated into herself, into new hobbies, anything to keep her mind off of reality.

"I had to kill the queen bee a few days ago," she said.

"Kill her?"

"The hive was getting aggressive."

"What does that mean?" he asked.

"They kept swarming me the second I went by in a suit. That shouldn't happen, you know. The expert who helps me tend them told me I only had two options. Kill the entire hive, or replace the queen."

"Not even a queen's safe, huh?" said Oliver.

Just then, his father walked over to the patio. Phillip lifted up his shirt to wipe his face, exposing his taut abs. He looked better in his fifties than men half his age. His wiry brown hair had advanced into a distinguished gray and he'd shed his softness, having traded benders with his poker buddies for lessons with a tennis pro in a skirt.

"I'm beat," he said. "Don't know the last time I got in such a good workout."

"Poor you, such a tough life. Regards to Bianca," said Marlene.

"Remind me—how much did we just fork over to your bee guy?" said Phillip.

"He's an apiologist," she said.

"So this new queen bee," said Oliver, "she's going to save the hive?"

"Trevor said it's possible," said his mother.

"Well, if Trevor says," said his dad.

His mother ignored him. "The queen can affect the mood of the workers. She'll calm them down."

"What if she doesn't?" Oliver asked.

"She'll repopulate the hive with less aggressive bees."

"You think it works like that?" said his father. "That aggression in bees is hereditary? Didn't realize they were such complicated creatures."

"I guess we'll see," said his mother.

"I'm on the edge of my seat," said his father.

Then Daisy called from the kitchen. "Lunch is almost

ready!" Through the sliding glass door, Oliver could see that she was filling up a tray with silverware and plates.

The three of them went inside to wash up as Daisy began to set the table.

They had lunch in the dining room. Daisy had laid out the dishes before going back into the kitchen to eat her portion. The dish that he had spotted before turned out to be portobellos in gravy. A close-enough mimicry of steak in brown butter sauce. There was also a spaghetti Bolognese with lentils and walnuts, a cream-free butternut squash soup, and a side of miso-glazed eggplant.

"So you're vegan now?" asked Oliver.

"I've always been passionate about animal welfare!" said his mother.

"I don't think honey is vegan."

"It's on the line," she said. "It's better to be an imperfect vegan than not to try at all."

His dad nodded along. "This animal stuff. It's a hot topic in the consulting business. Every client is asking—should I donate money to the Humane Society or ASPCA? I tell them to skip PETA. Nude modeling is going to backfire eventually." *Consulting.* His father liked to throw that word around like it meant something. Like it was a real job and not the sentence or two that he dropped in a conversation with an old friend during golf.

"What pool of animal rights expertise do you draw from for your *consulting*, Dad?"

Phillip didn't miss a beat. "The news. Talking to people. Knowledge is all around."

"Enlightening."

"How's your new girlfriend?" asked his mother. "I was so hoping you'd bring her today."

"Janna? No, not this time," said Oliver.

"Not even to celebrate your birthday?"

"She's on a long shift at the hospital."

"Bring her around next time," said his father. "We'd love to meet her."

"We wouldn't say anything," said his mother.

Oliver nodded, taking a long drink of Perrier.

"Your grandfather sends his love, by the way."

"Return to sender," said Oliver. "I can't believe you two still visit him." His parents went to Turpin Creek Correctional Facility every Sunday, like clockwork.

"He's my father," said Phillip.

Oliver took a small bite of the mushroom. "Not bad," he said. "Daisy did a good job on these."

"He's going to apply for compassionate release," said his father.

"On what grounds?" The courts would never free his grandfather. The man had embezzled millions of dollars from his own charity.

"He has a history of Alzheimer's in his family," said his father.

"Really? Who?"

"One of his uncles. Judges are more lenient on this disease. Those people would be too vulnerable in jail. Hard to give them the proper care."

"He never stops scheming, does he?" Oliver sighed.

"You could do it," said his father.

"Do what?"

"Sponsor his compassionate release."

"Me?" said Oliver.

"You have a law degree from Harvard, if I'm not mistaken."

"The press would love that," said his mother. "A grandson fighting for his grandfather."

"No way," said Oliver. "Have some other lawyer do it."

"I know that your grandfather did something bad, but it's time for forgiveness." She placed her hand over his. "You guys used to be so close."

Oliver's knife blade made a screeching sound as he cut into a piece of eggplant. That last part hit home. His grandfather had given him a golden childhood. They used to catch fireflies when Oliver was little, face off in hours-long Scrabble games in middle school, wander off on side adventures—just the two of them—on family vacations.

On their last family trip before the scandal broke, they had been jet-lagged, wandering the hills of St. Bart's before dawn. His grandfather waxed on about his future, his potential—Harvard, public service awards, SEC commissioner, foreign ambassador, senator, and beyond.

"What if I can't do it?" Oliver had said. "What if I can't be as successful—or as good—as you?"

"You have me," said his grandfather, grabbing his shoulders. "If nothing goes right, you come to me. Remember that."

In that moment, Oliver felt invincible.

"The world will soon be yours," his grandfather added. "I promise."

Two months later, he was in handcuffs.

"I can't," said Oliver. "What he did was horrible—he deserves what he got."

His dad lowered his voice. "You don't get to talk about my father like that. He did it for us." His eyes narrowed as he added, "He's even taking care of us now. Who's footing the bill for your precious co-op in The Rosewood?"

Oliver flinched. The trust that the judge carved out for his family was originally set up by his grandfather. They got to keep it because the prosecutor hadn't been able to prove that it was funded by any illegal dealings. The trust mostly paid for his parents' lifestyle, but it also covered Oliver's mortgage and maintenance fee at The Rosewood. But other than that, unlike his parents, Oliver made it a point not to use what he considered gray money. He didn't completely depend on his grandfather like they did. He became a lawyer, made his own money, and paid for all his food, vacations, and dates with his own bank account.

"You think on it," said his father, raising his voice.

"Nah, I'm good," said Oliver.

His father was about to say more when his mother put her hand up. "Enough," she said. "Oliver doesn't need a lecture. He knows what matters here."

"Yeah, justice," said Oliver.

His mother gave him a sharp look. "Family," she said.

They turned back to their plates, scraping the china with their forks.

"I have to head back to the city soon," said Oliver.

"Plans with Janna?" asked his dad.

"I'm giving piano lessons to my doorman's daughter."

"You're a teacher now?"

"I'm a musical *consultant*."

His father's face twisted. "What are you charging?"

"Nothing," said Oliver. "I'm giving my time."

"For free? I don't get it."

"Stop it, Phillip," said his mother. "Be supportive. I think it's a very nice thing for Oliver to do. He's played piano ever since he was five. He'll probably be a great teacher."

His father gave him a hard stare. "Yeah, you'll be a great teacher."

Oliver returned to The Rosewood a few minutes before the scheduled lesson. He was still dusting off the piano and straightening out the sofa pillows when the doorbell rang at exactly seven o'clock.

Tammy stood on the threshold, clutching a thick copy of Chopin's Études. She gave him a wave and said a soft "hi." He noticed how thin and long her fingers were, how delicate, fragile. He wanted to cover them with his hands to protect them.

She handed him a plastic bag and said, "Tangyuan."

"I've been meaning to try these," he said, placing them on the counter.

"They belong in the freezer," she said with a mature smirk.

Did she just see through his white lie? No, maybe she was trying to be helpful. Either way, she seemed precocious as she settled on the piano bench, carefully laying her sheet music on the rack and testing out the pedals. Satisfied at the setup, she began playing. Her fingers hit all the right notes, but the sound was dead and stiff. Her wrists were flat. Wooden.

"Who was your last teacher?" he asked, thinking about his strict instructors from childhood—all Juilliard graduates.

"It's only been my dad," she said.

Right, thought Oliver, remembering that Tony had mentioned something about that. It made sense. Doormen wouldn't have enough money to hire teachers or tutors for their children. Poor parents had to do everything and be everything for their kids. Oliver was impressed at that level of dedication, jealous even.

"Try it like this," he said, putting his hand under her wrist and propping it upward to make an arching bridge. She flinched and he immediately stopped touching her. He hadn't thought that she might take it the wrong way.

"Sorry," he mumbled. "I was trying to get your wrist to do this," he said, as he held out his own, making it go limp and hang over the keys.

She imitated him. "This feels weird."

He said to think of her hands as a puppet master and the piano keys as the marionettes. "It's less about pushing the keys down and more about pulling them up."

She tried again. Her first few measures sounded weak and plunky. She stopped, clearly frustrated, but then returned her fingers to the keys. After more rounds of the same plodding notes, she folded her hands in her lap.

"I hate Chopin," she said.

"Then let's play something else," said Oliver.

Tammy raised her eyebrows. "Really?"

"Let's see," said Oliver, flipping through his own collection of music. "We have some Beethoven and Bach."

Tammy pursed her lips.

"We've also got some Cher, Phil Collins, Celine Dion," he said.

"Celine Dion!" she piped.

He placed the sheet music for "It's All Coming Back to Me Now" on the piano rack. He was about to mention that it was written in C major, but she'd already started playing.

She stumbled through the first page, and then went over it, again and again. On the tenth or eleventh try, the sound turned, losing its brittle quality. Her small body rocked, moving closer and farther away from the piano to match the new rhythm that she found in her hands. Her lips mouthed the lyrics. At one point, he heard her whisper, "If I kiss you like this."

Oliver couldn't take his eyes off of her. It was as if his cold face had suddenly been bathed in warm sunlight. Something shifted inside him that he didn't know how to put into words. The way that Tammy lost herself in the music was the first thing that had moved him in years.

At the end of the song, her cheeks pinkened. "You're a great teacher," she said, her legs swinging above the pedals. *A great teacher.* The same words that his parents had said, but in her mouth, they felt different—real, genuine. She was grateful. She needed him, maybe even liked him. *She wasn't them.*

SEVEN

Tony

Today's not the day a train runs me over, thought Tony. A lanky Latino teen wearing a chain necklace and baggy jeans had just walked onto the subway platform. It wasn't only that the teenager claimed a spot too close to Tony. It was that the spot was behind him.

Tony froze in place, not wanting to bring attention to himself. Eyes bulging, he tried to stretch his peripheral vision. Failing that, he searched for a reflective surface to track the teenager's movements. Finally, he resorted to discreetly shuffling to the side so that he was closer to one of the metal beams near the stairs. If the teen shoved him, at least he'd have something to grab hold of. He heard on the morning news that there had been a recent string of subway pushings, three of which proved fatal.

Holding his breath, Tony stood next to the beam, praying that the 7 train would arrive soon. He half wished that it would shuttle him back to China.

In moments like this, he held tight to the memory of his first day in America. He'd never forget the squeak his sneakers made six years ago against the white glossy floors of John F. Kennedy airport. Beyond his excitement of landing in *Mei Guo*, he urgently needed to find a bathroom. Squatting over a hole was the last thing that his quad muscles wanted to do, but the twenty-hour journey did no favors for his weak digestive system. As he entered the men's room, he frantically searched his pockets for napkins. He didn't find anything except for his passport and a few cough drops.

He said to the man washing his hands at the sink, "Hello, sir, you have paper?" He couldn't remember the term for the specific kind of paper he was asking for.

The man gave him a weird look. "You mean toilet paper?" he said.

"Yes, yes," said Tony, making a mental note to write down the two words later.

"It's in the stalls," said the man.

"Stalls?" said Tony.

The man pointed at the row of metal partitions next to the urinals. Unlike the stalls in China, these had doors. Inside were aboveground toilets that he could sit on. Next to the toilets were full rolls of toilet paper. Public restrooms in China never supplied toilet paper because people would steal it. As he inhaled a gentle scent of lemon, he chuckled and released the most satisfying dump of his life. *This was Mei Guo*.

The 7 train whooshed onto the platform. Tony made sure to enter a different compartment than the one the Latino chose. He sat at the edge of his seat, trying not to touch anything.

He couldn't understand how New Yorkers had such a decrepit underground system. Trains in Beijing were pristine, fast, and completely safe. The ones in New York were unreliable—never on time and constantly stopping during transit. He couldn't even touch the handrails for fear of catching a disease. If it weren't for his tired legs, he wouldn't sit on the seats at all. Twice, he had seen a man taking a piss on them.

Even worse, the subway was a criminal's dream. Tony was mindful of pickpockets. He avoided riding too early in the morning or too late at night to avoid robbers. Then there were the crazies, the drug addicts, the homeless. Just last month, a woman with stringy black hair threatened to knife him if he didn't give up his seat even though half the train was empty. Naturally, he forbade Kim or Tammy from taking the subway without him.

An hour later, he was walking up the steep stairs in a cramped building in SoHo, wondering what he had gotten himself into. A few weeks ago at Clara's party, she'd told him that the *New York Post* wanted to do a cover story on them. "It's not just about my career, Tony. You did good. People should see," she had said. When he tried to say no, she pulled on his lapels with a genuine sense of purpose. "Do it for the other immigrants, then," she said.

"The immigrants?" he asked.

Her eyes softened. "After all, aren't we all immigrants?"

Kim hadn't been fully on board with the idea. "What if they ask you a question and you say something wrong?" she'd said. "What if you do something that Clara doesn't like and you're fired from The Rosewood?" She was still posing worrisome scenarios when Tammy said that it would be "really cool" if he did it. She sounded proud of him.

When Tony opened the door to the *New York Post* photo shoot, he quickly pressed his back against the closest wall. The sun-drenched loft felt like a war zone. Dozens of people dressed head-to-toe in black buzzed around frantically. Some held clipboards, barking orders.

"Get another lens."

"Tape this down."

One woman in a high ponytail held up a piece of circular metal like a grenade and said, "Found the speed ring!"

Even with their manic pace, they gracefully pranced through the maze of cables and equipment that threaded the floor like trip wire.

He didn't belong here. He couldn't keep up with these people. None of them bothered to look at him, and he wouldn't know how to talk to anyone if they did. He was eyeing the exit—it would be fine if he left, they probably preferred Clara on the cover alone—when a camera flashed a blinding light in his direction. As he brought his hands up to shield his eyes, someone grabbed his arm and pulled him close.

"There you are, darling," said Clara.

By instinct, Tony stepped away from her. He was still getting used to the American embrace. In China, the general rule was that physical touch was improper, especially with the opposite sex. A hug was out of the question. He didn't shake hands with women, much less have full body contact. He didn't even hug Kim in public.

Clara took his face in her hands and said, "You're not getting enough sleep, Tony."

This time, Tony relaxed to her touch. Her hands were so warm and soft. There was something youthful about her unpredictability, so thrilling about the way that she unapologetically grabbed at life—and him—with her bare hands. He had never met a woman like Clara before.

"We gotta get you straight to makeup and then changed into your cover outfit," she said.

"Cover outfit?" he said.

"I lobbied for a Tom Ford suit, but then they reminded me—this ain't *Vogue*."

Tony didn't understand half of what she said, but obediently followed her to the makeup station in the corner of the room. There, the makeup artist painted so much beige onto his face that it looked flatter than usual. She brushed some pink stuff on his cheeks and lightly swiped lipstick on him before he could pull away. Examining his eyes, she muttered, "How can we make these look bigger?"

The makeup artist took out a pair of thin scissors.

"What are you—" said Tony.

"Relax," she said, pushing him back into the chair. "Just trimming your eyebrows." After a few snips, she produced a small clamp, curled his eyelashes, then put something gooey on top. "That's all I can do." She sighed. "When you take the pictures, try to open your eyes wider."

Tony was busy trying out different expressions in the mirror with his new face when a man stomped over to him. "You must be Tongheng Zhang," he said, flicking his pen against his clipboard with self-importance.

The way this man said his name reminded him of all the times that interviewers, immigration officials, and some of Tammy's teachers attached a sneer to each syllable, as if to suggest these sounds didn't belong in America, and neither did he.

Before he could respond, Clara walked in front of him and said, "Tongheng is his Chinese name, but you can call him

Tony. He's the reason we're all here today." Tony realized everyone was staring at him, and his legs began to tremble. He couldn't remember the last time he was the center of attention. In China, sure—at parties and academic conferences—but never in America. In this country, he made it a point to be invisible. Immigrants weren't supposed to bother the police. Doormen weren't supposed to intrude. People with Chinese accents weren't supposed to talk too much. For Tony, invisibility was survival.

"Did you know Tongheng was my real name before now?" he whispered to Clara.

"I'm on the board of The Rosewood. Who do you think was the first approval vote on your job application four years ago?" She brushed her hand across his chest, sending an electric tickle to his brain. He grinned back his *thank you*.

After the photo shoot and a long subway ride, Tony was walking the last block home. He could feel his heart rate slow down. He was about to take his keys out of his pocket when he heard his neighbor from across the street, Biyu, call out, "Afternoon!" Once rosy-cheeked and happily plump, she now swam in her frilly, sleeveless blouse. The armholes were too large, exposing her lacy blue bra. She was on all fours, weeding her garden, dirt all over her hands. Sweat dripped down her face under the strong sun. Her skin was shades darker than when he last saw her.

He felt sorry for her, almost disgusted at her predicament. Women shouldn't have to do outdoor work. That wasn't where they belonged. His lips curled upward in revulsion at the thought of her next lover—how he would chafe against her calloused palms, taste the soil wedged underneath her nails.

Her next lover would own a broken woman. If a next lover ever came.

"Is Biyu still out there gardening? I saw her when I left for groceries and when I came back," said Kim as he walked into the kitchen. She was clutching a rolling pin, her hands covered in flour. She was in the middle of making noodles.

"Yes," said Tony.

"Did you talk to her?"

"She said hello first."

"I wonder if she's posting outside for a reason," said Kim, without blinking. She was in one of her moods.

Tony quickly added, "She looked horrible. *Tai shou le*—too skinny. *Ta bian hei le*—she turned black. Her lips aren't even pink anymore."

"What were you doing looking at her lips?"

Tony knew better than to respond. He felt like he was back at the photo shoot again. He hadn't been sure how to move, so he decided that he wouldn't. Clara had floated around him, leaning on his shoulder, posing against his back, eventually sitting on a stool. He just stood there like a streetlamp. "Chin up, chin up, chin up," the photographer kept saying. He got the sense that even the photographer didn't know what he wanted from him.

"I hope she'll move soon," said Kim, getting back to rolling out the dough. "Far away. Divorce is contagious."

Ever since Biyu and her husband, Ming, moved across the street two years ago, Kim had Biyu over for tea on the weekends. Tony had heard their frequent giggles from his room. He had wondered if they were talking about him. He used to go to the hardware store with Ming, swapping tips on how to fix a window or wallpaper a room. Sometimes, they would smoke secret cigarettes together.

That all stopped when Biyu came over after dinner one night and told Kim that she was getting a divorce. Tony was annoyed at the news. It meant the end of the two couples' convenient friendship. "She said that they both agreed to separate, but we know that Ming is leaving her," Kim had said to Tony. He nodded. The man always left the woman. "It's her fault," said Kim. He couldn't tell what she was thinking. Was she secretly happy that Biyu's life—which included a house with a yard—wasn't actually better than hers? Or was she scared that the same thing could happen to her? "It'll be okay," he'd said, rubbing her elbow. It wasn't lost on him that, for the next week, Kim would initiate sex every night.

Kim put down her rolling pin and grabbed a cleaver. She cut the dough into strips, sliding the knife so hard across the wooden board that it made snapping sounds.

"How was the photo shoot?" she said.

"Nothing bad happened," he said.

"Sit down. I'm almost done here."

Tony couldn't take his eyes off his wife as he slumped into a chair. Kim didn't look much older than when they had first met, and even without makeup, she looked more beautiful than everyone at the photo shoot. She had a small face with soft lines—a button nose, curved chin, and rounded cheekbones. He smiled at the serious way her eyes narrowed as she carefully cut the noodles into uniform pieces. His wife wasn't only beautiful. She was exacting and skilled. They didn't talk until she had finished and stored the noodles in an airtight container. "I'll cook them after Tammy comes home," she said.

It was only 5:00 p.m. They still had one more hour before

he had to pick up Tammy from Kumon and drive her to Oliver's for a piano lesson. It was only her third session, but Tony had already noticed a change in his daughter. She no longer needed his prodding to practice at home. The music sounded better than before, though he didn't recognize any of the songs. He even caught her smiling sometimes as she played.

"Come on," said Kim, taking off her apron. Tony followed her into the bathroom. She ran the tap until the water was warm. She brought her hands to his face and washed away his makeup. "They put mascara on you?" she giggled, as she wiped his lashes with a cloth and scrubbed off the lipstick. Finally, she patted his skin dry. "There," she said, "there's my Tongheng."

Without breaking eye contact, he picked her up and brought her to their bedroom. He pressed his lips against hers until they parted and let in his tongue. Even when he moved lower to kiss her clavicle, her breasts, her belly, he would always come up and meet her eyes again. Over the years, they had developed a natural rhythm, one forged by trust. And within their shared space, they could explore, transgress the boundaries of their structured lives, get messy. Be fully themselves.

Legs straddling both sides of her, Tony could feel her body pulsate. Her back arched toward him with a light moan. Her eyes darkened. She was ready for him. As he put her ring finger in his mouth, he sighed as he tasted the flour under her fingernails.

EIGHT

Tammy

2014

"I'm going to suffocate in this."

Vince tugged at the sleeves of his Loro Piana blazer. He was fighting off a tantrum, the same one that surfaced every time we visited the Briarcliff Country Club with his family. The cap-toe oxfords pinched his feet. The tucked-in shirts bunched around his stomach. He hadn't taken well to the club's restrictions on his behavior either. No swearing, soliciting business, or taking pictures. "We aren't even allowed to put drinks on the pool table. Where else am I supposed to put my glass during a game?" he would complain.

I smoothed out my dress—Rebecca Taylor, cocktail-length, floral silk—and clicked the heels of my nude pumps. Unlike Vince, I enjoyed dressing up for the occasion. More than that, I liked that Vince had to step it up with the collared shirts and turtlenecks. He looked so professorial. A handsome thinker. Out of habit, I reached for the phone in my purse to check for emails, but relaxed when I remembered Briarcliff's no screens policy. A classy excuse to get away from the constant barrage of messages from the law firm. Just another convention that belonged to a class I didn't inherit, but graduated into.

A server hovered over me and pointed at the cups on his tray. I knew now to say, "Coffee, no cream, please." He smiled and placed a filled cup and a chocolate-dipped madeleine in front of me.

My first few lunches at the club weren't so graceful. I didn't even understand how to order off the menu. I had pointed at the different dishes and asked Vince where the prices were.

"You just pick one from each category," he had said.

"So I pick four dishes?" I asked.

He nodded. "They're all included in the membership fee that my parents pay every year."

"I'll just pick two," I said. "I'm not that hungry." I had never ordered more than one entrée and a dessert at a restaurant before.

Vince sighed and said, "People will think that you have an eating disorder or you're ungrateful or something."

I decided on the plain vegetables and dip for my appetizer. "Crudites," I told the server, pronouncing it exactly how it was spelled. He looked confused.

Vince jumped in and covered for me. "She meant *cru-deh-tay*. She knows that it's French—she's just messing with you."

The madeleine tasted like a sugared cotton ball. Others at the table seemed to be enjoying it though. I followed their lead and dunked it into my coffee. It tasted like a bitter sponge. Maybe my palate hadn't blossomed yet. Vince tapped my leg and said, "Are you done? I want to go say hi to my Aunt Cindy."

The dining room's high ceilings were adorned with gold accents and wooden carvings. Silvery curtains with tassels framed the windows. Amber-hued landscape paintings hung against the opaline walls. I had wanted to closely examine them every time I visited the club and learn the names of the artists, but I could hear my mother's scolding refrain in my head. *Don't look around too much. Pretend it's nothing new for you.*

Once we reached Aunt Cindy, she greeted us with a hug wide enough to envelop both of us. We made frowny faces at each other when we talked about her mini Labradoodle, who was recovering from a broken leg. Then Vince and I moved on to Uncle Kevin, who had just made an investment in a new golf simulation start-up. He raised his eyebrows when I asked whether he had stipulated dilution protections in his term sheet. I could tell that Vince's energy was waning when his cousins, who were applying to law school, pestered him for the contact info of the tutor he used for the LSATs. I stepped in with, "You guys are smart enough to get into Yale without one." That slapped a sheepish grin onto each of their eager faces. I felt high on adrenaline. I was hitting particularly well today. Every laugh, every smile was another point scored.

When Vince huddled with his Aunt Liesel in the corner— no doubt discussing her son, who had OCD and only ate white foods—I went to take a breather in the bathroom. These events were a marathon, not a sprint.

I had hoped for an empty Ladies' Powder Room, but almost ran into a woman as I rushed through the door. I'd forgotten that the Briarcliff bathrooms had attendants. Flustered, and in an effort to regain my composure, I took a handkerchief from the basket swinging under her arm. Her polite face broke for a second, and then she said, "Sure."

Fuck. I was supposed to take the handkerchief *after* I used the bathroom and washed my hands. I wetted it in the sink and patted it against my forehead, trying to play it as if I had meant to cool myself off all along. I stole a peek at her in the mirror. She had pulled out a book. Relieved that I hadn't held her interest, I went into the farthest stall.

I put down the toilet lid and engaged in an illicit activity: cell phone usage. I scrolled through my Steinway & Appleton emails—the last-minute changes to disclosure schedules, the latest drop of documents into the data room that required diligencing—and calculated the hours I'd have to bill tonight and tomorrow. Saturday and Sunday. I had only been working at Steinway & Appleton for a year, though it felt like three. Oliver called it baptism by fire. My parents hailed it as a lesson in eating bitterness—success required sacrifice. Vince wanted me to leave. After a double all-nighter, he warned, "You keep going like this, you're going to get an ulcer."

I had just noticed that a partner placed my name ahead of a second-year associate's in the cc field of an email—was it a mistake or his subtle way of praising my work?—when a text message took up the screen. It was from my father: Hi. **Being deeply loved by someone gives you strength, while loving someone deeply gives you courage.** (that's Lao Tzu)

He had recently moved on from English self-help books—most of which were recommended by his coworker—to Chinese philosophy. For the last five years, he had been sending me corny quotes. The first twenty had been all different iterations of the *life is too short* mantra. Still, I appreciated that he was trying. Evolving. Somehow, these books and quotes persuaded him to rein in his temper. He hadn't lashed out at me since high school.

Of course, Vince knew nothing about my father's earlier outbursts. If he did, he would have a different opinion of him. Even worse, he would see me as a victim. Given his limited knowledge, Vince was actively supportive of my father's "commitment to vulnerability and self-realization work." He even gifted him a Brené Brown book last year. When I got irritated at receiving random quotes from my father, Vince would remind me that those phrases gave him the vocabulary to express his love in a way that he hadn't been taught in China. There was real truth in that, something I'd never considered.

The bathroom door opened and I heard a group of ladies come in. "There's only three stalls?" one said.

Break was over. My shift was starting. After washing my hands, I passed the attendant again. This time, I held out the inside of my wrist for a spray of perfume and took a mint.

Vince was alone in the great hall, one elbow on the marble mantelpiece, chewing his fingernails. When he saw me, he pulled me in for a quick kiss.

"Firm still standing?" he said with a wink.

"It's less stressful if I know what I'm facing later."

He took my hand in his and stroked it with his thumb. "What *we're* facing. I'll stay up with you. Get a head start on next week's voter suppression briefs."

"You're the best," I said.

I had met Vince during our freshman year at Harvard. I hadn't been particularly interested when he came up to me in our Rise and Fall of the Third Reich class, until he said, "Someone said I had to meet you." That someone was Oliver. *My Oliver.* The glow from Vince's shiny, pre-vetted halo was dazzling.

"What'd Oliver tell you about me?" I asked.

"He said that you were perfect."

I wasn't perfect, but Vince was. A Greenwich kid but you would never know it. He biked around Cambridge, pronounced *croissant* with a hard *t* even though he was fluent in French, and lived on the half-off-after-six ready-made meals at the grocery store. I didn't know he came from money until months later, when I met his family. "My parents are rich, but I'm just me," he had said after our twelve-course meal with them at Per Se. Generations of Van Fleets went to Stanford Law School, but he gave that up to join me at Harvard's. His father wanted him to go down the law firm path like I did, but Vince insisted on working at the ACLU. Holding hands with Vince felt like donning a shield. Everyone—including my parents—loved him. Respected and admired him. He was the validation of my own worth. A signal to others that *I must be good because someone extraordinary loves me.*

"Vince! Tammy!" His mother waved us over to the club's lounge. In a leather armchair next to a lamp with a pleated silk shade, she detailed the next family trip: Iceland, complete with a helicopter ride to see the northern lights. Before I dated Vince, the only places that I had vacationed with my family were the Jersey Shore and Washington, DC. Now it was shopping on the Champs-Élysées, New Year's fireworks outside the Sydney Opera House, and safaris in the Serengeti.

"We requested an office space at the hotel," his mother said to me. "In case you have to work. I know how it stresses you out sometimes." She gave me a small smile. I looked away, tears at the corners of my eyes. I had another family.

★ ★ ★

Later that night, after five hours of reviewing supply agreement contracts, I brushed my teeth and slid into bed beside Vince.

"Did you have a good time at the club?" he asked.

"Yes," I said, already feeling a heaviness in my eyelids.

"Peak and pit?" This was Vince's daily question. A tradition he wanted to pass on to our children, he had said. The rote quality of it annoyed me, but I played along. Vince would remember my highs, even simple ones like the mac and cheese at the Whole Foods hot bar, and made sure to add more of that into our lives. And he would try to fix any lows that I announced. He had spent hours last month researching fermented foods to help with my lingering IBS. His thoughtfulness papered over his predictability.

"My peak was hearing about the Iceland trip and my pit was when your Uncle Robbie asked me where my parents were from," I said.

"What do you mean?"

"I've always wanted to see the auroras. You know, when I was little, I dreamed that—"

"Wait—what's wrong with my Uncle Robbie?"

Vince had been there. It had happened during appetizers. It was my first time meeting his Uncle Robbie. He overdid the self-tan on his meaty face and kept rotating the chunky ring on his finger—Choate Rosemary Hall, class of 1975. He shoved two lobster puffs into his mouth, but side-eyed the edamame salad.

"You like these beans or peas or whatever they are?" he asked me.

"Yeah," I said, "but I usually only have them at a sushi place."

"Is that where your parents are from? Japan?" he said.

"My parents live in New York."

"Scarsdale," said Vince. "Right next to Yorktown. Practically your neighbor, Uncle Robbie."

The old man didn't look convinced. "What was wrong with the old stuff they used to serve? When did everyone become too good for deviled eggs and mini burgers?"

Vince sat up on the bed. "Come on, Tammy. He didn't mean anything by it."

"Sure," I said, closing my eyes. I had come to bed to sleep, not fight.

"He was just curious. He wanted to get to know you."

Now I sat up too. "Then why didn't you say that my parents are from China? That I'm from China? Why'd you say Scarsdale if you thought he was just being 'curious'?"

"I was taking your lead. I could tell you were uncomfortable."

"I don't need backup," I said.

"Maybe I would understand why you're being so sensitive if you told me more about your childhood."

"You're bringing this up now? I'm freaking exhausted," I said. But I knew he was right. To Vince, I was Tammy from Scarsdale. Harvard Tammy. Lawyer Tammy. I had been those versions of myself for so long that I sometimes forgot that I had ever been lived-in-a-basement-in-Flushing Tammy. Or even further back: foreign-born Tianfei. The only people who knew those prior versions of me were my parents and Oliver, and I saw no need for that to change.

Vince kissed me on the shoulder. "Why don't we do a food tour of Flushing next weekend?"

"Why? It's so dirty there."

"Because it's part of you."

"Just because I lived there doesn't mean it's 'part of me.' You don't even know me."

Vince's face fell. His big eyes watered and drooped at the sides. I felt like I had just smacked a puppy on the nose. "Tammy," he said, slowly, as though he was mustering up the courage to say something that he had been holding back for a while, "I love you. I want a life together, but I don't know how to get you to let your walls down. I need you to let me in."

"I want to," I said, staring at my hands. I wanted to so badly, but how could I share something with him that I hadn't quite figured out for myself? A history that I often blacked out. How could I tell him that my mother named me after a skinny blonde woman who won a car on *The Price Is Right*? Or that when my teacher let it slip that my legal name was Tianfei—which wasn't half as bad as Bong Mee or Wang— my classmates made slanty eyes and said, "*Ni hao*, my name is Tofu." Or that my father, for the gentle soul he was now, used to hit me across the face?

I didn't even realize that I was crying until Vince held me and said, "Shh, it'll be okay. We're going to be okay."

I kissed him, softly at first, and then more vigorously. "I love you," I said, pulling his shirt off.

"I love you more," he said, slipping his hand in my underwear. I could barely feel anything.

I ground against him and bit his ear, trying to signal that I wanted it rougher.

But he didn't get it. He never got it.

Losing my patience, I pushed him back on the bed and grabbed his cock. It was already hard. I climbed on top and slid him into me. He held on to my breasts with both hands.

A few minutes later, he was telling me to go slower. "Baby, I'm going to come," he said. I only moved my hips faster, hoping for a release or at least to get this over with. After he came, his eyes searched for mine. I clenched the walls of my vagina to pretend that I did too.

NINE

Oliver

1999

Oliver was in his office when his phone rang. It was the immigration law firm.

"She won't fit into any of the loopholes," they said.

"Nothing else you can do?" he asked.

"Sorry."

"But her visa expires next month."

"We know."

"Alright," he said and hung up the phone.

He had tried his best. He had hoped to keep her in the country. He even called the senator he'd met during a golf round-robin last year.

He punched in Daisy's number. "I'm so sorry," he practiced. The contrition in his voice sounded ugly. Almost feigned. Was it? Did he actually care that she had to leave for the Philippines? Startled by the thought, he hung up before the first ring.

Daisy was his earliest memory. He had been around three or four when he learned how to open the freezer door. Within minutes, he ate five fudge Popsicles under the kitchen table. Daisy dragged him out by his feet and scolded him, half laughing at the chocolate on his chin. Then his mother came home, toting a rolled-up yoga mat. He remembered backing away from the door. A cold burn hitting the top of his head—a mix of fear and brain freeze. Daisy met his eyes. She wiped his mouth with her shirt, stuffed the plastic wrappers down her bra, and went to wash the dishes at the sink. His mother hadn't noticed anything—she kissed him on the cheek and told him that he smelled good. *"Salamat,"* he whispered to Daisy. *Thank you.*

When he had a tennis match, Daisy was always in the stands with containers of brownies and cubed pineapple. She had taught him how to ride a bike, and then later, how to drive—automatic and stick. When he left for college, he promised to call her once a week. He kept that up for half a semester. Now he only talked to her when he visited his parents, which was once every few months. He still loved her, but more in his memories than in his present life—her role had grown obsolete.

His hand was still on the phone when the screen lit up, blinking green. Someone was calling him. His secretary picked up and mouthed, *It's your father,* through the glass pane between them. Oliver knew what he was calling about. His father had been ringing his landline and cell phone, leaving message after message over the past week, and was now resorting to trying his office line.

It had been two years since Oliver had declined to sponsor his grandfather's petition for a compassionate release. His father had done it instead, but the judge ruled against it. Every few months, his father dogged him about changing his mind. "We need to get creative. Give the judge an excuse to grant the petition," his father had said in his latest voice mail.

Oliver shook his head at his secretary and motioned: *tell him I'll call him back tomorrow.* Anyway, it was already past 6:00 p.m. on a Wednesday—the only evening he left work early, blocking off any meetings or client dinners. He had someplace to be. In fact, if he didn't leave soon, he'd be late.

But because the walls in the offices of Steinway & Appleton were made of glass, he had to first apply the appropriate window dressing to his office. On the one-floored panopticon, almost every lawyer could keep tabs on each other, see who was working and who was slacking, and that kept everyone busy, or at least outwardly so, typing away on their computers, flipping through paperwork, and juggling phone calls.

The panopticon used to be a popular prison format. The idea behind it was that it made the inmates feel watched at all times, even if no one was, which effectively compelled them to behave. Recently, most correctional facilities had abandoned the design, with activist groups calling it inhumane and degrading.

Oliver shuffled his papers across his desk, propping one over his keyboard as if he were in the middle of reading it. He draped his Burberry coat over the back of his chair and strategically placed his double canopy umbrella at the front corner of the desk. He had perfected the display that said, *I'm probably still in the building, visiting a partner's office, maybe getting coffee, or running out for a quick dinner, but obviously, I'll be back to work soon*. No one passing his office would think that he had checked out for the day.

It began to rain as he set foot on Lexington Avenue. He tried to flag down a cab, but after a series of occupied ones zoomed past, he gave up and bought an umbrella from one of the corner stands. He considered the fifteen dollars as a levy for his performative diligence. The wind kept blowing the umbrella inside out as he walked all the way from Midtown East to The Rosewood. He put his wet clothes into the laundry basket and took a hot shower. Afterward, he scarfed down leftover sushi from the weekend. The rice had gone hard and the tuna smelled fishy, but he drowned it in soy sauce and numbly ate it.

He put the kettle on the stove and took out a box of shortbread cookies. He'd been teaching Tammy piano for over two years, and they always started each lesson with hot tea and a snack. It had become the most consistent ritual in his life.

At seven o'clock on the dot, the doorbell rang. When the eleven-year-old came in, she immediately grabbed a cookie, polishing it off within seconds. He wondered how often she was allowed to have treats. She looked so skinny.

"How's the new house?" he asked. The Zhangs had moved from Flushing to Westchester the week before.

"Sucks. It's ugly and it's near the highway. I still can't fall asleep at night," she said, taking another cookie. "And the landlord said no dogs allowed."

Oliver had seen a picture of the house. Drab yellow siding and a lawn full of rocks, but just within Scarsdale township limits. "You'll be going to a great school though," he said encouragingly. "Your dad must be happy."

"My dad's never happy. He's always stressing about something. A promotion, our green card, my grades. He's already talking about how much he wants a bigger house in the center of town, and this time, he wants to *buy* it. Who cares so much about a house?" She ran her tongue over her neon pink braces, digging out lodged crumbs. "I'd rather be in Flushing. I miss my old friends. My new classmates only care about the color of their Coach purses."

Oliver wondered if this was Tammy's convoluted way of pining for a designer purse. A tactic that past girlfriends had used.

"We could go shopping for one together," he said. "It'd be your birthday present."

"I'd rather die."

Her spunk and comedic timing tickled him. He choked on a mouthful of peppermint tea, spilling some down his shirt. She lifted her eyebrows and smiled—delighted by his reaction.

"So what would you want for your birthday?" he asked.

"A car."

"Would a convertible be good enough?" he joked.

"Any car is freedom," she said, peeling off the price sticker on the cookie box.

They went over to the piano. After forty-five minutes of Mariah Carey songs, Tammy closed the lid.

"You nailed the chord progressions in the second section," he said.

"I know," she said. "I practiced."

"I'll see you in two weeks?"

"When you're in Bali, you should learn the lyrics to her songs. We can sing together."

"You don't want to hear me sing," he said.

She met his eyes when she said, "I do." The funny thing was, he believed her.

★ ★ ★

Oliver waded in an infinity pool overlooking the treetop canopies of Ubud's jungle. In the breeze, the leaves moved together in one giant, serene swath. A visual lullaby. He sipped on an overly sweet cocktail as Janna wrapped her legs around him, cuddling him like a koala. Her long hair fanned into the water. "Didn't I tell you that Bali was romantic?" she said, kissing him on the cheek.

He squeezed her ass. Bali was really wonderful, he had to give her that. Bali was no London or Florence or Ibiza—it was better. The past nine days felt like an escape to another world. Nature reigned the island with organized chaos. Motorbikes zipped down the dirt roads, unburdened by traffic signals. Wild monkeys dashed along the walking trails, stealing muffins from tourists. Mangoes dangling from the trees dropped at random, making for either a free snack or a blow to the head. Down a narrow, crowded street of small shops, vendors sold local beer brand T-shirts, bright batik-patterned sundresses, and brass figurines of Hindu gods. Inside an open storefront, Balinese women ground chilis and garlic with a mortar and pestle while children cleaned mangosteen and snake fruit. They operated in their own world, working in sync without much talk—an unaffected grace, a communal ease.

The next day, they skipped the resort buffet and ventured out to a vegan café that a girl from their sunrise yoga class had suggested. Every customer was white. "Australians," he said to Janna, picking up on their accents. The menu was avocado-everything and acai bowls. As he finished his latte, he stayed quiet. Not confessing to Janna that this had been his favorite meal.

On their way back to the resort, a Balinese woman in

a pink dress with a green sash across her waist grabbed his hand. She turned it over and traced a crease up his palm. "A forked fate line," she said, "the potential for two lives." He leaned forward, keeping his hand in hers. Her comment hit too close to home.

"Really?" he said. Her eyes locked with his—intense, shining with a light of knowing.

As he leaned in, she gave him a Cheshire cat grin. "Do you want a reading? Only twenty dollars."

After shaking her off, he walked in a daze. The palm reader was obviously a fraud, but how could she have known to say those words to him? Was it painted all over his face? He wondered who else could see. The plastic cup holding what remained of his iced coffee perspired in his hand, dripping water down his arm.

"Oh my God, what's that?" said Janna, turning around.

A thin, auburn-colored dog was following them, licking the trailing drops of water from Oliver's cup. It cowered at the sound of Janna's voice, but kept trailing them, hesitantly, at a distance.

"She must be thirsty," he said. He mimed to the local man peddling ice cream on the street and gave him five dollars in exchange for a bottle of water.

"How do you know the dog is a *she*?" said Janna.

Oliver shrugged. "She looks pretty. Like a fox."

The dog was still outside the resort the next day when they left for their jet skiing excursion. And she was there waiting for them by the front gate when they returned.

"Wow, this pup must be in love with us," said Janna.

"Probably," said Oliver. Dogs were attracted to kind people. People who they recognized as leaders and protectors.

Then Janna said, as if it were as casual as buying a pair of shoes, "Maybe we could adopt her." She stroked Oliver's hair. "She'd be like a trial run for us."

This was one of Janna's better ideas, ulterior motive or not. A story that could work for him. He went away on vacation and came home with a beautiful stray dog from a third world country. A dog that was clearly a mutt, couldn't possibly be mistaken for a golden retriever from a puppy mill. He'd bring her to a vet to cure her various parasites and fix up that patch of red skin on her leg. Give a shaggy street dog her forever home.

They asked the resort staff about the process. The receptionist said that he could arrange all of the paperwork for five hundred bucks and the dog would be cleared for US customs in a week. They had tickets to leave Bali in a few days. Janna couldn't stay any longer. She had a big nursing conference to attend, so Oliver offered to stay behind and bring the dog to New York.

"Taking your daddy duties seriously already," she giggled.

"What's the dog's name?" the receptionist asked them. "I need to write it on the application."

"How about Sadie? Or Cleo or Lucy?" said Janna. "Are those too basic?"

"Soga," Oliver blurted out. It was Agos, the original family name, spelled backward.

That's what I used to name the family trusts, his grandfather had told him. *Your funds are in Soga Trust III.* Oliver was supposed to hate his grandfather. He knew that. But the name hearkened back to a simpler time in Oliver's life, and no one would have to know what it really meant.

These days, his father took care of all matters dealing with the trust, and whenever Oliver inquired about it, he'd just say, "There's enough funds in there, if that's what you're worried about."

The last time Oliver brought it up, he had flat-out asked to see the documentation. "I need to plan for my life."

"You'll keep getting your checks."

"Maybe I'll ask the trustee. He's in charge of the distributions anyway."

His father gave him a frosty look. "I think you better drop this."

"But—"

"I can tell you everything or I can tell you nothing," his father said.

"What happens if you tell me everything?"

His father looked at him. Oliver could tell that he was assessing him, tallying up in two columns his strengths and weaknesses, his moral failings—his attachment to Daisy, his clumsiness on the tennis court, his driving. He was conducting a referendum on his character.

"Let's just leave it at nothing," said his father.

The dog moved into the private villa with Oliver and Janna that night. Soga slept on Oliver's feet, curled up in a ball. Even when he began to lose feeling in his toes, he remained still so as not to wake her. It had probably been years since she had a good night's sleep in a place where she felt safe.

Two days later, Janna flew back to New York.

"It's just you and me now, princess," said Oliver, as he scratched the snowy fluff underneath Soga's chin. She made a little howling sound and closed her eyes. She looked like she was smiling.

After sharing a banana for breakfast, they went for a hike

through the rice fields. Oliver didn't need the new leash that he had bought. Soga followed his every move, sometimes wandering off to sniff a rock or a piece of garbage but returning to his side within seconds. When a bicycle passed them, she scooted against his leg, afraid. She barked at a lizard that was crawling nearby. Oliver petted her behind her upright ears. "What a good girl," he said.

They were playing fetch on the beach when it started pouring. They ran under the nearest shop awning—already soaked. Lightning cracked through the sky, followed by a rolling thunder. Oliver was about to curse the weather when Soga swung her neck snug around his ankles and promptly fell asleep. He softly poked at her black nose and held her whiskers between his fingers. Their lives would be interlinked like this. Strolls in Central Park, runs around the reservoir, falling asleep on the couch together. His home would never be the same. Less clean but cozier. She even made him a better man. He could already feel himself becoming more patient, present, loving.

Back at the resort, Janna called him. He had forgotten that she had been in Bali with him at all. It seemed like a different lifetime.

"Is the dog too much work?" she said. "It's a lot to handle on your own."

He replied, "Soga is perfect."

"You'll have me to help you soon."

"Sure," he said.

Finally, the day came when they were on their way to the airport. He was in the back seat of the taxi with Soga on his lap.

"Sorry for the roads," said the driver. His English had a mix of accents—sounding airy and refined.

"The roads?" said Oliver.

The driver made figure eights with his finger. "Twists," he said.

"It's okay," said Oliver. "I don't even feel anything."

Two minutes later, the nausea hit. *It's just windy roads*, he thought. *It'll be over soon.* He was only a plane ride away from his apartment in The Rosewood. He would be sleeping in his own bed again and drinking tap water without risk of diarrhea. Everything was going to be okay.

His phone began to vibrate. They must have entered a data zone again. Signal was back. So was his real life. He scrolled through the notifications. Voice mails from Kip, the partners, clients, asking for certain documents. A long message from his mother with details about the farewell dinner they were throwing Daisy at Osteria Cotta. He thought about his calendar for the next week—meetings, piles of catch-up paperwork, dinner dates with Janna—and held back a gag.

He looked out the window. *Just breathe*, he told himself, trying to recall the technique that the meditation guru had taught him.

His pant leg was wet. The dog was peeing on the seat. He grappled for some napkins in his pockets, his fingers covered in urine.

"Fuck, fuck, fuck," he muttered.

The dog whimpered. She was sorry. "It's okay, it's okay," he cooed.

"We're here," said the driver, pulling up to the airport check-in area.

As he pulled out his cash, Soga jumped on him, knocking his wallet under the driver's seat.

"Get off me," he growled as she licked his face. Soga whim-

pered as he shoved her away. Still, she looked at him with
bright eyes, tongue out, tail wagging. He gently petted her
on the head. As her eyes closed, he kissed the top of her snout.
Soga was the tropical dream of Bali, but Bali wasn't real life.
He couldn't be the same person he was with her in New York.
People wanted things from him in New York. The firm barely
left him enough hours for himself as it was, and he wasn't about
to forgo brunch on the weekends for trips to the dog park, or
turn down nights out with friends to stay home with the mutt.
And he definitely couldn't imagine himself bending over on
the streets of Manhattan to pick up her shit.

He retrieved his wallet and got out of the car.

Soga tried to follow him, but he pushed her back into the
seat and closed the door.

"I'll give you five hundred dollars to take her," he said to
the driver.

"Excuse me?"

Soga barked from inside the car.

"Six hundred," said Oliver, emptying his wallet.

The driver looked confused.

"I give you money. You take care of the dog," said Oliver.
He kept his eyes on the man, determined not to look at Soga,
who was whining and pawing at the door now.

The driver glanced at the dog in the rearview mirror.
"Okay, I'll take her," he said.

"Take *care* of her, okay?" said Oliver, handing over the
money.

Oliver watched as the taxi drove away with Soga, her nose
sticking out of the crack in the window.

In the first-class cabin, he asked the stewardess to bring him
three vodka nips with ice.

"You're only allowed two at a time, but I'll make an exception," she said, putting an extra bounce in her step as she turned to get them. She hovered over him as he poured all the vodka into the flimsy plastic cup.

"That good of a vacation?" she said.

"Not bad."

"Traveling alone?"

He took a sip of pure vodka. He thought that he heard a whimper, but it was just the screech of the beverage cart.

TEN

Tammy

2002

My mother's head lolled on my shoulder as the train jolted. She snored faintly. Out the window, the Westchester brush grew thinner toward the city, broken only by station stops: Crestwood, Bronxville, Pelham. The names of quaint suburban towns.

The backyards of the run-down houses that sat along the tracks told another story. Some had meshed wire fences that shook as the Metro North rolled by. Others were littered with tree bark, two had broken trampolines, and one was filled with stacks of tires. These homes were on the outskirts of their towns.

Just like our house in Scarsdale. We had moved from Flushing to the butter-yellow house three years ago. Even then, the paint was flaked, exposing the gray wood underneath. Our backyard, which abutted a highway, was dry and filled with weeds. The endless sonic swooshing of cars kept me up at night that whole first year.

I hadn't wanted to leave Flushing. I liked my teachers at PS 164 Q, and I had finally established a cafeteria lunch table with Yumi and five other girls. We moved because, "better schools," my mother had said. What she meant was *whiter*.

On my first day of seventh grade, the classroom had erupted with giggles when the teacher introduced me. "Let's welcome Tia, wait, uh—Tianfei?"

"Tammy," I corrected her. "I go by Tammy."

"Oh, that's easier!" she said, relieved.

A curly-haired girl sitting in the front row said, "You can be Danny's girlfriend." She pointed at the Japanese boy a few seats away from her. He looked down at his hands while the entire class nodded in agreement. There were no other Asians in the room. No Blacks and no Latinos either, but there were three Stephanies and a William who actually went by William.

The school in Scarsdale had a black box theater and a computer lab. Everyone used mechanical pencils and erasable pens—the fancy kinds that only came in two-packs at the drugstore. The girls wore Tiffany chain bracelets and silicone wristbands debossed with pink ribbons for breast cancer awareness. The hipsters founded an Amnesty International club and the football players sold stale chocolate bars to raise funds for orphanages in Indonesia.

I tried signing up for the improv group, but it was full, so I had to join the Asian Heritage club instead. It consisted of the Japanese boy from my class, two Indian boys from a different grade, and a mixed-race Vietnamese girl whose father owned a pho restaurant in the center of town. The five of us wore clothes from Old Navy and Aeropostale. Button-down plaids and T-shirts without logos. All to say: *we're normal, nothing to look at here.*

Then there was Dani. With an "i." A natural blonde who colored her hair a dark red. She wore mismatched earrings and had a temporary tattoo of an Arabic proverb on her ankle that translated to: *If a wind blows, ride it.* A Canon digital SLR camera hung from her neck most days. She slipped some of her black-and-white photographs into lockers. Mine had received two pictures—one of my empty chair in science class when I was out sick, and one of me dozing off at a pep rally.

Dani wasn't part of any clubs or cliques. It only made her cooler and more mysterious. Everyone wanted to be friends with her. Everyone was curious about her. She seemed to know exactly who she was and didn't need anyone else's approval, and because of that, she got everybody's without even trying.

One day, I was behind Dani in the lunch line. She was wearing a violet T-shirt with a cassette tape printed on the chest. The tag was sticking out against the nape of her neck. It read: Urban Outfitters.

"We have to go," I told my mother, months later. It was still summer, but I would be starting high school soon. I needed to wear Urban Outfitters there.

"Is that at the mall?" she asked.

"It's in SoHo."

She perked up. "Manhattan? We'll make a day of it." She missed the city too.

And so, here we were, en route to Urban Outfitters on the Metro North. The train entered a tunnel and I turned to my mother, fast asleep in the seat next to me. Her long commute and grueling job were taking a toll. I felt guilty shaking her awake.

"Mom, we're here," I said.

She pulled at the bottom of her pilling cotton shirt, now a few sizes too small. Every weekday morning, she woke up at six, took the Metro North to Grand Central, and then the subway to Long Island City, where she worked as a software programmer at a consulting firm. She arrived by 8:00 a.m. and often didn't leave until twelve hours later. At night, her feet plodded, barely lifting off the ground, as she came through the front door. By that time, my father and I had already eaten our frozen dinners. Still a year from forty, she was already buying black hair dye to cover the white strands that had sprouted at her temples.

We got off the Metro North, and should've sailed downtown on the 6 train, but weekend maintenance meant we had to take the F and then the C. A man in a Yankees cap at the end of the subway bench was staring at my mother. I discreetly reached into my purse and clutched my house key like a dagger.

They hate us, my father had said to no one in particular a few weeks back. We were sitting at the kitchen table and his newspaper was open, with a coffee stain on it. A small headline about the raid of a massage parlor in Chinatown.

They hated Muslims for a year and now they're remembering to hate us too, he continued as he straightened out the American flag pin on his jacket. He didn't wear it because he was proud of this country. He wore it to say: *I'm with you guys and not them*, whoever *them* was at the time.

The subway train screeched to a stop and the Yankees fan walked toward the door. Then he turned around, smiled at my mother, said, "Ting Ting Ling Ling, I'll see you in my dreams tonight," and made a jerk-off gesture with his hand.

My mother put her arm in front of me and said, "Thank you." After the man walked off the train, she whispered, "If you aren't nice to them, they could get angry and hurt you." Her hands were shaking, so I nodded, pretending nothing had happened.

We exited the subway and walked straight into swarms of shoppers. At the intersection of Spring Street and Sixth Avenue, I coughed through a smoky waft of street meat. My mother took my hand. "This is nothing compared to Tianjin Street," she said. Back in her element, she led us through the teeming streets of SoHo.

As we made our way to Urban Outfitters, we passed by a long line of people waiting to get into Louis Vuitton. *Jiudian*, someone said. *Hotel*. Not expecting to hear Mandarin here, my brain took an extra second to register it. Upon closer examination of the line, I realized it was made up almost entirely of Chinese people. Doused in cologne, they wore shirts with garish logos and huddled under their parasols.

One of them stepped in front of my mother and said, *"Ni zhidao Xiang Nai Er zai nali ma?"* *Do you know where Chanel is?*

"Go down one block and then make a right," said my mother. She spoke in English, but gestured clear directions. She didn't like to be caught speaking Chinese in public.

My mother pulled me across the street. "Must be an empty tour bus nearby," she said, before telling me that those people were rich mainlanders. Here to spend their money to look more sophisticated in China. "As if those people could just buy class," she said. I wondered if *those people* included us too, but then I spotted the billowing black flags of Urban Outfitters.

The store had high ceilings and was air-conditioned to the hilt. The curated tables and racks were spread out, giving us plenty of room to maneuver around the other shoppers, which were older girls. College girls. They judged the clothing first. Price tags second. My mother shopped the opposite way. I touched the distressed flannel tops, flared corduroy pants, and Nirvana sweatshirts as I browsed through the racks. In the back section, I found two pieces that Dani owned—a tie-dyed racerback and a red bucket hat. I tested out the hat. My mother said I looked like a mushroom.

In the fitting room, I tried on a tank top with a tricycle riding over a rainbow. My mother rubbed the fabric in between her fingers and said, "I'm not paying forty dollars for polyester."

"But it's bohemian," I whined.

I put on a fluttery blouse with a dragon embroidered on the sleeve.

My mother traced the outline of the mythical creature and said, "Better quality, but this makes you look too Asian."

"I am Asian," I said.

"But not so much. You're lucky," said my mother, pointing at my features. "Slim nose. Big eyes. Even your face is getting less round."

"My what?" I said, rubbing my jawline.

"Someone once told me that you looked half-white," my mother added.

I looked at my face in the mirror and, for a moment, didn't recognize myself. What exactly did *Asian* look like? What did I look like? My mother liked to think that I looked white, but to white people, I was *other*. I would always be *other*. Even to myself.

After Urban Outfitters, I ushered my mother into nearby boutiques. I would feign interest in the clothes near the front, but then slip to the back—the sales racks—when the store's associates looked busy.

We carried four bags of clothes by the time we had finished shopping. Every item in them was for me.

It was only late afternoon. Instead of jumping back on the train, my mother wanted to go to Pearl River Mart—the last remaining Chinese market in SoHo. It sold bamboo steamers, traditional iron scissors with the big hand loops, and shiny brocade shirts. "Do we have to?" I said. She grabbed my wrist and pulled me through the throngs of shoppers toward the store.

I dragged my feet, wrestling from her grip in front of a nail salon.

"Please?" I said.

She was too tired to argue. She handed me some cash, said, "Get light pink," and made her way to Pearl River without me.

The salon was sparkling clean. Recess lights glared off the vinyl floor. At the polish rack, I thought of Dani. Her bangled wrists. Her lime-green nails—chipped in a cool way. I grabbed a green bottle and held it against my skin. Not quite right. I sighed as I picked up the light pink bottle and brought it over to the manicure table.

It wasn't until after my manicure girl had cleaned my cuticles and already painted three nails that I stopped her. I wasn't light pink.

"Sorry, can I change colors?" I said.

I went back to the polish rack, scrutinizing all four rows.

"This one," I said, handing a bottle to the girl.

"This will look good on you," she said.

I had picked Big Apple Red. It screamed bold, fiery, confident.

The girl next to her, who was clipping the nails of a Cameron Diaz look-alike, said, *"Ni you dei qing li le."* You have to clean her nails again.

My manicure girl scoffed. *"Zhen fan ren. Tiao le ban tian."* So annoying. She took half a day to pick a color.

My elbow twitched but she didn't notice.

Then the other girl said, *"Ta tiao le ge lao taitai de yanse."* She picked a color for old ladies.

My manicure girl snorted.

A lightning bolt of anger shot straight to my head. *These girls* had the nerve to mock me? *My own people?* Other people—I could brush it off, try to forget about it. But this. This was worse than any other offensive remarks I had swallowed. This was a betrayal.

Before I got up to make a scene with the manager, my manicure girl rubbed the back of her neck and said, *"Wo hao lei. Jintian you zheme duo keren. Wo hai meiyou chi dongxi."* I am so tired. There have been so many customers today. I still haven't eaten.

My indignation melted as I heard the ache in her voice. Saw the eye bags that she had earned. Felt her hands, flaky and dry from all the soap and chemicals they had to touch every day. She couldn't be much older than me. We looked like we could be sisters.

"Where do you live?" I said, settling on English so as not to embarrass her.

"Flushing," she said, eyes widening, meeting mine for the first time.

"With your family?"

She hesitated before saying, "Seven girls."

I stopped with the questions, worried that she might only be answering me because she thought that she had to be polite.

"I came to study," she said, after applying the first coat of polish. "But I cannot pay now."

"What do you want to study?"

"Law," she said.

"Wow, that's amazing," I said. "What made you choose that?"

"It's important that we know our rights," she said.

"So true," I said, nodding.

"I know it very hard. Okay if I be a little lawyer."

"A paralegal?" I asked.

She nodded. She had originally planned on working at the salon to save up money for night school, but then her parents got sick. "I send money to them in Shanghai," she said.

"You're a good daughter," I said.

She tilted her head and asked, "You Korean?"

"No."

"Oh, Chinese?" She put her hand over her mouth and blushed.

"It's okay," I said, having forgotten my anger. "My parents are Chinese."

"You been to China?" she said.

"No," I whispered.

An older woman came over, her hair pulled back in a severe bun. *"Kuai yidian! Laoban mashang dao. Ni hai de ca diban."* *Hurry it up! The manager is coming soon. You still have to mop the floor.*

My manicure girl nodded vigorously, glanced at my puka shell necklace, and looked back down, concentrating on my nails.

Not wanting to bother her, I turned my head to see what else was going on in the salon. But the entire place looked different to me now. The all-female staff stayed small, keeping their heads down except when they'd look up briefly, to meet each other's eyes. A secret acknowledgment of something that I couldn't understand.

I realized that the picture of the beach in front of me was a stock photo—the one that came with the frame. It had "8x10" printed on its shoreline.

In the corner of the room, near the door where the staff disappeared behind, I spotted a Chinese calendar that seemed to follow me everywhere in Flushing. It hung in my dentist's office, my favorite noodles restaurant, the post office. We had one in our kitchen even though it was too gaudy for my mother's taste. I had meant to ask my parents what was special about this particular wall calendar but kept forgetting.

A character was drawn with a heavy gold brush against a red background. 福. *Fu.* It meant *good fortune.* It filled up the whole page above the boxes with the days of the month. A girl working at a pedicure station wiped the sweat on her forehead and looked up at it.

福. It wasn't just a character. It was hope. A prayer for *good fortune.* For better luck.

ELEVEN

Tony

Tony breathed in the steam from his bowl of Biang Biang noodles—fresh from the pot, hand-pulled, practically bouncing. The scent of chili, garlic, and Sichuan pepper normally made his mouth water, but tonight, he couldn't even pick up his chopsticks. Kim barely touched hers either, save for an occasional stirring so the noodles wouldn't congeal. Only Tammy properly dug into the dish—hunched over, sucking it up like a vacuum, sauce slapping the sides of her mouth.

"Why aren't you guys eating?" said Tammy, finally coming up for air. "These noodles are your best batch yet, Mom."

"Your dad has his annual review tomorrow," said Kim.

"I'm sure he worked hard and it'll be fine," said Tammy.

Tony gripped his thighs. It wasn't fine last time. Last year, Elijah—his boss, the vice president of product at Iris Telecom—had said he was a "ten out of ten" but that other divisions of the company hit a few speed bumps, so he "had to be a team player." That meant no raise and no promotion. "Don't worry," Elijah had added, "we're still paying for the fees of that immigration lawyer." It wasn't a friendly reminder that the company was on his side. It was a threat that it could pull the rip cord on his naturalization process if he made trouble.

Kim tapped the side of his bowl. "Eat," she said. "Whatever happens tomorrow, we'll deal with it. Just don't lose your temper."

"I don't lose my temper!" he said.

"Not in the office," said Kim.

"Dentist and landlord," Tammy said. "And that was just this summer."

She was keeping score? Good thing she didn't see him yell at the mailman too. Those people deserved it. Even after he had told the mailman twice to make sure the door to the mailbox was completely closed, part of Tammy's *Elle Girl* magazine got rained through. The dentist kept suggesting he needed fillings when his teeth were spanking white. And the landlord wanted Tony to take care of the lawn. A lawn that didn't belong to him.

"I didn't hit anyone," he said.

Kim cocked an eyebrow.

Sure, he slapped tables and desks. The fire that accompanied his anger needed some outlet.

"It scares people," said Kim.

"Do that at work and you're going to get yourself fired," said Tammy.

No, losing his job wasn't an option, especially when he was so close to making it. He had been a Software Engineer III, a midlevel position, for three years now. Just one year with the salary bump that came from rising to senior engineer would give him enough for the down payment to buy a house closer to the center of town. "We're going to make it," he gritted.

"What did Curtis say?" asked Kim.

Curtis had started at the company a few years before Tony did. They had adjacent cubicles. Good-natured and a respectable coder, Curtis had his finger on the pulse of the company. He was always welcomed at the watercooler—a place where Tony never watched the right TV shows or read the trending articles. The only two minorities on the floor, their friendship may have begun out of an unspoken obligation to band together, but now Curtis was the only person whom Tony trusted in the whole damn company.

"Curtis said I'll get the promotion because I'm working as if I were already a senior engineer. Told me to puff myself up to Elijah. Remind him of my lead role on adding the data collection function on the product."

"They say data is the new gold," said Tammy.

"Curtis said that too!" said Tony, astounded with his daughter. She wasn't even in high school yet.

"If Curtis said it'll be fine, it will," said Kim, finally slurping her noodles with gusto. Though Tony had never said it in so many words, she knew that Curtis watched out for her husband. When another midlevel engineer took credit for a project that Tony had led, Curtis made sure everyone knew who had really done all the work. And Curtis was quickly moving beyond engineer and into the business side of the company. Last quarter, he had brought in his own account after sitting next to a TV executive at a Knicks game.

Lately, Kim had been copying Curtis's confidence-boosting trick: positive Post-its on the bathroom mirror. Tony thought it was silly at first, but he had smiled that morning when he read, "You are what someone looks forward to." Of course, Tony had never told Kim that Curtis was Black. He wasn't sure if that would change her mind about him, and whether that would eventually make him see Curtis differently too.

"Who cares what Curtis thinks?" said Tammy. "You're so valuable to the company. Just ask for the promotion. You deserve it."

"Your dad can't just ask for whatever he wants," said Kim.

"Why?"

"They're sponsoring his green card," said Kim. "*Our* green card."

Tony squeezed her hand. It was nice of her to acknowledge that he carried the entire family on his back.

"So they can just push us around?" said Tammy.

"They're doing us a favor," said Tony. "The company doesn't have to employ an immigrant. They're helping me out."

"But you're making them money," said Tammy.

"If I step out of line, they'll fire me, and then where will we be?"

Tammy made a disgusted sound. "That doesn't sound legal," she said, getting up from the table. "Be right back."

Tony and Kim emptied their bowls as Tammy pitter-pattered up the stairs, and then, fifteen minutes later, jumped the steps two by two on the way down.

She slammed a printout on the table with a triumphant, "See here? Employers have to pay their sponsored employees the prevailing market wage. Prevailing market wage. It's the law." She spoke slowly, repeating key phrases to make sure they understood. "Your equivalent—an American engineer with a master's degree—makes at least thirty thousand dollars more than you do. Thirty thousand dollars more. You need to ask for that."

Kim clutched at the printout. "Thirty thousand dollars?"

Tony squinted at the legalese. There it was: prevailing market wage. "Are you sure?"

Tammy put her hands on her hips. "It says it right there. You can't let the company bully you."

"A little lawyer already," said Kim.

Tammy sat back down and looked into her empty bowl. "We have rights. It's important that we know them."

The cubicles were humming the following morning. Incessant pen clicking, the jangling of keys and coins, panicked whispers. It reminded Tony of animals rattling in their cages at the zoo.

His coworkers poked their heads over the gray partition walls, shooting hushed questions across the pods.

"Are they calling us alphabetically?"

"You see who's in there now?"

The espresso machine churned and sputtered. "I'm going to throw this piece of shit out the window!" came from somewhere behind him. *A pump's burned out*, thought Tony, but at least it was no longer his job to replace it.

"Tim Bernard? Elijah's ready for you."

Tony peeked over his cubicle wall. A man, head down, dragged himself into the corner office and closed the door.

"They're only on the *B*s," said Curtis. "You've got some time."

"But they called Chad Sousa already," said Tony.

"Aw, they're just fucking with us now," said Curtis. He rolled his chair closer as he asked, "So, what's the final number you settled on?"

"Ten thousand dollars," Tony whispered, taking a sip of his third cup of coffee. The caffeine jitters had already kicked in, but he still felt more grounded with the drink in his hand.

"That's it? I'm asking for double that."

"Twenty thousand dollars for a raise?" said Tony. "Would they do that?"

"Don't know till I try," said Curtis, disappearing behind the gray wall between them for a second, before flinging a neon orange book onto Tony's lap. *Ask for What You're Worth*, by Jerry Solomon. The cover art was of a man's smiling face, except where the teeth should've been, there were dollar bills. "You can have it if you promise to read it," said Curtis.

"I don't know if I have time," said Tony.

"Excuses, excuses. One day, you'll see. You can learn more than programming and how to invest for retirement from a book. A book can teach you all sorts of things. Important life things," said Curtis. He was the king of self-improvement. The stack of books on his desk included *Powerful Habits for a Powerful Life* and *Getting Your Teenager to Say More Than "Fine."*

Tony wasn't wired like that. He didn't *think* about his feelings, much less *read* about them. They were just there, like breathing, and he had been born knowing how to handle that.

Elijah's assistant popped her head into his cubicle. "Tony Zhang?" she said.

Curtis jumped and said, "Already?"

"Follow me, please," said the assistant.

Curtis fist-bumped him and whispered, "Twenty thousand dollars."

The glass door to Elijah's office squeaked as it opened and shut. Elijah said, "Make yourself comfortable," with a smile— the same one he used to deliver both good and bad news.

"Hi, Eligah," sputtered Tony, already fumbling syllables. The "juh" sound had a way of coming out as "gah" when he was nervous. He glanced at the two computer monitors on his boss's desk, each sleeker and bigger than the one Tony had at his desk, even though Elijah didn't even code anymore. The screens were blank, save for the Lance Armstrong wallpaper and a minimized tab for Solitaire along one of the bottom ribbons.

Elijah opened a manila folder and flipped through the papers.

Tony cleared his throat, not sure if he was supposed to speak first. "This year, I led the data—"

Elijah put a finger up and said, "Give me a minute. Need to read your review."

He hadn't read it yet? Did that mean that reviews didn't actually factor into the promotion, or had they already decided against it? Tony's mind was still reeling as Elijah read out loud the highlights of the feedback.

"'Workhorse.'"

"'Surprisingly strong technical execution.'"

"'Polite.'"

"'Irreplaceable.'"

Elijah covered the side of his mouth with his hand and whispered, "That last one was from me."

A childlike smile spread across Tony's face. That had to be a good sign, right?

Elijah set the papers aside and leaned forward. "What I'm more interested in is—are you happy here?"

"Very happy, oh yes, yes," said Tony, flustered, but still telling the truth. Over the last year, he had moved up from owning small product features to more critical ones. He even enjoyed leading the data project, which was insanely tricky and tedious. He forfeited more weekends and grew more white hairs than his coworkers did, but those trade-offs were worth it. He got to call the shots. A return to his old self in China, where he managed a team at the university. After years of grinding under the radar, he finally felt valued at Iris Telecom.

"You have a bright future here," said Elijah.

Tony beamed, waiting for Elijah to deliver what had to be good news.

Instead, Elijah said, "Based on the structure of our team now, management has decided that if you commit to a few more years, you'll be promoted to senior engineer."

"A few more years?" said Tony, shifting in his seat. He felt queasy, regretting the copious amounts of coffee he had downed on an empty stomach.

"Only two, I think. Almost there, man. Congratulations."

Tony felt his anxiety explode into fury. *Congratulations?* That burned. The company didn't care that he worked harder than any other engineer. Or that his opinions didn't get respected at meetings because he didn't have the right title. They just cared that he was their workhorse. Their green-card captive, who said "yes" and "okay" to everything.

His hand twitched—the way it did before he lashed out at Tammy. The dentist, the landlord, the mailman. He gripped the chair handle. Kim had warned him. *Don't lose your temper.* He had to control himself. He should thank Elijah and walk away, but he couldn't. *Ask for what you're worth.* Curtis would support that, but the company thought that he was worth nothing. He was never going to get enough money to buy his own damn house! Just as he felt a rush of rage bubble up his throat, he heard Tammy's voice. *We have rights.*

Tony stood up, towering over Elijah.

"Thirty thousand dollars," he heard himself say. "I want my salary to increase by thirty thousand dollars. That is the market prevail wage."

"The market what?" said Elijah.

"The prevailing market wage." Tony unscrambled the words, trying to remember everything Tammy said last night. "The data project I led was important. Data is the new gold."

Elijah rolled his chair backward.

"Thirty thousand dollars and senior engineer," said Tony.

"That's a lot of money and responsibility," said Elijah.

"I talked to a lawyer," Tony bluffed. "She said those are my rights as a green-card-sponsored employee."

"Okay, okay," said Elijah, putting his hands out in front of him, "I feel you, but senior engineers are in charge of a staff of five. Do you think you're ready for that?"

"I ran a team of ten engineers in China."

"In China," said Elijah. "Things are different here. You can't just be a great coder. You have to attend meetings with the execs. Answer to them. Take it from me—they're not an easy lot to please."

"I can do that," said Tony, but inside, he was beginning to worry. Communication—written or spoken—wasn't his strong suit.

"I don't know," said Elijah, scratching his head. "I wanna help you, man, I really do, but it's a bit above my pay grade."

Tony's nerve was slipping. He had been gaining ground, but Elijah was slowing the momentum.

"How about a $10,000 raise?" Elijah offered.

That was the number Tony had originally wanted. But now,

all he could hear was Tammy's voice. *You can't let the company bully you around.* She wouldn't want him to stand down.

His eyes welled up from the pressure. He bit his tongue and mustered every ounce of courage he had left. "Thirty thousand dollars and senior engineer. Tell management that it's the law."

Elijah raised his eyebrows and then gently nodded.

Tony got the feeling that Elijah was kind of proud of him as he exited the office.

His knees buckled as he marched past his desk to the lobby. A blur of words and noises surrounded him—none of which he comprehended. Was this what a concussion felt like? The sinking feeling of the elevator's drop to the ground floor only intensified his daze. Stomach still turning, he bought a ginger ale from a hot dog cart. What had he just done? What had come over him? Was he losing his mind? He tried to replay the conversation with Elijah in his head, but like a dream, it became harder to grasp the more he tried to remember the details.

An hour later, he was behind the wheel of his gray minivan, pulling out of the transit center parking lot. It was almost one o'clock. He shouldn't be back in Scarsdale already, but it was the only place he wanted to go.

He turned off the highway at the intersection of the plaza with the discount supermarket and fast-food tacos. Not ready to go home yet, he made a left instead of a right, passing by a different neighborhood. He noted a Mazda and Subaru parked along the block. He sat up straighter. At least he was driving a Toyota. Not a German car, but one of the better Japanese brands.

He took his time weaving through town, discovering side

streets and businesses he never knew existed. With each mile, his muscles loosened, releasing the morning's angst. Before he knew it, he was close to town center. In the presidential neighborhood. On his favorite street—Coolidge Lane. He rolled down his window as he admired the earth-toned Colonials. With their strong symmetry and crisp white trim, they gave off a stately, no-nonsense demeanor. And their landscaping gave them a classic, almost royal feel. Some flower beds were planted in a ring around tree trunks. Others crowded the front door, a most colorful welcome committee. *How rewarding it must feel to have your very own front lawn.* Like his promotion, it would come with more responsibilities, but it would be a challenge he had earned. An elderly man rolled his garbage can down the street, eyes glued on Tony's car. Someday, thought Tony, as he drove away. Not today, but someday, he'd belong here.

It was half past two already. Tammy should be home from school soon. They had moved to the suburbs for her. While Kim missed the bustle of Flushing, Tony settled in—as his idioms book taught him—as snug as a bug in a rug. The peace. The space. Scarsdale calmed him down. Soothed him in a way that Dalian or Flushing never could. And as he pulled into the rental house's gravel driveway, he realized what he had been fighting for at Iris Telecom: a home.

"Hello?" he said as he entered through the front door. No one replied but he heard the television.

He found Tammy in the living room.

"Dad? What are you doing home?" she said, eyes darting to the zipped backpack at her feet. "I was going to start my homework in—"

"Keep it on," said Tony, sitting on the couch next to her. "What are you watching?"

It was a rerun of a courtroom drama. She pointed at the different people on the screen and explained, "She dated him, and then he dated that girl, but the two girls are best friends and didn't know that they are in love with the same guy, and then his mother got into trouble with the law, and the first girl has to defend her. Get it?"

He didn't.

"I can explain it again."

"It's okay. I just want to sit with you," he said.

She snacked on a handful of pretzels. "Do you want some? You look hungry."

Pretzels to him were just hard, dry pieces of wiry bread. He could think of a dozen Chinese snacks he'd rather have. But he stretched out his hand anyway, letting Tammy pour a few into his palm. "Delicious," he said.

"Uh-oh, the judge didn't like that argument," said Tammy, "but here comes Lucy Liu. She's good. She always wins."

Tammy laughed, her feet lifting off the floor. Her head nodded backward. She only did that when she found something actually funny.

"You're not watching," she said, slapping his knee.

Her warm touch almost broke him. "Need water," he said, darting off the couch. He was crying by the time he got to the kitchen. *What had he done at the review?* If he got fired, what would happen to Tammy? Nothing else mattered except having the job and the green card. Who cared if he got to own a stupid house? All that mattered was Tammy. He hadn't come to America for his future—he had come for hers.

Just as he was about to pick up the phone to call Elijah and apologize and say he'd be happy to take the $10,000 bump and wait for the promotion, the phone rang.

"Hi, this is Elijah. Can I speak to Tony?"

"Yes, this is he."

"I spoke with the bosses upstairs. I fought for you, told them you were integral to the company, the whole nine yards."

"Thank you," said Tony, uncertain as to where Elijah was going with this. "I wanted to say that I'm sorry—"

"You're being promoted," said Elijah. "Senior engineer, like you asked for."

"Oh my God," said Tony.

"But the raise is $20,000. Nonnegotiable."

"That's very generous," said Tony, collapsing onto his knees, fist clenched against his forehead, not believing what was happening.

"Congratulations, man. You really have something in you. See you back here in the morning," said Elijah.

Tony sprinted back to the living room. "Tammy! You did it!" he said, blocking the TV.

"Did what?" she said.

His heart swelled so rapidly that he lost his breath. He wanted to tell her about the entire day, what she had made possible, every one of her words that had come out of his mouth during the review. But only one thing, a memory buried deep in his bones, almost someone else's voice, spoke through him. *"Ni shi wo de xin gan."*

"What'd you say?" said Tammy.

How could he explain it? The phrase didn't translate well. His mother had used it sparsely. Only when the moment warranted it, when no other words would do. A sweet phrase that meant *you are the parts of me that I can't live without.* She had whispered it to him when she hugged him outside the airport before his virgin flight to America.

"Dad?" said Tammy. Her eyes shone, unblinking.

"You are my heart and liver," he said.

She craned her head back to the TV. "Dad, that's so gross," she mumbled, as she put more pretzels into her mouth.

TWELVE

Oliver

2006

The black, iron-wrought gates stood open. Two brick piers held up its flowery crown. To the students hurrying through it, Johnson Gate was nothing more than a passageway from the street to Harvard Yard. But Oliver paused before it, taking in its majesty, its sense of foreboding. To him, the gate was a portal to the past.

As he wandered through campus, the world peeled away. Here, he was no longer thirty-five, the youngest partner at Steinway & Appleton, invited back to Harvard to join the board of the Crimson Pride Alumni Association. He didn't live in The Rosewood or even New York. He wasn't a Wright yet. A key turned and he became eighteen-year-old Oliver Agos, his first year away from home, when the only things that mattered were grades and girls. He still remembered camping out on an orange velvet couch at Singing Beans when he couldn't stand the quiet of Widener Library. He could still feel the hard metal bar of the bench press he devoutly lifted every week at the gym. He hadn't realized how gloriously carefree his small world had been, and how much he'd miss it when it was torn away from him. Harvard was one of the last places that acknowledged his potential; a place that taught him that the world was full of possibilities and that he only needed to stretch out his hand to claim it.

As he walked the perimeter of the great lawn, trying to remember which hall Tammy said she lived in, memories dropped from the folds of his brain. The time he hooked up with a senior from Stoughton North, which had earned him a standing ovation from the boys in his freshman hall. The ultimate Frisbee games on the south lawn where he could've sworn one of his errant throws smacked Matt Damon in the forehead, leaving a shallow scar that he always fixated on in the movie star's films.

Across the Yard, he caught sight of Grays Hall. His junior-year dorm. It looked like every other red-bricked building on campus, but it was where he had experienced the worst night of his life. Oliver could still hear it—the rapping of knuckles on his dormitory door. The digital clock flashing 4:14 a.m. His roommate murmuring in the dark, "What chick did you piss off now?" Bleary-eyed, Oliver had opened the door shirtless. It wasn't a girl. It was Kip, wearing a sweatshirt and jeans. He never wore that.

Crawling into the back of a black SUV, Oliver hadn't realized that he would never see his dorm room again. That he was hours away from being hated. Hunted. That he'd be living in hotels for the next year, changing cities every few weeks. That the family doctor would goose his mother with diazepam and his father would buy a gun. That they wouldn't read the newspaper for months, unable to face the grim mug shot of his grandfather on every cover. That he'd never be an Agos again.

He checked his watch. Three minutes past noon. Tammy said to meet at the John Harvard statue. Just then, from his right—"Oliver!"

Tammy was only a freshman, but she seamlessly fit into the fabric of the school. In a plaid vest, leggings, and UGG boots, she could easily grace the cover of a Harvard brochure.

Oliver felt something catch in his throat at the sight of her. She wasn't alone. "This is Sang-tae," she said, tilting her head at the boy with his arm around her shoulders.

With porcelain skin and a Roman nose, Sang-tae was objectively beautiful. He kissed Tammy on the cheek and said, "Text me later. Whenever." As he left, he gave Oliver a once-over.

Oliver hugged Tammy gingerly, surprised that Sang-whatever's obvious jealousy gave him an odd thrill. That boy viewed him as a threat. As though leaving Tammy alone with him might not be the smartest choice. *I could take Tammy away from him.* A pleasantly dark thought.

"Boyfriend?" he asked.

"It's early days," she said.

"What's wrong with him?"

"I don't know if there's a spark."

"Don't tell me you believe in that," he said.

She shrugged. "I'd like to."

"Sparks don't always start a fire."

She elbowed him in the stomach. "That's so corny!"

"Okay, fine. If I were to scour the campus for your perfect man, who would he be?"

"Someone with kind eyes."

Oliver frowned. He had expected an answer like six foot, athletic build, and funny. What did *kind eyes* even mean? "I'll keep a lookout for that," he said. They were standing so close that passersby shot curious glances at them. Not that far apart in age, they made a handsome picture and Oliver knew it. Before this moment, he had only ever seen her as a little girl who came to him for piano lessons and college advice. A little girl he had grown to love. But now he saw the curve of her hips, the dewiness of her skin. As her hand swung close to his, he had to fight off the urge to hold it.

"You sure you still want to eat at Annenberg?" said Tammy. "They always have the same shit," she said. "They just change up the labels. As if we couldn't tell that the Chinese sesame noodles were the exact same dish as the Japanese stir-fry."

"I see that Harvard isn't living up to expectations," said Oliver.

Tammy paused. "The people are normal."

"What do you mean by that?"

"I came here thinking that everyone was going to be some kind of model-slash-genius."

"And you got?"

"Just average, smart people. Nothing special. Except for the entitled donkeys who throw around money like they earned it themselves."

"I'll make sure to pass along your complaints to the alumni association," he laughed. His first board meeting was later that afternoon.

"Just tell them to have more classes like the Rise and Fall of the Third Reich. The professor is bomb. He actually cares to give a good lecture." She pointed at the John Harvard statue and added, "Also, would be good if they tore this fraud down."

Oliver flinched. For a second, he thought that she was talking about his grandfather. But she didn't know about Matthew Agos. "What's wrong with the statue?" he said. The inscription underneath it read: *John Harvard, Founder, 1638.*

"One—it's not even John Harvard. Two—John Harvard was a donor, not the founder. And three—actual founding year is 1636."

"Oh come on—he's a landmark!" said Oliver. "People even rub his shoe for good luck. He's good for morale."

"Students pee on that shoe at night," she said. "Probably after they've just thrown up in a bush."

"That's for morale too," said Oliver.

"Did you do it?"

"Of course not," he lied.

A few minutes later, they entered Annenberg Hall. Oliver smelled the familiar matrix of odors: clam chowder soup, overcooked burgers, and unwashed sweatshirts. It made his eyes water with nostalgia. Tammy swiped him in with her card.

"I'll pay you back," he said.

"That sounds like fun," she said.

Oliver tilted his head as he picked up a tray, wondering if she was flirting with him.

The Crimson Pride Alumni Association meeting was held in Sever Hall. The heat was cranked up, intensifying the scent of old people and Chanel N° 5. Oliver had arrived ten minutes before schedule, but most of the chairs were already taken. A quick survey of the chattering table—gray hairs, growing guts tucked in Brunello Cucinelli cashmere, and Botox. Retirees. People who didn't have much else to do or anywhere else to be. Oliver was easily the youngest person there. He gave a small wave, slid into a corner chair, and pretended to check his phone.

A couple of months ago, when Kip suggested that he join the association, Oliver had cautiously declined. His grandfather had been a prolific collector of luminary positions. Head of the fundraising committee of The Met, on the board of directors of Dow Chemical, and a senior adviser to Ronald Reagan's two presidential campaigns. All honorable titles to hide what Matthew Agos really was.

"You know I want you to eventually take over my clients," said Kip, "and Jimmy Van Fleet is head of the association." More importantly, Jimmy was the CEO of the third-largest oil company in the world.

"I'll schedule dinner for the three of us at Cipriani," Oliver counteroffered.

"Nah, that'll reek of desperation. You need an excuse to interact in a less formal setting. It's not just about professional deals with these people—you got to run in their circles and become their friend, or at least make them think you are."

"Yeah, I don't know. Seems like a lot of effort for it all to be fake."

"Then make it real. Do it your own way, but get it done," said Kip. "Why else did I call in every favor I had to get you into law school there if not because it would benefit the firm?"

"What?" said Oliver.

"Come on, don't get all butthurt," said Kip. "You're a partner now. It's your firm too."

Oliver shrugged. "I guess I could do it." At least it gave

him an excuse to visit Tammy, who was about to start at Harvard that fall.

Suddenly, a flurry of excitement swept through the Crimson Pride meeting room. Jimmy Van Fleet had arrived. He made his way through the crowd of CFOs and SEC directors, making small talk. When Jimmy got to Oliver, the silver fox swatted away his hand and went in for the hug. "Kip told me you're the guy to know. That you'll be taking care of me and the company soon."

If Oliver hadn't known better, he would've fallen for the man's charm. But Jimmy had a reputation. A screamer, demanding timelines, 6:00 a.m. calls. Kip was the only partner who could handle him. "He'll treat you like his whore but he never disputes the bill," Kip had explained.

Instead of taking the empty chair reserved for him at the head of the table, Jimmy hoisted himself on top of the storage cabinets. "The gang's all here," he said, all casual and cool. The room went silent. Everyone attentive.

Jimmy made swift work of the agenda. He welcomed Oliver to the board, spitting out his credentials—double Harvard, partner at Steinway & Appleton. "Plus the kid looks like a JFK Jr. knock-off," he said, and then, after glancing at his reflection in the glass bookshelf, added, "but not as good-looking as yours truly." The Deloitte VP gave an overview of current financials, and the General Motors CEO discussed organizing a fundraiser around the upcoming Harvard-Yale football game—maybe a casino night. Then the group unanimously passed an amendment to the association's bylaws—adding "promoting diversity within the alumni community as well as the general campus" to its mission statement.

Last item on the list: start an alumni Facebook group. "Oliver, you want to take charge of that?" said Jimmy. "My son's an undergrad here. He can give you social media tips."

"Sure, I know Facebook," said Oliver, thanking God that it didn't exist when he was in college. Not only would he have been skewered on it when his grandfather's scandal came out, but no way would he have been able to fly under the radar in law school. Someone would've been able to piece together that the newly minted Oliver Wright was the same person as the hated grandson of Matthew Agos.

At the end of the meeting, Jimmy approached him. "Do me a solid?"

"Anything," said Oliver.

"I have to catch up with a few of the people here. My son Vince is in the hallway, waiting for me to take him to a late lunch. Can you check on him? Make sure he's okay?"

"Of course," said Oliver, with a strained smile. Jimmy was testing him. Would Oliver do as he was told? Would he not only be the man's lawyer, but also his son's babysitter? What else would he do for Jimmy?

Oliver found Vince reading a book on a bench in the hall-way. He had a *Save Darfur* button on his backpack. "Sorry," said Vince, "no need to worry about me. You probably have better things to do."

"No, no," said Oliver, sitting next to him, "it's good to meet you." The boy's eyes were a brilliant blue, making Oliver feel as though he were looking into his own. A pair of kind eyes.

Vince faced him and shut the book he had been highlight-ing. *Inside Nazi Germany.*

"Light reading?" chuckled Oliver.

"It's for my Rise and Fall of the Third Reich class," said Vince.

"I heard the professor is bomb," said Oliver.

"Make sure you tell my dad that. He doesn't get why I'm even taking the class. He keeps saying that it's irrelevant. 'The Third Reich already fell.'"

"I get you," said Oliver. "Gotta learn from our history and all that."

"That's the thing though," said Vince. "We haven't. It's still here. White supremacy has just become so systemic that no one bats an eye at it anymore. Racist sentencing, hate crimes, housing discrimination." There was no hint of bravado in his voice. His outrage was genuine. This kid wasn't cut from his father's cloth. He was an idealist who reminded Oliver of his younger self. The self who used to raise money for his grandfather's charity work—promoting clean water initiatives and drilling wells in Uganda—until it came out that it was all a hoax. No filtration systems were installed, no hygiene educators were dispatched, and no wells were dug, other than the one staged for the donor pamphlet. Maybe Vince would be strong enough to stick to his convictions.

"But who am I to talk about racism? Look at me," said Vince. "I'm the Aryan ideal. Maybe people like us can only understand it theoretically."

"I have brown hair," Oliver said, deflecting.

"Want to hear what the professor calls the latest iteration of the Third Reich?" laughed Vince. "A dirty old man. So privileged, so convinced of his own superiority, that he takes whatever he wants because he knows he can get away with it."

Oliver's stomach turned. *A dirty old man.* He wasn't even that old, but would people label him that way if he were with

Tammy? A predator? He flushed at the thought of kissing her, his lips crawling down her neck. He felt his mouth go dry—partly with lust, more with revulsion. His hands gripped the bench. He could never do that. She was only eighteen.

"I have someone you should meet," Oliver announced, louder than he had expected.

Vince raised his eyebrows.

"You'll definitely like her. Trust me."

THIRTEEN

Tony

2009

"Not yet," Kim said. "There's a car."

Tony held the wheel of the minivan steady. He could only see highway pavement in the side-view mirror. The car must be in his blind spot. After a few seconds, he saw a blue Lexus appear and pass him.

"Okay, you can go now," Kim said, looking over her shoulder.

He merged the minivan onto the Henry Hudson Parkway. At the exit for West 96th Street, he slowed down.

"Not this one—we're looking for 79th," she said.

As Tony pressed the gas, he wondered who was really doing the driving. He glanced at his wife, her eyes intent on the road ahead. His director.

They had met at a summer workshop hosted by his uni-

versity. Schools from all around the region were invited to
the lab, including the medical school. Kim hadn't been the
lab partner he wanted, but she was the one he needed. On
their first day, in a cramped room of fifty students, a professor with a face stippled like an old potato assigned partners.
Sitting in the front row, Tony swiveled around and scanned
the classroom. He locked eyes with a girl with a heart-shaped
face and a jade clip in her hair. He had hoped that she would
raise her hand when the professor announced his partner—
Li Kuan-yin. Instead, a girl in the back corner with sticks for
arms gave him a wave. That was Kim.

The next day's experiment was on translational equilib-
rium. He tugged at the pulleys of the force table apparatus.
The ring on top kept veering off to the left. "Ours must be
broken," he said. Anybody else would've taken his word for it,
but Kim leaned forward to examine the device. She adjusted
each string and added a thin weight to a pulley. Her touch was
calibrated in degrees. A moment later, the ring settled right
in the center of the surface.

The other students strained to see how she'd done it, but
she just continued filling out the worksheet. She acted as if
nothing out of the ordinary had happened, as if she never met
a problem she couldn't solve.

In the car, he glanced at those same fingers, relaxed across
her lap. They were stubbier, darker. Clumsy some mornings
when she knotted his tie. The weight of age, or the weight
of her wedding band. Did she ever wonder about how her
life would've turned out had she stayed with her high school
boyfriend? The way Tony wondered, sometimes, about the
girl with the jade clip.

Traffic from Scarsdale had been uncharacteristically light,

and they pulled into a parking spot near The Rosewood with twenty minutes to spare. Tammy—a junior in college, back home for spring break—was reviewing her law school application with Oliver. She had taken the train into the city, and had planned on taking it back out, but Tony balked at the suggestion. "The sun would set by then," he had said.

"I guess we'll wait," said Kim. She futzed with the radio. A disapproving crinkle in her brow that wasn't directed at the static.

"The GPS said forty minutes. An hour if we hit traffic. We didn't want to be late, did we?" he said.

"Can't ever be late," she said. "The sky might fall down."

Tony stayed silent, holding space for the irritation to wash out of both of them. Kim, of course, shared his strict adherence to punctuality. They both considered it a principle to their success. It wasn't him or their early arrival that she was chafing against. He was just a stand-in for her frustrations with a slacker colleague, the exhaustion of household chores on the weekends, the lack of any time to simply live for herself. She needed an excuse to let off some steam. A release. Tony understood that all too well.

She pulled out a copy of Tammy's essay and scribbled in its margins with a red pen. "'A group of students and I mobilized a fundraiser for inner-city schools,'" she read out loud.

"'I spearheaded a fundraiser,'" he suggested.

"*Spearheaded*—that's good. More proactive," she said.

As his chest swelled, he felt a sting of pain. It went as quickly as it came. He relaxed into his seat, massaging his sternum.

"I'll make a note," said Kim.

"Don't bother," he said. "She won't use it." Tammy didn't care for their advice anymore. Not when they told her that reading while lying down would worsen her eyesight. Or when they insisted that she wake up before noon on Saturdays or stop using the floor as a laundry basket. All leading indicators of future unproductivity. On criticizing their daughter, Tony and Kim were a united front. It was their duty as parents to point out her shortcomings so she could correct them.

Kim untied the plastic bag at her feet. "You get her," she said, handing him a foggy plastic container of dumplings. "I didn't have time to dye my hair."

Tony strode through the revolving doors of The Rosewood. It had been almost a decade since he had worked at the building, and other than the artwork in the lobby having changed from pastoral landscapes to colorful geometrics, everything was the same. He could still see the flickering lights coming from the black-and-white video feed behind the desk. The soft matte cover of the incident report log next to the SABRE pepper spray. And he was still greeted by Magic, in the same silly doorman uniform, complete with white gloves and the brimmed hat that used to dig into his scalp.

In fact, the only real change in the place that Tony noticed over the years was in Magic himself. The Polish man had gradually and happily piled on the pounds—as though his life had become a perpetual feast celebrating his eldest daughter's pregnancy and his younger daughter's wedding. Tony's body had, by contrast, adapted to his new responsibilities—raking, mowing, shoveling, planting, mulching—leaving him with not much more than a bundle of aching muscles.

The two of them had both improved their English—Tony picked up on how Magic didn't stumble when switching from past to present tense anymore—but Magic's accent had smoothed over much more than Tony's had. That was to be expected. Magic's job was blue-collar, but it was more social. Even though Tony led meetings now, he still spent most of his days sitting in front of a computer in a box with gray walls. With his white skin and blond hair, Magic could pass as an American in a way that Tony never could, even though he had a master's degree and earned six figures.

Magic was in the midst of sorting the mail. Tony noticed that Clara's slot was completely full and took the opportunity to casually inquire, "Someone's popular. How's Clara these days?"

The woman lived a childless, husbandless life—not only unconventional to Tony, but shameful, almost a waste. Yet he sometimes found himself daydreaming about what she was doing. He imagined her at a rare wines auction at Christie's, bidding paddle in hand, teacup dog in purse. Jetting off to Paris and Milan when the shops at SoHo grew too dull. Her life only belonged to her, and she could do with it whatever she wanted. He had long convinced himself that he didn't need those things, not even the luxury travel—his trips back to Dalian every other year to see his family were enough—but on the occasional Monday morning, as he stirred an instant coffee in his cubicle, he thought of Clara and envied her freedom.

"Didn't you know? She's been in Kathmandu for months," said Magic. "Decided last year she was done with the extravagant stuff. There was the silent retreat in Thailand. Then living in a fishing village on Vanuatu."

"She's going on vacations *to be poor*?" asked Tony. The words sounded wrong coming out of his mouth.

Magic rolled his eyes. "I told her she's welcome to switch lives with me. I'll take the penthouse. She can have Greenpoint."

"Interesting," said Tony, shaking his head. Maybe it was true that life was a circle, not a ladder. That once you had it all, all that was left was to return to the beginning. Clara was proof. People with everything wanted to experience living with nothing.

After some more small talk with Magic about the building's new residents, Tony said that he had better go pick up Tammy. Magic grabbed the phone and said, "Let me give Oliver a buzz first."

"No need. He's expecting me," said Tony, already walking toward the elevators. He ignored Magic's call to "hold on." Magic had seen him come into the building as a guest dozens of times at this point, but still somehow made him feel like he needed permission. When he had complained to Kim about this, she had told him to ignore it. She said, "You moved on and up. People don't like that."

The brass doors of the elevator opened, but right before Tony could walk in, Magic caught up with him.

"Could you give these to Oliver?" said Magic, passing him a stack of envelopes from the mail cubby. And then, in a low whisper, "The one on top. They've been arriving for years."

The sender was marked as Turpin Creek Correctional Facility. "Jail?" said Tony, the container of dumplings wobbling under his arm.

"I don't know," said Magic, "but I see Tammy coming and going. I have two daughters myself."

The doorman pressed the button for the elevator again, held his arm out against the open door, and motioned for Tony to get in. "Have a good day, sir," he said, tipping his hat as the doors closed between them.

Tony looked down at the white envelope. Had Oliver been in prison? Or was someone he knew in prison? Neither of those scenarios made sense. Oliver wasn't the type of person who would break the law or keep in contact with someone who had. Oliver was good—actually, better than good—he was the Zhang family's lucky charm.

Over the years, Oliver had provided an education for Tammy that Tony couldn't have afforded. It wasn't just the piano lessons. Oliver made introductions to Ivy League counselors and went with the family to tour campuses. Whenever the Zhangs needed help with anything—from their citizenship application to finding affordable Broadway tickets—Oliver showed up for them. He represented the best of Americans—helping those with less without expecting anything in return.

Looking back at the envelope, Tony muttered, *"Hushuo."* *Bullshit.* Not only did Tony know Oliver, he knew Magic. This was the type of conspiracy that gave Magic a hard-on. His version of detective work was uncovering Mrs. Lachey's affair with her concierge doctor and Mr. Friedman's asshole bleaching sessions. Magic wanted these letters from prison to mean something dirty about Oliver. It made the doorman feel better about himself.

By the time he rang the doorbell, Tony was thinking straight again. Oliver must have done some legal work for a wrongly accused prisoner—probably pro bono—and the letters were official paperwork for the case.

Oliver opened the door and saw the stack of mail in Tony's hands. "Thanks, man," he said, taking the envelopes and magazines from Tony.

That threw Tony back in time to when he was a doorman, when he should've been handing over the mail to Oliver. When Magic had given him Oliver's mail, he had taken it on instinct. It was so rote from his past life—offering a hand to the residents whenever he could. To Oliver, Magic, everyone in the building—would he always be the doorman? Was that how he saw himself as well?

"Where's Tammy?" said Tony.

Oliver pointed to the balcony, where Tammy stood, looking out at the skyline. "She's packing up her stuff," he said. He waxed on about how strong her personal statement was, but that it needed a little work. "She's got the grades and scores, but she's got to convey an authentic purpose. Law schools these days aren't in the business of training lawyers anymore. They're looking to build leaders."

Tony placed the container of dumplings on top of the mail in Oliver's hands. "Thank you. Please take this as a token of our appreciation."

Oliver tried to refuse the gift. "I don't want you to think you have to bring me something every time. It's too much—"

"It's important," Tony said firmly. He had rolled out the dumpling dough himself, and Kim had mixed the shrimp-and-pork filling. They were his great-great-grandmother's secret recipe. Oliver couldn't get these dumplings anywhere else. Not from a store and not even from another Chinese family.

An annoyed voice cut through the mini standoff. "Oliver, just take them or else we'll never leave," said Tammy. She let out a sigh that was meant to be heard.

Tony realized he should have brought an American gift. All along, all those years, he should have been gifting wine or flowers. Tony frowned as he stared at the dumplings, which suddenly looked shriveled—small and insignificant.

"Turn on the air-conditioning," said Tammy, buckling her seat belt.

The windows were open. It was only March. A little humid

due to the impending rain, but no need to waste gas. "It'll get breezy when we pick up speed," said Tony.

"Can you stop being so cheap? Aren't we past that?" said Tammy.

"We're not being cheap," said Kim, as she pressed the button for the lowest A/C setting. "It's just not that hot today."

"Turn on the radio," said Tammy.

Tony hesitated. "Why don't we talk more about your law—"

"Z100," said Tammy, head down, scrolling on her phone.

He hit the button for that station. A bouncy beat came on, with a raspy voice that rapped so fast that it made him question whether it was English. Tammy was bobbing her head, mouthing the lyrics.

He just wanted to talk to her, but he didn't know how to get through. He wondered if he ever would.

The gravel crunched as Tony cut the engine. They were home. Tammy ran up the porch—a soft creak of hollow wood. The screen door swung shut as she and Kim disappeared inside.

On his way to the front door, he bent down to inspect the grass. Not one blade of yellow. His dedication had paid off. He had spent all month top-dressing the lawn with compost, turning the sprinklers on before 10:00 a.m. on the weekends, and repositioning them whenever he spotted any runoff. He took a deep breath. It smelled of spring.

But then he noticed the hydrangeas. Their thin stems, flopping outward. They needed mulch. He had bought them earlier that week at the local garden shop. Pink and purple—Tammy's favorite colors. But when he planted them, a dizzy spell had stopped him from finishing the job properly. Kim had prescribed rest and two glasses of salt water. He made a mental note to wake up early the next morning to tend to the flowers.

Dinner was quiet. Kim eyed the baskets of clean laundry in the living room. The ironing board, already set up. Tammy moved her food around her plate and kept checking the time on the microwave. He was going to ask her about her law school applications again when she said, "I liked the pink and purple flowers outside."

"The flowers?" he said.

"Yeah, they're nice. Love the colors."

"I'm not done with them yet," he said, looking at his plate to conceal his smile. *She noticed the flowers. She noticed his hard work.* "I'm mulching them tonight. You'll like them even more tomorrow."

"Tonight? It's so late," she said.

He cleared his plate in three bites. "No, no," he said, still chewing, "I have energy."

Tony shouldered two thirty-pound bags of mulch from the garage to the front lawn. Ripped them open on his knees. Carefully surrounded the leftmost flower bed with wood chips, shoring up the stems, brushing off any that covered the leaves. The operation reminded him of handling transistors in his engineering lab in Dalian. The rush that he got from working with his hands, the satisfaction that he earned from fixing something. Now the most he worked with his hands was typing on a keyboard. Coding was nothing compared to working with metal, wires, real materials—the earth.

By the time he finished propping up the flowers, his shirt was ringed with sweat. He couldn't wait for Tammy to see the hydrangeas in their full glory tomorrow, drenched in sunlight. He sat on the grass to catch his breath. Reclining on his elbows, he took in the sight of the house. *His house.* It had taken years of saving, but they had finally made it. A milestone of his success in this country. Back in Flushing, when they visited all the open houses in the suburbs, this had seemed like a distant, if not impossible, dream.

The house had looked perfect—with its royal blue door and lush lawn—the first day they had moved in. A week later, he noticed cracks along the window frames. The next month: a strip of shingles that flailed in the rain. An invasion of weeds and a dying rosebush. Everything was always in need of replacement or repair, and though he made weekly trips to the hardware and gardening stores, he felt like he was barely keeping up. Sometimes, he thought about putting the house back on the market.

After padding in the last of the mulch, Tony went to the kitchen for some orange juice. Through the open doorway, he saw Kim ironing a pair of jeans in the living room. The ticking clock of the *60 Minutes* introduction played in the background. Ice rattled out of the stainless-steel fridge, an appliance beyond their budget, but he'd had to have it. Kim had suggested a cheaper one—white, plastic. "It's not even made in America," he had countered, "and this one has a five-year warranty."

As he opened the fridge and reached for the Tropicana carton, a screw twisted in his chest. An immense pain tore through his rib cage. He caved into himself, but remained standing, arm frozen in midair. He felt urgently afraid, as though he had forgotten something very important. The pain shot up his neck, radiating to his jaw.

His eyes scurried across the room, but he didn't know what he was looking for. The fresh scallions on the top shelf. The red cap on the gallon of milk. The strawberry yogurts that Kim liked for breakfast. The colors pulsated; they glowed. Had life always been this beautiful?

He staggered backward and saw the list for Meixin Super-market, pinned to the fridge by a magnet. The Post-it next to the telephone on which he had written the numbers of Tammy's friends in case he couldn't find her. The chipped counter—his next project. He still had responsibilities. He needed more time.

He heard footsteps and thought of Kim and Tammy. He was desperate to see them, touch their faces. He had to tell them something. Was it to check the stove? To drive carefully? He couldn't find his mouth.

As he hit the floor, he felt the chilled air from the fridge wrap around his face, his neck, all the way down to his weary ankles. It was nice. Like a cold towel on a hot day. *This must be what the breath of God feels like*, he thought, before it all went black.

FOURTEEN

Tammy

A scream.

I was out of my room and down the stairs before I even realized it was my mother's voice.

In the kitchen, the refrigerator door was open. My dad's legs rested flat across the floor. His chunky Reebok sneakers. Mulch caught between its shoelaces. A series of dull thuds. My mother's fist pounding against a broken drum. "Tongheng," my mom yelled. "Tongheng!" Her voice trembling as she tried to shake his body awake again.

It was me who dialed 911. The operator sounded like she had just woken up from a nap. I repeated my address twice. "Hurry, my father is dying," I said.

It took the paramedics thirteen minutes to arrive. They rushed into the kitchen with a gurney. My father had stopped breathing and my mother was performing CPR. I winced at the cracking sounds as she pressed down on his chest. A paramedic peeled her away. "We'll take it from here," he said, bending down to take my father's vitals.

"I'm a doctor..." my mother said in Mandarin, her voice trailing off.

I sat her down on a chair as we watched the paramedics work on my father. Minutes later, we heard him gasp for air. Then my mother began to cry.

Outside, the wheels of the gurney scored my father's beloved lawn. The red and white flashing lights had drawn an audience. Neighbors huddled in their robes and collared pajamas, forming a semicircle around the ambulance. Curious, solemn faces—all ghostly white. They never accepted my family—gave us weird looks and Stepford smiles when we moved in. Many offered to have us over for coffee to "welcome us to the neighborhood." None followed through. My mother excused their behavior. "They're afraid we might lower their property values," she had said.

I stared at the gardening hose on the lawn. I wished I could turn it on and spray the false concern off their faces.

After loading my father into the ambulance, a paramedic said, "Only one family member can ride with us."

My mother squeezed my hand, nodding for me to go.

As I was about to hop into the metal box, the paramedic said, "You need shoes."

I looked down at my bare feet, covered in damp grass. I must have lost my slippers somewhere between my room and the yard.

"Here," my mother said, holding out the Velcro sneakers she'd just been wearing.

As I adjusted the straps, I said, "We'll be okay, Mom."

A neighbor whom I didn't recognize took off her robe and wrapped my mother in it.

I braced myself as we drove off. The back bay of the ambulance was a moving cage. Every time we turned down another road, the medical equipment inside the overhead cabinets clinked and clattered like wind chimes.

One paramedic hovered over my father. Two sprays under his tongue. An oxygen mask over his nose and mouth. My father fogged up the silicone with his breath. "Blood pressure and pulse are holding steady," said the paramedic. He brought out a medication kit. Announcing each as he gave it to my father: aspirin, nitroglycerin, clopidogrel. I memorized them immediately. My mother would want to know.

"Breathe," the paramedic said. "You. You have to breathe."

He was talking to me. I was dizzy, but I shook my head. Each inhalation hurt. Oxygen turned into daggers in my lungs. I clutched my own chest and heard my own heart beat—strong and pounding, wildly alive. I wanted to rip it out. Lend it to my father for the night.

I took my father's hand. He looked past me with a far-off stare. His body jostled like a rag doll every time the ambulance hit a bump. The way it moved—almost rippling—was frightening.

I met his eyes again and began counting his blinks. Ascribing meaning to them. One blink meant *hello*. Two meant *don't worry*. Three: *I love you*.

Then the blinking stopped. His eyes remained shut.

"Dad!" I shouted. "Wake up!"

"What's his name again?" asked the paramedic. "Tong-something?"

"Just call him Tony," I said.

"Tony," said the paramedic, "Tony, my name is Greg. You're going to be okay. We're in an ambulance now, and we're on our way to the hospital. Your daughter is right here. Hang in there. You're going to make it."

That was the moment my mind snapped open. A slice of time that I'd remember forever. I can still hear the paramedic's steady voice. The straightforward, unadorned way that he addressed my father as Tony. Not a doorman, not an engineer, not an immigrant. But just a man.

I stared at my father, the man whom I had wished dead hundreds of times before, and felt the fog of my hatred for him burn off. He hadn't been the ideal father. He hadn't been the American dad I'd longed for—the one who read Harry Potter to you at night, cheered from behind the chain-link fence during tennis games, or chaperoned field trips to the Bronx Zoo. I'd never reached for him when I'd felt stressed or sad or lost. When I'd been confused about exams or school applications or my career, I hadn't sought his advice. At my most cynical, I hadn't seen our relationship as parent and child. I'd seen us as a transaction: he was the investor, and I, his speculative stock.

But when the paramedic talked to my dad, I was suddenly pushed back. Out of myself, out of my body. And with the shift, a new perspective clicked in: my dad wasn't just my dad. He didn't simply exist in relation to me. He was larger than that. He was Tony. He was his own person, and when I thought of the integrity of his life as a whole, I finally recognized it for what it was: a miracle. A foreign transplant who had toiled for years as a handyman, plunging toilets, then as a doorman, sorting mail. Bottom of the melting pot. Look at him now. A United States citizen. Leader of his own engineering team. Homeowner in a wealthy zip code. Daughter at Harvard. The true manifestation of the American dream.

I had thought that I didn't need him. Was better than him, knew more, was smarter. But now, as I gazed at his face—soft and fallen—I could see that everything I was, everything I could one day become, was only possible because I was standing on his shoulders.

Time tugged me backward and I was two or three years old again. I looked up at my father's face. I was in a bicycle basket. We went over humps in the road. Little bumps. Big bumps. I bounced. I heard myself laugh, a soft, feathery coo. I saw my father smile. I felt the tears in my eyes, tears of laughter, falling on his hands, which were still brown with dirt and splinters of mulch.

Every day when my father overworked himself—in the office, taking care of our home, supporting my tuition—that was him conveying love. Every day when he got mocked for his accent, laughed too late at a joke, or was passed over for a promotion. Every day that he allowed himself to live in a country that took every opportunity to remind him that he was and always would be *other*.

I kissed his hands. "Daddy," I said, tears in my throat. "Daddy, please don't go. I'm sorry. I'll do better."

For what felt like forever, the only response I received was from the beeping of the monitors. High-pitched sounds accompanied by flashing dots of light.

But then his hand twitched. A wave coursed through his body. A strong breath. His eyes fluttered open and found mine.

"Daddy," I kept repeating, "Daddy, I love you."

FIFTEEN

Tony

Something was wrong. There was acid in his mouth. His chest was pounding. No, the pounding was on top of his chest, reverberating in his bones. Someone said, "You're not pushing down hard enough."

"Stop it," he tried to say. They were always pushing him down.

But his mouth went slack.

His body was deadweight.

Thick ropes tightened around it.

He was moving but he was still.

Was he going somewhere?

No, no, he couldn't go. He had to tell someone before it was too late. "I forgot to close the refrigerator door," he wanted to say. "The food is going to spoil!" He hated wasting food. His father hated it more. In the village, there were no scraps. Even rotten food found a stomach.

A man's voice said, "Aspirin."

I don't take medication, he thought, as his mind drifted off.

Beeping, beeping. An alarm clock?

Time for work.

He tried to sit up, but there it was again—that weight on his chest. He had carried it for years, but when had it become this heavy? When had it begun to hurt? Had he grown too old, too weak, to persevere?

"Let me up!" he wanted to scream.

Daddy.

A honeyed voice that sent a spark through his body.

He reached for a blurred face as he felt the world disappear again.

The next time he woke up, a man with glasses was touching him.

"It's okay, Tony," said the man in a stern voice. "I'm Dr. O'Leary. You're at Hillcrest Memorial Hospital. We're taking care of you."

Kim came into view. *"Wo jiu zai ni shenbian."* *I'm right by your side.*

"Your eyes. They're red," Tony said to her.

"We're going to take you in for a minimally invasive operation to fix an artery in your heart," said the doctor.

"My heart?" said Tony.

"You had a heart attack, but your ticker's still pretty strong. A quick angioplasty and stent placement should be all you need to live a long, healthy life."

He had a heart attack? The beeping on the monitors picked up the pace. "No, no, no," said Tony. His whole face had grown sweaty. "No, it's not me."

"Take it easy," said the doctor.

"Call Dr. Leung," said Tony, reciting a 718 area code. Since coming to this country, he'd only had his original doctor from Flushing.

"We already did," said the doctor.

"Dr. Leung knows Chinese! I'm Chinese!" said Tony, trying to get out of the bed.

Kim grabbed his hand and squeezed it. *"Bie pa. Jiu shi ge xiao shoushu." Calm down. It's just a small surgery.*

This was all wrong, he thought, looking past the two round faces in front of him, settling on a chunky TV box with antennae on it. It looked like it belonged in China in the eighties. That must be a totem. A sure sign that this was only a very vivid dream. He tried to pinch himself, but his fingers fell limp against his arm. Weariness took over again—his eyes grew hot and sunken. Each blink took three to four seconds. "Clara was here, not me," he said, closing his eyes.

"Daddy." There it was again. That honeyed voice. "Dr. O'Leary is going to help you. You won't feel a thing. Don't worry."

The voice sounded sure.

She was here. She would protect him.

He melted into the bed. Each breath lulled him more into the deep.

"Don't worry," he murmured. "Irish is good."

Exhaustion pulled him under.

The sharp smell of *bai jiu* tickled his brain. Was that his father, handing him a drink? Where was his mother? He missed her. It took a minute to get his head on straight. No, it wasn't *bai jiu*—it was disinfectant.

He slowly opened his eyes.

Kim and Tammy stood at the foot of his bed.

He looked around at the room's blue-and-white color scheme. "I'm in the hospital," he said, more to himself than to them.

The doctor came in. "Oh good, you're up. The angioplasty was a success. How are you feeling?"

"Tired," he said. But this wasn't mere exhaustion. Not the kind of fatigue he could sleep off. It was a terrifying, yet surprisingly satisfying, fragility. He had never been so connected to his body—the delicate ligaments in his leg, the timid gasps of his lungs, the soft throb in his shoulder. He could trace each inhalation to the corners of his existence—healing, soothing, reawakening. The pulse in his thumb, the rise and fall of his tongue. He focused on his breath—it was all that mattered. And when it left him, he felt a flash of fear. Would it return? His body deflated. His chin slumped forward. And then, by some miracle, the next breath was on its way.

Tony had finally slowed down enough to recognize it, to be grateful for it: the simple joy of being alive.

"Hungry?" asked the doctor, placing a juice box and a bag of pretzels on the table in front of him.

"Try to eat," said Kim.

Eating. The concept seemed foreign at first. But then he remembered he had a stomach. He palmed the pretzels into his mouth. "Where's the salt?" he said.

Dr. O'Leary laughed. "You'll have to lay off that stuff for a while. You'll also have to find a way to reduce your stress too."

"I don't feel stressed," Tony said.

"How's work been lately?" said Dr. O'Leary.

"Work doesn't make me stressed."

"It sneaks up on us."

"How long do I have to stay here?" said Tony, wishing he were in his own bed, wearing his own socks.

"When was the last time you rested?"

"You mean took a vacation?"

"Truly rested. No plans, no nothing."

"You mean when I'm sleeping?"

Dr. O'Leary gave a chuckle. "We're keeping you here under observation for three to five days. Maybe you can get some rest here."

"I'm going to visit you every day," said Kim.

"Visit?" said Tony.

"They only allow one person to stay overnight with you," said Kim.

"I'll be here," said Tammy.

Tony tilted his head toward the doctor. "She's at Harvard. She'll be in law school soon." He said it with a smile, but everyone in the room understood it as a veiled threat. There would be no misunderstandings with Tammy around. No question she couldn't ask, no request she couldn't make. She would demand the highest standard of care for her father, and she had the smarts, the foresight, and the ferocity to ensure that he got it.

"All good," said Dr. O'Leary. He passed some papers to Tammy for review and left the room.

The hospital room wasn't exactly peaceful. Incessant bedside monitor noises—some coming through the thin walls of neighboring rooms. Creaking sounds his bed made every time he moved. Intrusions by nurses checking on his vitals every few hours. Bleating of phones, dinging of elevators, clunking of wheels. Tony wondered how he'd be able to fall asleep, but within minutes of Tammy turning off the light, he was out cold.

Ten hours later, he woke up again.

"Bravo," said Tammy. "That was the best medicine you could've taken." She was lying in a makeshift bed, with the top half of her body on a single-seater couch and her legs curled over a wooden chair. She didn't look like she had slept a wink.

"Are there more pretzels?" he asked.

"I think we can do better than that," she said. She got up and went over to the nurses' station.

Thirty minutes later, Tony scarfed down a dish of skinless chicken, steamed spinach, and sweet potatoes. It was the best worst thing he had ever tasted.

The day was a revolving door of doctors, nurses, and nutritionists.

Dr. O'Leary arrived midmorning to give him the rundown of his at-home care. The regimen of pills, recommended eight hours of sleep, 150 minutes of activity a week, methods to reduce stress. "Box breathing. Sounds silly, but it works. Even on CEOs." He spoke directly to Tony, but kept Tammy in the corner of his eye, not moving on from each topic until he saw her nod.

Then it was the nutritionist, who looked the same age as Tammy. She wore her hair in a bun, and Tony spotted a small star tattoo behind her ear. "You need to commit to heart-healthy eating," she said. "Vegetables, fruits, whole grains, no processed foods."

"I told him to eat oatmeal," said Tammy, sighing, "but he keeps at it with the Frosted Flakes."

"Too much sugar," the nutritionist said.

"I don't eat a lot of it. One bowl at most," said Tony.

Tammy's cell phone buzzed. She screened the call.

"Was that your mother?" he asked.

"No," she said.

"Who?"

"Vince."

"Why didn't you pick up?"

"I'll call him later," she said.

"I like him," said Tony. "He's good for you." The young man and his blue blood family were going to take Tammy places—places she couldn't reach on her own. It was another introduction he should thank Oliver for.

Tammy rolled her eyes. "You like him so much, you be his girlfriend."

An hour later, Kim finally arrived to relieve Tammy. "I spent all morning cooking," she said, unloading bags of Tupperware containers.

"Don't be mad," she said.

"Why would I—" he started. But then he saw the contents. A steaming egg custard—too pale to contain yolks. A naked flounder devoid of crispy skin. He touched the plump dumpling. "Shrimp and pork?" he asked.

"Just shrimp," said Kim. "You know the new rules."

Shrimp without pork. Unthinkable.

But like a good husband, he devoured the dumplings with a smile, and then excused himself to nap.

Kim fluffed his pillows every time he woke up and even stole an extra pillow from somewhere.

Later, Dr. O'Leary cleared him for light movement. "Just a few laps around the floor," he said.

When they were alone again, Kim shook her head. "You're too weak for that."

"My legs want to move," said Tony. "My body wants to move."

She laid a hand on his chest. "You need rest."

Before he could object, she said, "Are you being nice to Tammy?"

"Of course," he said.

"You should be grateful. Not every daughter would do this," she said.

"She's on spring break."

Kim's eyes narrowed. "Even if she weren't, she'd come take care of you. You know that, right?"

With his teeth, he peeled off a piece of dried skin from the top of his thumb. "I don't know," he said. "I don't think she likes me."

"I didn't know you cared about that," said Kim.

In the evening, Tammy returned, freshly showered, backpack full of books.

She studied for her British poetry and ancient political thought courses as Tony picked at his dinner. A platter of chicken, green beans, and brown rice. Tammy spruced it up with a perfectly ripe avocado that she brought from home.

The nurse came in to ask whether he'd had a bowel movement yet—*no*—and if he'd tried walking—*also, no.*

"I can walk with you," said Tammy.

"Your mom didn't like the idea," said Tony.

"You always listen to Mom? What do you want to do?"

"I don't know," he said. Over the years, he had defaulted to Kim's counsel. After all, she was usually right.

"I want to try," he heard himself say.

Tammy held out her arm.

Together, they slowly trod up and down the hallway. His body felt liberated. He could feel his intestines unfurling. Not too long after, he finally had that bowel movement.

The second day passed without much fanfare. He tried oatmeal for the first time. It reminded him of the rice soup he'd had as a child. "I'll eat *anything* else but this," he said, as he pushed away the bowl.

People came in to check on him. All his vitals looked good.

In the afternoon, Kim helped him walk around the floor. She seemed almost offended when she heard that he had taken his first steps with Tammy instead of her.

By the third day, Dr. O'Leary announced that one more night of observation should do it. Tony was elated. He couldn't wait to return to the peace of his own home. Take in fresh air, do laps around his own block. Regain the independence of his own life.

He even missed his cubicle at Iris Telecom. How lucky he had been to be there all these years instead of in this hospital bed. Curtis had sent him flowers and a jumbo card that his colleagues had individually signed.

Get well soon, Tony! We need you back!

The office isn't the same without you.

Salads on me when you return.

His absence was noticed. He had the privilege of making money and providing for his family at a company that made him feel wanted and valuable.

"That's nice of them," said Tammy, reading the card.

"They didn't have to do that," he said.

"They care about you, Dad. You know that, right?"

"They really didn't have to do that," he said, blinking back tears.

That final night, he was on the wrong side of sleepy. Too stirred up, thinking about returning to his renewed, shiny normal.

"Not tired?" said Tammy, bringing her chair next to his bed.

"I must have slept too much during the day," he said. The past few days, actually. So *that* was rest. That was what he needed. He had run at one speed for so long, he forgot how to turn back the dial.

"Obviously, I wish you didn't have a heart attack, but I'm kind of glad you did," said Tammy. "We haven't spent this much time together—ever."

"We used to live together," he laughed, but he knew what she meant. He patted her arm. "You'll have to get some sleep soon. I know it can't be easy for you. Squashed up on the chair at night."

"Why don't you tell me a story," she said.

"A story?"

"About your life in China," she said. "Before me."

She had never asked about that. "Before you," he said, slowly, clawing backward into what felt like lifetimes ago, "your mother and I were just kids."

"Kids?" she said, leaning forward, a giggle in her voice.

"We didn't save one penny of our salaries. Spent it all on movies and dinners—even bought a keyboard! I used to play

your mom love songs." Those were the days. He couldn't remember ever losing his temper then. It had all been so easy.

"How?" she asked. "What about rent?"

"The university I worked at paid for our housing."

"Saving for retirement?"

"The government pays for that separately. We would get
eighty to a hundred percent of our salaries once we retire."

"What if you lost your job?"

"Zero chance of that happening. We'd basically have to
steal money or kill someone."

Tammy knit her brow, steeped in thought. "If you had all
of that in China, why'd you come here?"

"Why did I come?" said Tony, questioning his own logic
in that moment. Then he saw the ugly TV on the wall. "For
that thing!" he laughed. "Life in Dalian wasn't perfect. It
would take us a year and a half to buy a TV smaller than that
one over there. Two years for a fridge. Even making a meager
wage in America, we could afford those luxuries."

Tammy didn't find any humor in what he'd just said. "You
left for a *TV*?"

Of course she didn't get it. How could she? She hadn't lived
in that world. To live in a house in China, you practically had
to be one of the twenty members of the Politburo. Where job
security also meant job immobility. There was no switching
to a better role. There was no climbing the ranks based on
your merits. You had to wait your turn—for the person above
you to retire. "That TV meant something. It meant living.
Not just surviving."

"Surviving?" Tammy countered, waving an arm around
the hospital room. "You're working yourself to death here."

"I couldn't live in a country where my head already hit the ceiling," he said.

"But you've hit a ceiling here. If you were born in America, with your skills, you'd probably be CTO of Iris Telecom right now. No way would you still be working for Elijah."

He took Tammy's hand in his. What she said was true, but there was a greater truth that she had failed to see. "There was always going to be a ceiling for me. Whether I stayed in China or came to America. But here, in America, there's no ceiling for you."

Tammy trembled. "Daddy," she said, streams of tears rolling down her face.

He could feel her pain mixed with his. He bent his head down, remembering every time he lashed out at her, every time her face scowled at the sight of him. That wasn't how he wanted to be a father. He swore that he would be better than his father had been to him, but he couldn't escape his upbringing. He had become a monster all the same.

"No," he answered himself out loud. "I'm still young," he declared. "I'm young enough to change."

His mind flashed to the title of the latest self-help book that Curtis had recommended. *Change Your Mind to Change Your Life.*

He would read. He would study. He would master self-help like he did his engineering courses. This work was no different from the work he had already done. Except that it was far more important.

Change Your Mind to Change Your Life.

And his life was Tammy.

SIXTEEN

Oliver

2015

"We need to reopen the comp issue," Kip said into the speaker-phone in the center of the table.

Oliver held back a sigh. He couldn't believe that Kip was going through with this. Pepsi had already agreed to a generous compensation package for the exiting C-suite at Lemonatta. They were even buying out their stock options at two times their strike price.

When Kip had revealed the details to Lemonatta yesterday, the entire executive team had been pleased. Wyatt Kellerman, the company's CEO, even said, "I know we rode you hard on this one, Appleton, but you nailed it. You're done."

It was some random VP's offhand joke that rankled Kip. "You know, I thought the package would've been larger. I'd heard the legendary Kip Appleton would flip you over and shake you until there wasn't anything left in your pockets but lint. And then he'd come back for the lint." Everyone laughed. Kip did too, through a clenched jaw.

After the call ended, Oliver immediately advised against upping the ask. "You heard Kellerman. We did good," he had said.

Kip stared him down. "Did that sound like a happy client to you?"

Tammy hurried into the conference room. She was late—not a good look in front of Kip. Oliver pulled out the chair next to him. She gave him a quick smile and shuffled through her papers.

"Where were you?" Oliver whispered.

Not looking up, she gestured with her index finger—*hold on*.

"We'll need a twenty percent bump on the current package," said Kip.

"That's out of the question," growled Martin Fishbein, the opposing counsel. Fishbein had a naturally gravelly voice, and the static of the speakerphone only made him sound more like the Crypt Keeper. His firm—which already cornered the market in Chicago—had recently opened an office in New York and swiftly poached two clients from Steinway & Appleton.

When Kip had found out last month, he had thrown a chair at his assistant. She barely looked up, then went back to typing out his billables. "Fran knows I never aim directly at her, just in her general direction," he had explained.

Tammy tapped on the table and passed a report over to Kip. As he drank in the highlighted portions, the edges of his mouth curled. She had given him a winning hand.

"We took it upon ourselves to do a little survey," said Kip, leaning into the speakerphone. "The last ten mergers of this size."

Tammy leaned back in her chair, waiting for him to deliver the blow.

"The executive payout was, on average, eighteen percent higher. So really, we're just looking for the market rate," said Kip.

"I'm guessing that comp package was mixed. Stock and cash," said Fishbein. Pepsi offered Lemonatta an all-cash deal, and cash was king.

"Overall value is what matters here," answered Kip. "And just between us, Kellerman wasn't pleased when he saw this report. Thinks you guys are trying to scam him. I tried to talk him out of it, but he's not going to sell for anything less."

Oliver shifted in his seat, uneasy with the old man's bluff. If Fishbein called him on it and the deal imploded, the client could sue for malpractice. But Kip lived and died for this shit. Kip was a wire walker, a Viking, a guy for whom the deal itself wasn't enough—he always had to turn it into a zero-sum game.

"I'll take it back to Pepsi," said Fishbein, "but I will say, if you're really hell-bent on going down this path, it might reduce the purchase price for the whole deal."

"If that's what it comes to," said Kip.

"So your execs are okay with the shareholders getting less money as long as they get more? The press is going to love that."

Kip rolled his eyes and made a jerk-off gesture. "Well, Fishbein, who worked to make the company this profitable in the first place? I can tell you who didn't—the lazy-ass shareholders, shoveling in their dumb money and crossing their fingers."

After a long pause, Fishbein replied, "You have a way of looking at things."

"Ring back when you have good news," said Kip, hanging up the call. He swiveled in his chair, his gaze landing on Tammy. He made a show of evaluating her outfit—a slate gray Theory sheath dress with a cinched belt at the dips of her waist. Finally, he said, "Look who came in and dropped a bomb."

"I'm glad it helped, Mr. Appleton," she said.

"No, no, slugger. You can call me Kip."

Tammy nodded and locked eyes with Oliver.

Oliver kept his connection to Tammy a secret from Kip. He had told her that it was to protect her reputation by avoiding accusations of nepotism at the firm. But really, it was because she was special to him, in a way that he couldn't yet understand himself. He wasn't ready to invite Kip to interrogate their relationship and pry out how he really felt.

Oliver even warned her not to bring up her connection to the Van Fleets. He didn't want to give Kip a reason to swoop her under his wing. Who knew how he would use, change, or corrupt her.

"You don't want people to treat you differently because you're engaged to a client's son, right?" Oliver had reasoned. "At least wait until you're married. It'll give you time to earn a reputation on your own merit."

After a moment of mulling it over, she had said, "Plus it'll look extra bad if we ever break up."

"Break up?" said Oliver. The two of them had been dating for eight or nine years.

She shrugged. "Forget I said anything. I'm just stressed from the wedding planning."

"You're getting married," he said. "Come on, get excited. It's only the rest of your life!"

"Yeah, I'm excited," she said.

After the conference call, Oliver stopped by Tammy's office. "You didn't want to let me in on your idea?" he said.

"I only thought of it an hour before the meeting and was trying to pull together all the stats—"

He waved her off. "I'm just pulling your tail. It was a smart move."

She frowned. "Close the door," she said.

"Did you get more goss about whether Covey is actually dating that paralegal who draws in her eyebrows at her desk every morning?" he asked.

But Tammy's face had turned serious. "What Kip did in there." She winced.

"What are you talking about?" he said.

"Obviously he didn't have time to show the precedent compensation report to Kellerman. I just handed it to him at the meeting."

Oliver chuckled. "That's Kip. You'll get used to it."

"He negotiated in bad faith."

"*Bad faith?* Please don't ever say those two words in front of him. He'll think you're a pus—" Oliver stopped himself.

"A what?" she said.

"A girl," he said. "Listen. Kip plays a little dirty. It's not illegal."

"Not exactly honorable either."

"Where's the honor in losing, *slugger*?" he said.

"That nickname better not stick."

"We'll print it on the back of your marathon shirt."

"Fucking try it," she said, finally smiling. "Last eight miler in the morning."

"See you bright and early," he said.

It was September already. Only three weeks until the big day.

"You're almost rid of me," she said.

"I'm counting down the minutes," he said.

The truth was, Oliver looked forward to marathon training with Tammy. It was the high point of his day. When Steinway & Appleton had announced their pro bono marathon challenge the previous spring—sponsoring every runner with a $5,000 donation to a charity of his choice—it was assumed that he would partake. His head was one of the only ones in the partner pool without a single gray hair. "You have to represent the M&A group!" said a particularly unathletic partner in his fifties. All Oliver heard was: *more work for you.*

It wasn't the marathon itself that had worried him. Even though he was in his midforties, he reckoned that he could muscle one out that very weekend. It was the commitment to training—or rather, Tammy's rigorous five-month plan—that caused him pause. When she synced the schedule to his Google calendar, merely reading it made him grimace. He should've expected this when he had suggested that they buddy up for training. Now that he thought about it, maybe part of him did.

The first couple of runs were torturous. When his alarm went off at 5:45 a.m., he'd barely managed to drag himself out of bed. He blasted EDM into his headphones to push his legs forward on the Central Park trails. All while watching Tammy bounce around like a bunny in her Lululemon outfit that molded to every curve of her body like a layer of butter.

Their favorite songs fueled their runs until the relentless replays permanently burned them out. Halfway through the second week, they swapped playlists. He had her romantic Brits between his ears—Adele and Ed Sheeran. Her knee drive turned more aggressive on his AC/DC and Guns N' Roses. By the fourth week, though, they had completely ditched the music. "Distract ourselves by talking instead?" he had said. And so, the traditions began.

Tuesday's mornings were reserved for goal setting, or, as millennials called it, "manifesting." Oliver usually wished for new clients. For two weeks in a row, Tammy "asked the universe" for a shout-out in the firm's public deal announcement, which listed a select group of associates that the partner had considered most vital to the transaction. "I want to send it to my parents," she said.

Wednesdays included midrun fuel of gummy bears and swapping childhood stories. It started with cute nuggets about how their mothers used to dress them and what their favorite snacks were—his were ants on a log, and hers were koala biscuits with chocolate inside. Then they began to tell each other stories that they had hidden from others. The time she stole a Beanie Baby—Zip, a black cat—from the pediatrician's office by placing it inside her hood. When he had cheated on calculus tests in high school by writing equations on the undersides of Band-Aids.

Thursday's training session was reserved for brainstorming where they'd go for lunch that day. "Chipotle?" she had said on their tenth week.

"Hard pass on the diarrhea," he said. "Hot bar at Green Harvest?"

"I'm not spending fifteen bucks on a turkey sandwich."

"I'll pay for it," he said. "Come on, how can you say no to organic bacon?"

"I think organic bacon is probably just normal bacon," she said. "How about Indian food—Ashoka?"

"What'd I just say about Chipotle?"

"You're useless," she said.

They ended up sharing an order of samosas and the Tandoori platter at Ashoka.

Saturdays were reserved for long runs and a movie afterward. The blockbusters were out in full force that summer. *The Avengers*, *Fast & Furious*, *Jurassic World*. Every other weekend, he obliged when Tammy picked an indie release at the IFC Center. He was surprised how quickly he forgot about the itchy seats that didn't recline and popcorn-strewn floors sticky with spilled soda. The documentaries on the Stonewall uprisings, conditions of detention facilities near the Mexican border, and impact of glacial melting on villages in the Zanskar Valley pulled him into another world.

The only day of training when they didn't see each other was Sunday. Cross-training day. Tammy usually went to hot yoga. He didn't understand how cat-cowing in a hundred-degree room "healed" the body, but he almost offered to get them memberships at a studio near The Rosewood when he learned that Vince was accompanying her to classes. As for Oliver, he told her that he cycled. He didn't even own a bike. Every man deserved some rest.

As Oliver walked down the hallway from Tammy's office to his own, his hands pulled on his belt. He had tightened it by one notch already, but it was time for two. As he opened his closet to get a good look at himself in the hanging mirror, he surveyed the heap of worn-out knee sleeves, Nike shorts, and Dr. Scholl's support pads and swelled up with a sense of pride, and then—panic. Tammy's voice rang in his head: *You're almost rid of me.*

Three more weeks. That was all that was left before the daily structure she'd grafted onto his world would disappear. The structure that had pulled them closer together, that had turned her into his partner, his confidante—his best friend. It also hadn't escaped his notice that, in the last four months, he had landed three more clients, smoothly juggled five signings and seven closings, and even inspired the night-shift janitor to register for a 5k race on Thanksgiving. He liked the man he had become. As he tightened his belt, he struck a Superman stance. This evolution, this shinier Oliver. It wasn't a development of self. It was the intervention by a force of nature.

Then it was November 1, race day.

Before he knew it, they had sailed through Staten Island and Brooklyn. Their pace slipped in Queens, but they found a second wind in the Bronx. Through it all, Tammy stayed by his side. They were keyed into each other's rhythms by now. When they needed to zone out to music, when they had to complain away the pain, when the other needed a reassuring smile and a pack of Gushers. Now they were nearing the finish line—poetically, back to their training ground: Central Park.

Oliver could feel his organs jostling. His face was flushed and sunken, simultaneously dried out and covered in sweat. A rhythmic pain cracked in his ankles. He couldn't quite trust his vision, which sometimes told him he was jogging in place, other times, like the ground was slipping out from under him. But he kept on pushing through the vertigo, even as the pavement tilted beneath his sneakers. He leaned forward, just as Tammy had coached him to. Forward propulsion.

She was running a few meters ahead. A New York City Marathon number—3011—flapped on her back with the slogan: *Women Can Run…for Government too!* Her French braid bounced above it, with strands threatening to come loose. One glance at her long strides and he knew that he was holding her back. His leg muscles were locking up, but he could see that hers still had a spring in them—another gear.

A man in a traffic-cone-orange sweatband jogged past him. Oliver had noticed him way back at the starting line. "No grown man wears a headband. He might as well have tattooed *virgin* on his forehead," he had whispered to Tammy as they waited for the pistol blast.

Tammy slowed down. "Come on! That's your favorite virgin. We can't let him beat us!"

"Go on without me," he gasped back.

"We promised to finish this together."

He couldn't even catch his breath to argue.

"Look how close." She pointed to a distant spot. He squinted. Did that sign say that they had 1.5 miles left or only 0.5?

She slapped him on the back. "Let's go, old man." She sped up, teasing him to catch her. Every few paces, she turned around to check that he was still there.

The crowds behind the metal barriers were growing larger and louder, screaming out the bib numbers of the runners. An archway made of red and silver balloons—the finish line was in sight. His cadence quickened for a moment before almost flatlining again. The world looked blurry and shiny. He reached out for balance and found Tammy's hand. An intense hold that triggered a dumb smile across his face. She practically tugged him over the finish line.

The blaring of horns. Cheers. Faces, morphing together. A rush of emotions poured through his veins—relief, joy, accomplishment. And something painful too—a familiar feeling he couldn't ascribe a shape to.

People were patting him on the back, but where was Tammy? He had lost her in the mess.

"Tammy?" he yelled. "Tammy!"

Someone wrapped a sheet of foil around him and said, "Walk it off, walk it off."

He looked around for her, on the verge of tears, but she found him first, diving right under his arms and hugging him. Their bodies, sticking together. His lips accidentally grazed her forehead and he tasted her sweat. Suddenly, he had the urge to kiss her.

"Pizza," she called out, breaking away from him. A volunteer in a T-shirt was handing out free slices. Tammy came back with one for Oliver too. He ate that piece, another, and her leftover crust. Anything to suppress the impulse he just had.

They stumbled through the crowd, joints aching, collecting oranges and pints of chocolate milk. On the 72nd Street finisher's exit, they both glanced at the remarkably empty medical attention tent before grabbing two waters from an open cooler.

"You feeling okay, slugger?" said Oliver.

"Honestly, I feel like I want to cry," she said, looking at the pavement.

"We read about that, remember? Lots of people get emotional after crossing the finish line," he said.

"Do you feel emotional?" she said.

He shrugged. "I'm just glad it's over."

They passed a line outside Van Leeuwen. "Ice cream?" he suggested.

After twenty minutes of waiting and a few samples apiece, they sat on a bench on Columbus Avenue to enjoy their eight-dollar scoops of ice cream.

"We could've bought a gallon of Turkey Hill," she said.

"But *this* is vegan," said Oliver, spooning a bite of honey-comb ice cream.

"My parents would die if they knew," she said. "I thought of them at the finish line."

"How come?" he said.

"All those hours, those miles," she said. "Getting up and getting it done even when we didn't want to. The sweat, the calluses, the cramps. All that planning and dedication. The sacrifice. Pushing everything to the back of our minds. Tunnel vision, running toward the end." She looked at him, eyes welling with tears. "Do you think my parents will ever feel finished? Do you think they'll get to rest one day, relieved that they made it?"

"I think," said Oliver, not sure of what to say, "I think they're proud of you."

"They did it for me, you know. Everything," she said.

"They did it for your family," he said.

"I hope one day, I can make enough money so I can take care of them forever. They'll never have to even think about working again."

"That's really noble of you," he said.

"It's not about being noble," she said, breaking off a piece of her waffle cone. "Or, I don't know, maybe it is."

"You love them," he said. "Reminds me of how I used to love my own family."

"Used to?" she said.

There was that feeling again, rising up like it had after he finished the race. "My family," he croaked, "they're complicated."

"Isn't every family?" she said.

"Well, not every family has my grandfather in it."

"Your grandfather? You've never mentioned him before."

Oliver felt a dam burst inside him. That was the thing with secrets—no matter how much you pushed them down, they longed for freedom. And when the right person was in front of you, when the right time came, they sprung in search of the light. "My grandfather's in jail," he said. "He's in jail."

"What?" said Tammy.

"His name is Matthew Agos," he said.

He let it sink in.

"Oh my God," she said. "The Wellspring Foundation?"

Wellspring. To this day, it still sounded like a beautiful waterfall, a sea spray, a fountain full of magical pennies.

"Yes," he said, clearing his throat. "One hundred million dollars in donations. Do you know how many wells they actually dug in Uganda?"

She stayed silent.

"Well, technically, they *did* dig one. For a photo op. And my grandfather embezzled the rest of the money," he said.

"Your grandfather is Matthew Agos?" she said, mostly to herself. "But your last name."

"My parents changed it," he said. "I don't really know if they knew about my grandfather's crimes before the SEC did.

Sometimes, I think erasing the Agos name was their way of
erasing their guilt."

Tammy nodded. "Yeah," she whispered.

"I was twenty when I found out," he said. Tears flowed
freely down his face. He didn't bother hiding them. They felt
good—a cleansing relief.

"I'm so sorry," said Tammy.

"It's okay," he said. He meant it. He had released himself.
Telling Tammy the truth made him feel powerful, in charge
of his own path for the first time in years. Now she had the
chance to know the real him—to love the real him.

He admired the concern on her face—it wasn't about him,
it was for him.

"When was the last time you saw him?" she asked.

"Years ago. He didn't really want to see me much after I
didn't sponsor his release."

"How come you never told me?" she said.

"I didn't tell anyone."

"Why?"

"I'm his blood," said Oliver.

She nodded.

For a while, they both focused on the people passing in
front of them. A group of teenagers, huddled together, completely immersed in their own world, blocking the street. The
deliveryman, weaving around them by skipping into the cy-
cling lane.

"I'm glad you told me," said Tammy.

"I am too," he said.

"You know, I'm nothing like my dad," she said.

Oliver shook his head. "It's different. I even *look* like my
grandfather."

She slid toward him on the bench, closing the distance between them. Her hand rested on the side of his face, turning it to meet her eyes—soft, brown, full of conviction. "Doesn't look like that to me," she said.

He held his breath as her eyes fell on his lips. A moment later, he felt a kiss on his cheek. He was a little disappointed until she said, "You know I love you, right?"

"I love you too," he said.

She used the ball of her thumb to wipe away his tears.

He clutched her hand.

He wished he could hold it forever.

SEVENTEEN

Tongheng

1987

Tongheng met Kuan-yin at Dong Feng diner near Qingniwa Bridge. He had barely slept the night before, and even now, the anxiety that had weighed on him all week continued to clamp around his throat.

"What time's the car coming?" he asked, flattening his hair.

"Not until six this evening," she said. "Father tried to schedule it for earlier, but the driver was booked out for the entire day. Another official wanted him on hand to tour some locomotive factories." She filled his plate with a fluffy *mantou*, salted duck eggs and sliced turnip.

"I shouldn't eat," he said. "Saving room for my mother's cooking." He tried to sell it with a smile.

She studied his face. "No," she said. "You're nervous."

"I'm never nervous," he said.

"I know," she said, picking up the *mantou* and shoving it into his mouth. "That's because you have me."

She always knew how to make him laugh.

He took a big bite of the plain steam bun and paired it with the rich umami of the duck egg.

This was considered the simplest of meals in the city of Dalian, but he could've only dreamed of eating it when he was little. In the fishing village of Shui Long—*Water Dragon*—roughly a hundred *li* from Dalian, it had been rice soup for breakfast, lunch, and dinner.

"I can't wait to meet your parents," said Kuan-yin.

"Soon," he said. That depended on whether he could argue his father into submission. Tongheng was traveling back to the village to ask his father to ask Kuan-yin's father for her hand in marriage. It seemed like a very roundabout way of doing things, but he had to follow the family law.

"What are you worried about?" said Kuan-yin. "My father's going to say yes."

Tongheng already knew that. At the young age of twenty-four, he had just been promoted to assistant professor at the Dalian University of Technology. A rare feat, a testimony of a bright future. Kuan-yin's father hadn't been completely sold on him, but upon the good news, he said, "Next time your parents are here, I would like to treat them to dinner." He was suggesting *hui qing jia*. The first formal step toward a wedding.

"I'm not worried about *your* father," said Tongheng.

Kuan-yin opened her mouth to speak, but then took a bite of *mantou* instead. Like any wise soon-to-be wife, she knew when to stop prying.

Shui Long village was only an hour's car ride away from Dalian. When he told the driver the destination, the old man fell out of politeness for a moment. *"Nongcun?"* he said. *The countryside?* He recovered with a stiff nod and said, "It'll be a scenic ride."

Tongheng said, "Doing a favor for a friend."

"I need more friends like you," said the driver, puffing on a Zhonghua cigarette.

Tongheng kept his head down, pretending to read the newspaper that had been left in the back seat. He shouldn't have listened to Kuan-yin and taken the bus instead, even though it would've meant billions of stops, overcrowding, and hard seats.

"My father can ask his company to borrow the driver for the day. The high ranks do that all the time," she had said when Tongheng first brought up the trip.

"I'd rather not," he'd replied.

"One day, my father's going to be your family too," she said, already picking up the phone.

Tongheng wondered what his father would say if he saw his son arrive in a car—the unearned luxury of it, the message it sent: *I'm better than you.* But Tongheng let Kuan-yin schedule the car anyway. He was a man now. He couldn't be afraid of his own father's reaction. Still, he shuddered. He could already hear his father's voice if he saw the car or heard through the grapevine about it. *"You're not fooling me,"* his father would sneer at him. *You're not fooling me,* thought Tongheng, clenching his fists.

The driver pointed out the window. "The fashion show is coming to town!" The exhibition building—five stories high—was draped with a long red cloth that said those exact words in white lettering. "I gotta ask the boss for tickets."

Tongheng scanned the surrounding bank buildings—tall, stately, one higher than the next. The streets were evenly paved, punctuated with lampposts and clear signage at every turn. Buses, trams, and a few cars filled the roads, but most transportation was by way of bike. Men in dress pants and women in long dresses effortlessly balanced their briefcases and purses as they rode in an organized procession. Tongheng squinted at the glint of a passing cyclist's gold watch. A reminder that he shouldn't be here, that he didn't belong. He had arrived not by way of birth, but by way of grit.

Dalian was one of the nation's crown jewels. In the last century, the city ping-ponged from rule under Britain, Japan, Russia, Japan, and back to Russia, before finally returning to China in 1950. Foreign control had left the area in a much better state than when they found it, modernizing the city beyond its original means, building it into the country's largest foreign-trade port, intermixing Chinese and Western styles into its blueprint, and making it the Paris of the Far East. Shui Long village—a tiny fishing hamlet—unfortunately, had no such overseas intrusion. It had stayed distinctly Chinese.

Near the entrance of the village, Tongheng got out of the car and thanked the driver with a jar of candied hawthorn that Kuan-yin had prepared the day before.

The driver took it with glee. "My wife loves these." He peered into the village and looked back at Tongheng. "What a shithole," he said. "You really are a good friend."

Walking into Shui Long, Tongheng felt a pang of nostalgia. The village and its inhabitants barely changed over the years. Since he was a child, he had wanted to escape to the city, but now he recognized that the village had a tranquil simplicity. It was ugly, but at least to him, a familiar ugly. Like every fishing village, the ground had the look of day-old rain with

patches of crusting soil. The clothes hung to dry in front of
the houses, underwear billowing in the breeze. The crooked
door of Old Yang's place, the wood planks in the windows of
Little Chen's. Roofs were fortified with tarps and tin up and
down the street. He knew the inside of each individual house,
the single room for everything—eating, sleeping, cooking,
drinking, dying—everyone in the family living body to body.
He could smell the whiff of the communal pits for shitting,
could almost hear the buzzing of the swarming flies, but even
that reminded him of how open, freely, and unabashedly he
had used to live.

Making his way through the maze of houses, Tongheng
bowed his head to a middle school classmate who was clean-
ing bushels of clams in a plastic tub. Neighbor Zhu tramped
down the street, carrying buckets of bait and trash; his boots,
clad with mud. Zhu must've just finished setting out the fishing nets for the evening. He stared ahead with a glassy, vacant
look, exhausted after a hard day's work. Everyone made way
for him. No small talk. Just respect.

That old man had earned his solitude, but something different was going on with Tongheng. The villagers left him
alone for another reason entirely. When Tongheng had first
left for Dalian, people were excited and cheered him on. After
all, he was the first kid from the village to test into college
in years. And every time he returned, they wanted to know
about how he was doing, what endeavors he was pursuing,
what he had seen. But as his accomplishments grew, the distance between them did too. The villagers approached him
less and less, until slowly, they barely talked to each other at
all—him, too embarrassed to tell them about his successes,
and them, too embarrassed to ask.

Tongheng turned a corner onto the stretch where his parents lived. A hard-faced woman sat on an upside-down bucket, eating a bag of sunflower seeds. She placed the shell in the middle of her teeth, cracked it, and caught the liberated kernel on her tongue. "Here, city boy," she said, offering him some sunflower seeds from her palm.

Did he know this woman? Her leathery, tan face, pocked with dark spots, looked pinched, as if every feature gravitated toward her nose. Even the gullies of wrinkles seemed to spiral inward. He couldn't place her—had his memory begun to blur the faces in the village? "Hello, Auntie," he said.

She spit out an empty shell into the small growing pile next to her feet. *"Ben dan,"* she mumbled. *Idiot.*

"Tongheng!" His mother was waving at him from down the lane.

"Ma!" Tongheng said, breaking into a run toward her.

As they embraced, he surveyed the state of the house. Concrete, sturdy, and with a new tiled roof that he had paid for. The ratty burlap curtains had been replaced with the embroidered cotton ones he had brought on his previous visit home. But there was no mistaking it as a fisherman's house. A pair of boots were tied to a window railing, hanging upside down to dry out.

"That lady who was talking to me—who is she?" he asked.

"Oh, her? Be glad you haven't met her before. Grumpy fool. She's from Xitang village. Moved here a few months ago to marry Lao Sima when her first husband died. Now Lao Sima wishes he were the dead one."

"I wonder how she knew where I was coming from," he said to no one in particular.

"Your father is already asleep," said his mother, ushering

him inside. "He has to wake up at three to check the nets. The merchants are coming to buy their hauls earlier and earlier these days."

Tongheng was relieved. He glanced at his father's back, perfectly still on the *kang* bed—a concrete box, framed with wood and topped with layers of blankets. The stress of dealing with him could wait until tomorrow.

Next to the bed were a bamboo back scratcher and two packets of playing cards. Tongheng had lost his interest in card games long ago. The one time he beat his father in *zhao pengyou*, the old man had slapped him upside the head in front of everyone. "Why did you hesitate to play your last card?" he said.

"I wasn't sure what you had in—" said Tongheng, before feeling the brunt of his father's hand again.

"You should've known you won the game before even playing the card," his father spit. "If you counted the trump cards like any monkey could do, you would know that you had the only one left."

The neighbors playing with them fell silent. One meekly pushed the clay bowl of winnings—counterfeit cigarettes, no Zhonghuas here—toward Tongheng.

"Luck isn't winning," said his father, kicking the bowl. It rolled down the road, tinkering before breaking apart. Seemingly out of nowhere, three children had sprung toward it and scooped up the contents.

His mother lit the small wood-burning stove at the far end of the room. Soon, Tongheng smelled the clam broth bubbling in the pot—briny yet sweet—not one note different than it had been when he was a child. As his mother stirred thick, handmade noodles into the soup, they spoke in hushed tones, as to not wake his father. Tongheng told her about his promotion, the latest hydraulic system he was working on, and that Kuan-yin had recently finished her internal medicine rotation. "Can you believe we'll have a doctor in the family?" he said.

"Only the smartest girl for my *baobei*," his mother said.

He puffed up every time his mother called him *baobei— my treasure*.

Everything he said to his mother sounded grander. His news visibly delighted her. Maybe this was what it was like to be a parent, thought Tongheng, to feel the joy of your child's triumphs in multitudes.

After they ate the hot noodles, they sipped on the remaining broth, lifting the bowl to get every last drop.

As Tongheng suppressed a belch, his mother laughed. "How polite! You've really become a city boy."

Later that night, she laid out a clean blanket on the *kang*, right next to her. He hadn't slept that soundly in months.

A rough shake of his shoulder woke him up. "Huh?" he said into the darkness.

"Get up, *Xiao Tong*," said a gruff voice. *Little Tong*. His father handed him a padded jacket.

"Now?" said Tongheng.

"The traps," said his father.

"What happened to Jiping?"

"I gave him the day off. Why pay someone when my son's back home?"

"Happy to be a bargain," Tongheng joked.

It was late in the fourth month, just on the cusp of spring. The sun wasn't due to rise for more than an hour. But the quarter moon was sufficient. Its light glanced off the waters and the smooth rocks of the shore, illuminating everything they needed to see—the skiff, the engine, the floating beads in the water that signaled where the nets were.

At least thirty boats were docked at the harbor. They were rudimentary—motors on slabs of wood. Each boat had a lucky red ribbon tied to an errant piece of wood that jutted upward. They floated in waters littered with instant noodle buckets and drink cans. His father's skiff was a mere ten meters long. As Tongheng boarded—stepping on the ribs of the vessel to avoid the wet trough—he immediately caught a splinter in his palm.

"Here," said his father, taking off his own gloves.

"Thanks," said Tongheng, slipping them on. He planted his hands against his thighs. Those gloves had to stay as far away as possible from his nose.

His father started the engine and steered them out to sea. All things considered, the morning was peaceful. But the clanging of the motor reminded Tongheng of why he couldn't live this life.

As they passed a set of buoys, Tongheng gripped the side of the boat. It had been a couple of years since he'd last been out on the water, and he didn't know if it was the rocking or his anxiety that was making him nauseous. He stared out in the darkness, making sure his father didn't see the sick look on his face. He'd better ask about the marriage to Kuan-yin now, before the nausea got any worse, before he was in an even weaker position.

Three years ago, when he had first told him that he was dating the daughter of two architects at the development bureau, his father had scoffed, "I bet all the back scratchers in the world that this won't last more than a year."

When Tongheng had objected, bringing up his own list of

successes, his father retorted with four chosen words: *"Men dang hu dui." Matching doors and parallel windows.* The philosophy that marriages only lasted if the pair came from families of equal socioeconomic standings.

"The world is different now," Tongheng had said.

"It will never change enough for parents to throw away their prize daughter to you—a country boy with a shit inheritance," his father had said with a tone of finality. As the words cut deep, Tongheng noticed a flash of pain in his father's eyes. He felt it too—shame.

The engine banged.

"Ba?" Tongheng said. "I need to ask you something."

"Are you happy?" said his father.

"Happy?" said Tongheng. "I didn't know you believed in that."

"Your mother says I'm getting soft in my old age."

"I have a good job and a good woman. What is there to be unhappy about?" said Tongheng.

"You know, I was certain you weren't meant for this village the moment you were born. Never heard a baby scream so loudly, like you were outraged at where you'd landed," said his father. He pointed to a nearby set of floating beads. Together, they hauled the net onto the boat. The catch was better than average. A few yellow croakers, fat greenlings, and a dozen prawns.

As they moved on to the next net, his father said, "It's hard being a parent."

"So I've heard," said Tongheng.

"You're handed a sacred duty. One you can't understand until you have it. And it makes you push. Makes you push and push until you forget who it is you're really pushing, or what it is you're pushing for."

His father had never been this candid with him. Tongheng stayed quiet, in hopes of hearing more. Of maybe even getting to actually know his father as more than the commander of the family—more than merely his implacable supervisor and enforcer.

His father said, "But the pushing doesn't matter in the end. When you die, you're dead. Whether you made a million *yuan* or were a beggar."

Incredible. This, coming from a man who lashed him with a belt for playing an extra hour of basketball with his friends instead of studying algebra. "Right," said Tongheng. "I'll stop working so hard and just go panhandling."

"What are you trying to prove?" asked his father.

"What do you mean?"

"I'm proud of you for the promotion at the university. But what's next? A professor with a better title?"

"I could invent something," said Tongheng. "I have a few ideas."

"All the invention happens overseas."

"I could go there."

"They won't let you invent anything there. At best, you'll work for them. Maybe your child, I don't know," his father said, trailing off as they pulled up another haul. "Look, *Xiao Tong*! Sea cucumber!" he said, cheering. "My buyer has been chasing me for this."

"*Ba*, what are you trying to say?" said Tongheng.

His father stopped the motor. "Come sit with me," he said, motioning to the small deck on the bow.

For a while, they sat side by side, gently rocked by the water, warm sprays of the sea misting their faces. Finally, his father said, "I'll ask her father."

"You will?"

"I want you to be happy."

"I love my life," said Tongheng. It was true, but even he had to admit that it sounded unconvincing. "Why don't you visit me in Dalian? You'll see."

"Some people belong at sea," said his father.

"Some in the city," said Tongheng.

His father pointed above them at the influx of birds stirred by the dawn. "And maybe, some, in the sky."

EIGHTEEN

Tammy

2016

My phone screen lit up. Four missed calls from my father.

"Can you *not* look at your phone right now?" Vince said.

"My dad called—"

"He can wait." By Vince's standards, everything ranked below the wedding. It was a few months away. A spring fete on the rooftop garden of Rockefeller Center with the pillars of St. Patrick's Cathedral in the background. Then a few floors down for the glittering reception in the Rainbow Room. Since Vince's family was footing the bill for the wedding— my parents' contribution of $20,000 might account for a fifth of the floral arrangements—I deferred to them on wedding decisions.

And there was no doubt in my mind that they would make it the envy of every bride. The Van Fleets were the type of people who knew how to have a good time. Their adventure vacations—helicopter rides into the northern lights and night skiing in Japan—left me fatigued and thankful to be sitting at my office desk again. The tasting menus at Eleven Madison Park, the coins of Moulard duck foie gras and delicate mounds of creamed arrowleaf spinach, just left me constipated. While I clinked glasses with John Legend at a charity event at the Whitney Museum, my ankles twitched in four-inch heels, my body drained after a twelve-hour day at the firm. The wedding would be draining too, I was sure of it, but it would be tasteful. All I had to do was show up.

I put down my phone.

"What is it about now?" I said. "Didn't we already fix the seating chart?"

"It's not that. Listen, I thought about not telling you, but I know how you feel about surprises," said Vince.

That made me nervous. His surprises never quite landed with me. Mine never went over well either, especially with my parents. At least not last year, when I said we were going to a noodle shop in Midtown but then surprised them with a table at Sushi Yasuda.

"I can't get full on sushi," my dad had grumbled.

"I don't want to pay this much money for uncooked food," said my mother.

"I'm paying for it," I said, not that there was any confusion about that. I had paid for all of our meals out since I'd started working at Steinway & Appleton.

"Your money is my money," my mother had said.

They grimaced through the omakase experience, picking up sashimi with their chopsticks and turning them this way and that, as though inspecting them for flaws. The waiter looked sorry for me.

"What is it?" I asked Vince. "Your mom wants to commission an ice sculpture of the two of us?" I was joking. His mother had immaculate taste.

"I want to make a toast in Chinese at our wedding," he said. "I've been learning Chinese for the last few months."

"You don't have to do that," I said.

Vince was visibly disappointed. "What's wrong?"

"Nothing, it's fine."

"I wanted to do something special. Make our wedding really *us*. Chinese American."

I felt my throat close up. "Chinese American?" I croaked.

"Exactly," he said.

"Who exactly is the *Chinese* person here?" I said.

He scratched his head. "I don't know what you're getting at."

"Am I Chinese?" I said.

"Is this a trick question?"

"Check the flag on my passport."

Vince put both hands up in a conciliatory gesture. "I'm sorry, I'm sorry. I thought it'd be cool."

He thought it'd be cool. That about summed up his privilege. Vince thought that being bilingual and being born in a different country was *cool*. That growing up in Flushing, where people rolled down metal shutters in front of the storefronts at night, added *character*. That not being able to afford a trip to Disney World, and instead, hoarding quarters for the two-minute ride on the mechanical Donald Duck that did nothing but jerk back and forth outside Xing Long Supermarket, was *cute*. That overseeing my parents' medical procedures and writing up their wills was *admirable*. Vince could never understand me. It wasn't his fault. How could he understand my past experiences when I had packed them into neat sound bites? The past that I tried to shake off, but that tagged along like fleas.

"Do whatever you want," I said. "I just don't like you hiding things from me."

"*I'm* the one hiding things?" he said.

I froze, trying to keep my face expressionless.

"Don't think I haven't felt something's off," he said.

"Define this *something*," I said. Why was I challenging him? I knew what that something—or rather, someone—was, but I wasn't ready to confront it yet.

Since the marathon, I had been spending more time with Oliver. While he could leave the firm by seven, it was rare for me to escape by ten. That meant that my dinners consisted of takeout at my desk. It had started slowly. Just once a week, and then twice, and now almost every day, he had been staying at the office later to have dinner with me. He established a routine of picking up our orders from the delivery boy in the lobby, knocking a made-up tune on my door, unwrapping my plastic utensils for me, and surprising me with desserts—banana pudding, fig mascarpone Cronuts, and Chinese almond cookies.

"How sweet," I said, biting into the almond cookie with a satisfying crunch.

"Me or the cookies?" said Oliver.

"The cookies, obviously."

"I remember your dad snacking on them when he worked at The Rosewood."

"Yeah, they're his favorite. Says they remind him of China."

"You ever been back?"

I shrank at the question. My parents had returned to China every year or two since we moved to Scarsdale, but I always had an excuse not to join them. Academic summer camps for talented youth. Preseason tennis practice. Internships during winter break. Sometimes, I enrolled in something intentionally, after I learned about their trips. In high school, I had chalked it up to needing space. I lived with them every day. Let them have their vacation and let me have mine. And then later, I had dreams of going elsewhere—Maui, Marrakesh, Dubrovnik.

Dalian was at the bottom of the list. My parents waxed on about the stunning seaside and tree-lined streets, the new buildings that had gone up in Zhongshan, its financial district, and of course, its unparalleled seafood. To this day, my father refused to eat conch anywhere else.

"But isn't the traffic horrendous there?" I countered. "You can't even go on Google."

They told me about my cousin's pregnancy, how she glowed at eight months, and my grandfather's birthday, when they surprised him with the new iPhone. I feigned excitement. I barely knew their names.

I felt nothing toward Dalian. Maybe I never would, but this wasn't the time to explain all of it to Oliver.

"You imbeciles got me too busy to go anywhere!" I said.

"What's got you stuck here this week?" he asked.

"Dougherty's trucking client," I said.

"That Dougherty. He's a lucky guy."

Vince shook his head. "I don't mean you're actually hiding something." He shrugged as he searched for words. "You feel different. I dunno. Maybe we just haven't spent a lot of time together lately."

"I know," I said, "but that's firm life. Do you want me to quit?"

"Of course not," he said. "It's not about your job."

I wiped the screen of my phone with my sleeve.

"Are you happy here?" he asked.

The phone went off again—my dad was calling for a fifth time.

I locked eyes with Vince, but picked up the call.

"Hello?" I said.

"Where are you?" said my father.

"Home," I said. "I was away from my phone."

"Your grandfather's dead."

"Which one?"

"My dad," he said.

"I'm so sorry."

"He was eighty."

"Do you want me to come home?" I said. It was already half past ten at night. I probably wouldn't get to Scarsdale until midnight.

"Actually, he was eighty according to the lunar calendar. Seventy-nine in America." My father's voice broke.

"I'll call a car now," I said.

As my Uber slowed down on our street in Scarsdale, I said, "It's the white one with the blue door."

The driver spotted it. "Nice," he said, nodding at the house.

I noticed that the siding had been cleaned and brightened with a power wash. The lawn was neat and lush. The flower beds flourished in orderly rows, each a different pop of color.

After his heart attack, my father had finally hired professionals to tend to the house.

"How much should I tip them?" my father had asked me.

"Ten percent? Fifteen if they did a good job?" I said.

"Eighteen percent, then," he said. The extra bucks were what he called "the minority tax." A payment for equal respect and treatment.

I got out of the Uber at the bottom of our driveway, near the garbage can and recycling bin, which stood shoulder to shoulder like a pair of black and blue brothers. The porch light was on—one of the only not dimmed on the street. I was about to ring the doorbell when I glanced at the coffee table, spotting a red pack of Zhonghuas and a plate rimmed with ashes and butts. I had never known either of my parents to smoke.

I followed my mother into the kitchen. My dad was at the table, his hands cupping a Harvard mug. He looked like a wilted flower. He stayed sitting as I hugged him. "I'm really sorry, Daddy," I said.

He nodded, bottom lip trembling. "I can't even fly home until morning." He placed his elbows on the table and covered his face with his hands.

"I can help you pack," I said.

"I already did it," he said.

I stood behind his chair. I didn't know what to do with my hands. I looked to my mother for instruction, but she was busying herself with cubing a snow melon. *My grandfather died,* I told myself. I thought I should cry but I felt nothing. I was told that my grandfather had held me as a baby, but I had no memory of that. I only saw the man's face in photographs, heard his voice from our short conversations where I wished him Happy Chinese New Year. Still, he was my blood, and I thought that when the time came, I would feel *something*.

What I did feel was sympathy for my father. I sat next to him and touched his arm. "I'm here if you want to talk."

His hands fell on the table, and he picked at a scab of dried sauce. "Your grandfather was a fisherman. Even in his old age, he tried to go out to sea once a week."

"He loved the water," said my mother. "One time he visited us in Dalian, we took him to the most expensive seafood restaurant in the neighborhood."

My dad laughed. "After one bite, he put his hands on his hips and said, *My sea cucumber would've had more taste than this piece of jelly!*"

"Sounds like he took a lot of pride in his work. We must take after him," I said.

"How would you know?" said my dad, sighing.

"I wish I knew him," I said.

"Well then, how come you never came back to China with us?" he said, picking at the table again.

"I'll go," I said. I meant it. I had my excuses, but they were just a cover. And look at where they'd gotten me. My grandfather was dead and I felt no grief, no sorrow, only remorse. And shame. My cheeks flushed, and I felt the welling of tears.

"It's too late," said my father.

"Eat some melon," said my mother, sliding a bowl in front of him.

I checked my phone. A string of text messages from Vince. Tonight had been just great—everywhere I went, I fucked things up. And now I couldn't say or do one right thing to comfort my father. I wished that I were eating takeout with Oliver.

A loud clang. My father had hit the edge of the dish with his hand, sending it clattering onto the floor. The fallen melon pieces looked like upside-down mahjong tiles.

"You think you can ignore me? *Ni zhege hunqiu.*" *You bitch.*

I looked over at my mom. Was he talking to me?

"I asked you a question!" he yelled. He lunged, knocking the phone out of my hand.

"What the hell?" I said.

"Just because you make so much money, you think you can ignore me? Not picking up my calls earlier, and now, looking at your phone while I grieve my dad?"

"I'm sorry," I said. "I was just checking—"

"If you add up all the money I've made in my life, it's more than you've ever made!"

As I snorted at that ridiculous statement, I caught my mother's eyes. They were filled with fear, but I knew that mine weren't. "That comparison doesn't even make sense," I said, retrieving my phone from the ground.

"Right, because you're *so* smart. You think you're better than me. *You came from me! You came from your grandfather! From China!*" He smacked his hand against the table in a threatening strike and leered at me like a feral animal. I met his stare, not wincing or moving away from the table.

He hadn't blown up at me like this in years. He had been dutiful in reading self-help books, filling out anger management workbooks, even journaling his emotions. His pleasant demeanor disarmed me. I'd let my guard down. But now, the beast was back.

"You're a real piece of work," I said.

He looked at me, blankly.

I stood up, towering over him. "Don't know what that

means, huh? Guess you're not so smart either, then. Twenty-five years in this country. How many more do you think you need to understand English?"

He moved to stand up.

I backed up a few steps. "Come any closer and I'm calling 911," I said.

Everyone in the kitchen stayed still. My dad, with his hands out at the ready. My mother, hunched in her chair. And me, standing over both of them, daggers in my eyes.

After a few moments of holding my breath, I sensed a cord loosen in my father. His body slackened, deflated.

"I'm leaving. Don't follow me," I said.

As I walked to the front door, I heard my father shout after me: "You're not fooling me!"

NINETEEN

Oliver

The DJ played techno bangers at an ear-shattering volume. That was the saving grace of Cielo Club. There was no possibility for small talk. No need to fake conversations. All Oliver had to do was nod, fist-bump, and down shots of Don Julio.

Tonight, Kip was entertaining Paul McNickle—a current client of Martin Fishbein's. Their night had started with steaks at Smith & Wollensky's and a layover at an invitation-only speakeasy hidden behind a Laundromat. In the car over to Cielo Club, Kip and McNickle snorted lines of coke for a pick-me-up. "Get ready to go hard tonight, fellas," said McNickle. For him, that had meant turning into a slovenly, suburban teenager—untucking his shirt, swinging his hips wildly off the beat, and dancing with his finger in the air. Kip mimicked the finger dance in solidarity. Seconds later, he pocketed his hand with a shudder. Even he had lines he wouldn't cross to land a new client.

Oliver nursed a gin and tonic while Kip and McNickle did shots with a waitress in a keyhole leotard. Kip's table was surrounded by twentysomething girls—a roster of models pumped into the club by shady promoters. Oliver recognized some regulars. They giggled as Kip rested a hand on their lower backs. The new ones tried too hard, woo-ing and shim-mying their tits whenever the DJ said to make some noise. The scenes at the tables around them weren't that different: older men in suits and ties, swiping their corporate cards, swarmed by an entourage of girls in dresses each tighter than the next. Two empty tables in the corners were roped off for a Mets shortstop and a low-tier Kardashian who may or may not show.

The flashing lights stopped strobing for a moment and la-sered over a single table. A blare of horns announced a march of waitresses waving sparkler-topped champagne bottles. Mc-Nickle clapped for the show and then shouted something into Kip's ear. Oliver didn't need to read his lips to know that he was asking when their table would receive the same treatment.

For years, Oliver had indulged in this lifestyle, bypassing the long line outside because Kip paid off the bouncer. Yes, he had enjoyed it, but lately, it began to feel like something that it was objectively not: cheap. Buying this orchestrated happiness for a night cost thousands. These days, he'd rather split truffle fries with Tammy in her office.

Thirty minutes later, Kip granted McNickle's wish. A string of servers arrived at their table, with the sparking vodka bot-tles. McNickle gazed around the group like a peacock in the moonlight. His face said it all: Kip had just stolen Fishbein's client.

Oliver sat down, hoping no one would notice. This wasn't where he wanted to be, but at least it was better than being alone, in bed, staring at the ceiling. For a solid month, he'd had trouble falling asleep, tossing and turning with a pit in his stomach, thinking about Tammy. He'd been captivated by her, even from the very beginning, when he first found her playing the piano at Clara's. Through the years, he'd watched her grow up, making small discoveries about her along the way, each one shaping his new reality: he loved her.

But he had no idea if she felt the same way. If she didn't, then telling her the truth would destroy their relationship. Could he risk it? He finished his drink, wincing as the liquor burned the back of his throat. Could he have chosen a more complicated person to fall in love with?

"Get into it," said Kip, sliding next to him. "Need help?" he said, revealing pill capsules in his hand.

"Another night."

"Somewhere else you'd rather be?"

Oliver shrugged. "Tiring week. Late nights at the firm."

"Who's keeping you there?" Kip leaned in.

"What?" said Oliver. Did Kip know?

"Which client," said Kip. "What'd you think I meant?" His Botoxed forehead didn't move, but Oliver knew he'd picked up the scent.

Before Kip could press the matter, Oliver grabbed a pill. As he swallowed, he felt Kip's gaze. The man was examining him like someone who was admiring his own creation.

The chemicals swept him away sooner than anticipated. Before he knew it, the bustling crowd and kinetic music went from nuisances to extensions of himself.

"Good?" yelled Kip.

Oliver nodded, his teeth grinding in a comforting motion. A fire crawled through his veins, wiping his mind, lighting up his senses. The alcohol smelled sharp and sweet, the beads of sweat on the moving bodies glittered. The music matched the beating of his heart, every song seeming like it was being played just for him. His world morphed, the colors grew more saturated with every passing minute.

"There we go!" said McNickle, raising a glass to him.

Oliver had an urge to hug the man, who suddenly didn't seem out of place at the club anymore. If anything, McNickle seemed to be the type who belonged here more than anyone. He was probably a nerd in high school, doughy and pimply-faced, never picked for any sports teams, didn't even bother trying with the girls. But he didn't let that get him down. Instead, he worked with what God gave him: brains, discipline, and patience. Pulled himself all the way up to CEO of a Nasdaq-listed company, and even more impressively, a client that Kip lusted for.

Oliver shouted, "You're a good one, McNickle!"

The crowd surged as if in support of his declaration.

"This is the Oliver I know and love," said Kip.

Oliver pushed away the model he was dancing with and gave Kip a kiss on the cheek. "You're family."

Kip's face flushed red and he pulled Oliver to his chest. "You're like a son to me, you know that?"

"Ride or die," said Oliver, feeling a closeness he had never felt with his parents. There was one other person who could compare. With his chemical clarity, he couldn't deny it anymore. He loved Tammy. They should be together. It was fate. He could run to her right now.

"This stuff is magic," said Kip. "My dealer wasn't lying."

The music kept pulsing, tying the night together. Oliver felt like he could go on forever like this.

And then, with no memory of how he got there, he was in the back seat of Kip's Aston Martin, windows down, a throbbing bass on blast. "Where are we?" he said.

"Scarsdale. Dropping McNickle at home," said Kip. "We're a full-service firm."

"Scarsdale," said Oliver. Maybe he could visit Tammy. But no, she was living in the city. With Vince. Disappointment washed over him, sobering him up a little.

"Those girls were so hot," slurred McNickle. He slumped in the passenger seat, head flopping around like an infant's.

"We'll go to an even better place next time," said Kip.

"Vegas!" said McNickle.

Suddenly, the brakes locked. Oliver flew forward, almost hitting the center console. Time stopped as he stared at the furry hunchback in the middle of the road. A raccoon. And then, as if it sensed Oliver, the animal turned toward the car, with a sinister, yellow eyeshine. He could see that its humanlike fingers were curled around a metal can.

"Kill the fucker!" roared McNickle from the passenger seat.

"How's this for community service?" said Kip, backing up the car to get some more runway.

"No!" shouted Oliver. "Are you guys fucking insane?"

Kip revved the engine.

"Stop!" said Oliver, gripping Kip's shoulders.

They heard a crunch under the wheels. But it was only the metal can. The raccoon had scurried away, watching them from the sidewalk.

"You shouldn't even be driving!" said Oliver, putting on his seat belt.

"Pussy," said Kip.

"It was only a raccoon!" exclaimed McNickle.

After weaving along streets bearing the names of fruits, they dropped off McNickle at Plum Tree Court.

"Sweet dreams," said Kip.

"Vegas," murmured McNickle, stumbling across his lawn. The front yard light turned on. His wife—ethereal in a billowy white robe—opened the door and let him in. As she waved at the car, mouthing a *thank you*, Oliver almost threw up.

"Come up to the front," said Kip.

Oliver pulled himself together and scooted into the passenger seat.

"Successful night," said Kip, "minus the raccoon fail. Thought you were going to fucking cry."

"I wasn't," said Oliver.

"Your grandfather would've slapped you into next week."

"Can you not lecture me right now? I'm barely thinking straight. How are you even driving?"

"A man can do anything if he puts his mind to it," said Kip.

Oliver chuckled. "You and Gramps. Two peas in a pod."

Kip tensed, focusing on the road in front of him. "Bronx River Parkway."

"You okay?" said Oliver.

"Where's that road we turned onto?"

"Kip!" said Oliver.

Tears were streaming down the old man's face. "Shut up," he said. "It's the fucking drugs."

Oliver had no idea Kip was capable of crying.

"Your grandfather is my best friend," said Kip. "He's my ride or die."

"I know," said Oliver.

"You don't know shit," said Kip. "Matthew—he found me.

I was a young, dumbass associate on a deal he was working on, but he saw me. No one believed in me like he did. I still visit him once a week in that disgusting facility that he has no business being in."

No business? thought Oliver, but he stayed silent.

"He taught me everything I know," said Kip. "I love him."

Oliver reached for Kip's hand, and to his surprise, the man held it. "I'm sorry," said Oliver, realizing that Kip was just another victim of his grandfather. That he had learned about friendship, loyalty, and love from the older man. Maybe Oliver could show him there was another way. A way that Tammy had shown him.

"I'm here for you," said Oliver. "You'll always have me."

Kip wiped his nose.

"Come on," said Oliver, trying to lift his mood. "Is this the fastest you can go?"

Kip turned to him, eyes gleaming.

"Let's see what this car is made of!" said Oliver.

Kip switched the headlights off.

The car jolted as it went from 25 to 50 miles per hour.

"Apple Lane! Peach Street! Apricot Road!" said Kip, naming the streets they were zooming past. He kept squeezing Oliver's hand, his energy—pure, contagious.

"Cranberry, Orange, Eisenhower!" said Oliver.

"Jefferson! We're running with the big boys now!" said Kip.

The Aston Martin passed 60, hitting 70 and rising. Oliver threw his head back, his other arm floating out the window. *This was a ride he never wanted to end.* The roar of the engine against the quiet night, Kip's warmth amplified by the chemical euphoria.

"Lincoln! Coolidge!" said Kip.

Coolidge, thought Oliver. *Wasn't that the street where Tammy's parents lived? Wasn't that the address on their annual Christmas cards?*

And then.

He opened his eyes just in time to see something collide with the windshield.

TWENTY

Tony

Tony heard Tammy's car door slam shut.

"Good riddance," he said, getting up from the table. He bent over the mess of fruit on the ground. "How dare she," he said. "I mean, can you believe that? My own daughter."

Kim stared at the wall with a stony expression.

"My dad died and she can't even stop looking at her phone," he said.

"You always have an excuse," said Kim.

"What?" he said. He was kneeling, cradling melons against his chest.

"The two times, years ago, when we had been late on paying rent. That year the residents didn't tip you well at Christmas. When you got flustered at the callback interview. You bring it all home—every stress the world puts on you—and you put it right on Tammy."

"This is different. My dad—"

"I would have left too," Kim said, her voice barely above a whisper.

Tony slowly stood up, staring at the plate of melons in his hands.

"*'I don't lose my temper anymore, my temper is even better than yours,'*" she mimicked him.

"I didn't lose my temper," he said.

She took a deep breath and said, "You are *so* idiot." She paused between every word, hammering them like nails.

"The floor's clean now," he said, bringing the plate to the sink.

"Always going on and on about how you've changed. How your temper is so much better than your father's."

"Did I use a belt? A broom? My fist?" he said, raising his voice. "Compared to other Chinese dads—"

"We're not in China."

"Well, maybe we should be!" he said. "If we were, she wouldn't dare talk to me like she does!"

Kim glared at him. "Coming here was your idea."

He didn't have a comeback this time. She was right.

Lately, he'd been wondering what life would've been like had they stayed in Dalian. Why had he fought so hard to forge a new life in the States? *But you did it*, he thought. *You succeeded where others couldn't. It all worked out the way you planned. You own a house, a lawn, a refrigerator. But did you lose more than you had gained?* When he had left China, he knew that he was walking away from the only home he'd ever known. He didn't realize that he would also be sacrificing a daughter—giving her away to another culture.

"It's all my fault, then," he said.

"Tongheng," said Kim, sighing. She got out of her chair

and took his face in her hands. "Tammy *is* better than us. If you weren't busy being so mad about it, you'd be proud."

He dropped his head, kissing her palms. "My dad died. He *died*. After everything he did for me, he's *dead*. She didn't even care." He had known, the second he'd heard his mother's voice, calling from around the world, that his father was dead. And he hadn't been there. He had left his father behind, just like Tammy was slowly doing to him.

"Your dad did a good job with you," said Kim, "and you did an even better one with Tammy. Look at her. Could you wish for more?"

"She's perfect," he said. Tammy was his little girl. Once, finding her a piano teacher had been his biggest problem. Now, when she came for dinner, she barely touched the baby grand piano they'd gifted her for her sixteenth birthday. Mostly, it sat silent, a reminder of her absence, but sometimes, he could talk her into playing. And when she did, even though she said it was too sappy, she would play "My Heart Will Go On," his favorite. And every time, a desperate swell of emotion washed over him, opening and breaking his heart, even though he barely knew the lyrics.

"I need to make things right," he said. "I have to go see her tonight."

"This late?" said Kim. "It's almost two."

"I'm flying out for the funeral in the morning. There's no other time."

"Just call her."

"I'll drive. It'll be fine," he said. A call wouldn't do. It had to be face-to-face. He couldn't allow anything to get lost in translation. Tammy had to know that he didn't mean any of what he'd said to her.

"At least there won't be any traffic," said Kim.

As he fetched the car keys from the drawer, Kim wet a paper towel and wiped the section of the floor where the melons had fallen. "It's sticky," she said. "The mess is still there even if you can't see it."

Wasn't that the problem with everything, he thought.

As Tony locked the front door behind him, he took out the pack of leftover Zhonghuas from his pocket. Kim considered smoking to be practically suicidal, but after a couple of dragged-out exhalations, he felt lighter—his jaw loosened, his shoulders relaxed. It wasn't that different from box breathing, he mused.

The neighborhood was still, quiet and dark. Even though it was February, some houses still had their holiday decorations. Tony had packed his away weeks ago. Before he'd moved into the presidential neighborhood, he'd aspired to be just like its residents. But the people on the street weren't perfect. The Brosnan kid next door smoked pot when his parents were out of town, sending the skunk smell right through Tony's kitchen window. The Kleins never picked up after their dog unless someone else was out on the street. Last year, when Tony fixed the hardware connection on the Gutmans' doorbell camera, he spied a "PAST DUE" envelope on the hallway table. Scarsdale was just a place where everyone was trying to do their best with what they had. In that way, it wasn't so different after all from all the other places he had lived—the village, Dalian, and Flushing—all the places he had worked himself to the bone to escape.

He put out the cigarette. Crisp, cold air cleared out his lungs. The stars were out, shining more brightly than usual, or maybe that was only because he had never stopped for long enough to really notice them. Tears gathered at the edges of his eyes as he searched for a sliver of moon. The moon that used to be the first light his father woke up to, the moon he'd never see again.

Tony slid onto the leather seat of his new Toyota Highlander. He had only upgraded from the minivan a few weeks ago.

What was the plan here? He couldn't be that far behind Tammy. He would go to the door of her apartment, say he was sorry and that his anger wasn't about her—it never was. He would share with her stories about his own father—the morning they caught an unopened beer can in the fishing net and passed it back and forth, chugging it on the boat; the time they almost died of laughter after setting off fireworks for Chinese New Year and accidentally lighting a cranky neighbor's roof on fire. Sweet memories that had been overshadowed for too long. Why was it that the bad ones had edged out the good?

Maybe he could convince Tammy to book a trip together back to China. They could walk past the hospital where she'd been born, visit the preschool where she'd gotten in trouble for hogging all the toys, the lake where they'd taken her to feed the ducks. He could show Tammy her roots.

The gas tank indicator arrow pointed at three-quarters empty. As he tried to remember which gas station on Post Road was the cheapest, he backed out of the driveway a little crooked. There was a light tap and then a rumbling. The trash can had rolled out into the middle of the street.

"Seriously?" he said out loud.

He shifted the car into Park.
He jogged out into the street.
He grabbed the garbage can.

TWENTY-ONE

Oliver

"Stop!" said Oliver. "Stop right now!"

Kip slammed on the brakes.

Oliver clambered out of the car.

"Close the fucking door! The light!" said Kip, fumbling for the button to turn off the car's interior lights.

"Oh my God," said Oliver.

Lying in the street, half a block away, was a body.

"That's a person," he said.

"Get back in the car," said Kip. "You're going to fuck everything up."

The body rolled over.

Then, from somewhere on the street, a woman screamed.

Oliver immediately ducked back into the car.

Without looking back, Kip made a quick left and accelerated through the neighborhood. Houses and trees flashed by, mailboxes and lampposts were there and then they weren't.

Time pulled apart, everything felt far away. A cold shock had taken over.

Oliver left himself and floated, as if watching the scene at a remove, suspended above a stranger, seeing everything happen as if it were happening to someone else.

He was numb, and then all at once: fear. A devastating, inescapable fear. He couldn't speak until they reached the highway.

"We have to call the police, don't we?" Oliver said.

They passed a speed limit sign. Kip touched the brakes.

"What was that person doing out in the street in the middle of the night?" said Oliver. He clasped his hands together to stop them from shaking. "This isn't happening, right? This can't be happening to us."

The highway was mostly empty, but Kip kept checking the rearview mirror.

Oliver searched his pockets for his phone. "Should we call a lawyer?"

Kip didn't answer. The whites of his eyes glistened in the dark.

"Should I call Covey?" said Oliver.

"No," said Kip. "Covey's been waiting for something like this to happen. He's been champing at the bit to scrape my name off the letterhead."

"Who do I call?"

Kip was silent for a moment. Then he exploded into hysterics.

"Oh my God, oh my God," he said, bursting into tears. "What just happened? I didn't see anybody! I couldn't see."

"What do you mean you couldn't see?" said Oliver.

"I can barely see at night anymore," said Kip.

"You can't?" said Oliver. "You drove all the way out here."

"I'm seventy years old!"

"We just celebrated your sixty-eighth birthday last—"

"You don't understand," Kip said. "You don't know what it's like to be old." He gripped the steering wheel. In the glow of the dashboard, Kip looked frail, vulnerable, his wrinkled hands thin and tremoring.

"It's okay," said Oliver. "It wasn't your fault. It was just an accident."

"Like you said, what was that person doing out there in the middle of the night?" said Kip. "No one could've seen him."

"That's your defense," said Oliver. "That's what you can say to the police."

"No one can find out," Kip sputtered. "The police—you know what they'd do to me."

"What do you mean?" said Oliver.

"They hate guys like us. They'll string me up! They'll want to destroy me. All because of who I am, what I've built, what I've earned. It wasn't even my fault, but they'll want to make an example of me." He grabbed at Oliver's hand. "If you say anything, my life would be over. That would be it. You know that, right? You wouldn't let them do that to me."

The car began to drift from the lane.

"Kip!" said Oliver.

The old man put both hands back on the wheel. "I couldn't see!" he gasped. "I didn't mean to hit anyone."

"Of course you didn't," said Oliver. "No one would think that." He rolled down the window. "You need some air."

"No," said Kip, "what I need is *you*. You can protect me. You're the only one who can."

Oliver put his hand on Kip's shoulder. The old man reached up and squeezed it. Kip was in trouble. This was Oliver's opportunity to take care of him. Kip hadn't meant to hurt anyone. But this one mistake, it would ruin the rest of his life. Oliver couldn't lose him. The man was more of a father to him than his own ever was.

Saving Kip was wrong. But it was right too.

"No one else needs to know what happened tonight," said Oliver.

"I love you," said Kip.

"I love you too," said Oliver, tears in his throat.

They drove past a sign for New York City.

"What do we do now?" Oliver asked.

Kip pulled out his cell phone. "This happens more than you think," he said. "I know a guy who can disappear the car. He's done it for our clients before."

Kip was in the middle of dialing a number when Oliver pushed the phone down. "Wait—police," he said. He seized up, holding his breath until the patrol car passed them. He had never felt that way around the cops before—always been able to smooth-talk his way out of a ticket, strode past them at the court's security checkpoints without a second glance, and exchanged thoughts on the weather in the bodega's coffee line.

Was this what it would feel like every time he saw them from now on?

As if reading his mind, Kip said, "Don't worry. They can't touch us unless we let them."

TWENTY-TWO

Tammy

I was halfway back to the city when my mother called. "Your dad," she said, "he's been hit by a car. We're going to the hospital."

"Tongheng Zhang," I said to the man at the front desk of the emergency room. "Where is he? I'm his daughter."

The man typed something into his computer. "Not finding anything. Can you spell it?"

"It's spelled like it sounds. *Tongheng*," I said, before spitting the letters out.

"He's in surgery. You can go to waiting room number three."

I jogged down the long corridor.

Waiting room 3. It was the one I had been in for my father's heart attack, but now, it barely looked the same. Instead of scraping against a linoleum floor, my boots dug into the plush carpet, creating an instant imprint. Faux-leather chairs had replaced the stained wool-blend seats that had made me fear catching a venereal disease if I sat there too long. A series of woodlands photographs hung on the pistachio-colored walls. *Better Homes & Gardens* and *HGTV* magazines were displayed in a half-moon formation on the glass table. Two fish tanks gurgled softly in the background. The seating arrangements allowed for privacy from the clusters of other people. I snuck glances at their taut faces as I looked for my mother. The room was designed to dehystericize trauma. But my father just got hit by a car. No interior designer was going to calm me down with a picture of a fucking lawn.

Against the far wall of the room was my mother, sitting in a chair all by herself. Her head was down, gaping at her fingers with an intense fascination. As I got closer, I realized she was fixated on her wedding ring and was compulsively rotating it with her thumb.

"Mom," I said, walking up to her.

"Oh good, you're here," she said.

"Any more news?"

"No, but I have a feeling," she said, twisting her ring again. "It'll be okay."

"Why would he go after me?" I said.

"He felt bad," said my mother.

"I'm not a baby," I said.

She closed her eyes and sighed. "When you have children, you'll know."

I picked at my jeans.

"I don't blame you," said my mother.

I hadn't thought that was a possibility until now. Would other people see it that way too? *Was it my fault?* Rationally, I understood it wasn't. I wasn't driving the car. I hadn't told my father to go after me. How many times had I fought back and he *didn't* get hit by a car? It wasn't my fault, it couldn't be, but at the same time, in a twisted way, it was. My mother didn't blame me, *yet*. But once we were out of the waiting room, once we knew the outcome, her pain would bear down on me. If he died, it would be my fault. If he survived, it would be my fault that he was hurt. And she wouldn't be wrong.

"I'm so sorry," I said. "If I could do it again, I wouldn't—"

She put her hand on my knee. "He tried to say something to me. After I found him," she said, staring at the empty chair across from us.

I nodded. That was a good sign.

"Statistically," she said, "the likelihood of your father dying within a day of his own father's death is minuscule." She seemed pleased by the sturdy logic of her own statement.

"Are you hungry?" I said.

"No," she said.

"I'll get you something," I said. I just wanted a task, something to take my mind off my dad.

The vending machine was a grid of vitaminwaters, Clif Bars, and baked chips. Last time, it was filled with Cheez-Its and Famous Amos cookies. I chose the snack in the C4 position. I checked the label three times before entering in the selection.

I dropped the bag of trail mix on my mother's lap.

"This gives me gas," she said, but she ripped it open anyway and palmed a handful into her mouth.

"I'll stay with him during recovery," I said.

A nurse came out of the double doors.

Everyone in the waiting room straightened up and a dozen

sets of eyes zeroed in on her, stalking her until she approached the elderly couple a few seats down from my mother and me. The nurse's back was turned to us, but I could tell from the couple's faces that it was good news. Before she finished talking, the man checked his phone, scrolling through notifications. For him, the game of life was rolling forward again.

My focus drifted to the back of the nurse's head. Specifically, her French braid. She had clearly done it herself. The braid swerved off-center, and a rogue chunk of hair bubbled outward. The bottom pieces sagged—most likely the result of her arms growing tired during the weaving process. How sad that she didn't have someone to do it for her. My father would've properly tucked every strand of hair into place. The more I looked at the braid, the more irritated I got. I could fix it for her. Wasn't this the same as telling someone that they had spinach in their teeth? But before I could convince myself that it was, she tapped her clipboard and left through the double doors.

I didn't know how much time had passed when a surgeon in a long white coat and mint green scrubs marched through those doors. *Don't be my father's*, I begged. The surgeon was all wrong—soap opera good-looking, straight out of the cast of *Their Burning Hearts*. Surgeons weren't supposed to be curly-haired Adonises. I wanted a surgeon who was an old, stodgy as hell, stubborn asshole who would smite God himself in order to save my father.

He approached my mother and me with a drooping gait. And he couldn't meet my eyes. It was written all over his perfectly symmetrical face.

My mother had fallen asleep on my shoulder. I put up a

hand, telling him to wait. *Five more seconds*, I mouthed. My mother deserved it. I wished that I could let her sleep forever.

"Mom," I said, "Mom, it's time to wake up."

I held her as she screamed.

Hours later, I sat cross-legged on my bed, watching the sun rise. It seemed so cruel, a betrayal—that the sun still decided to do that. That it didn't know that my entire world had been razed to the ground. And I had been responsible for the razing. I looked at my walls, imagining them crumbling down around me. I would deserve it.

I picked up my boots and threw them at the sun. They bounced off the window with a thud. I went around my childhood room, collecting books, Beanie Babies, pens, socks, and chucked them all at the window. Every thud felt satisfying. I wasn't even sure who I was angry at—myself, my father, or the sun.

I hadn't called Vince. Telling him would mean it was real. I would have to comfort him, tell him I would be okay. The only person I had called was Oliver. He was in the inner circle. He didn't count. Or maybe, he counted the most.

My mother was across the hallway, phoning China. It hadn't seemed so noisy a while ago, but now, the sounds seeped through my walls. A stream of cries in between muffled Mandarin. "Shut the fuck up," I said, under my breath. I clasped my hands over my ears, but that only made the sounds echo louder in my skull. They drove me crazy. Right out of the house.

I sat down on the front steps, head in my hands. Finally— some quiet. No one was out. People weren't running to their cars yet, clutching their coffee tumblers and Longchamp totes, hair still wet. It would still be an hour or so before the schoolchildren scuttled to their bus stops, backpacks bouncing behind them.

"Tammy?"

It was Mr. Gutman, the neighbor two doors down. He was on the sidewalk in front of our house. He had rolled over a garbage can.

"I think this is your family's," he said.

I looked over at the lone recycling bin at the bottom of the driveway.

"I guess," I said.

"I think your dad was trying to pick this up when it happened."

"How do you know?"

"I have a security camera. Actually, it hadn't been working for a while, until your dad came over to fix it."

"Sounds like Dad."

"I checked it right after I heard what happened. Drove it to the police station myself," he said.

"Did you see anything?"

"I'm not sure," he said. "But the detective has it."

There was a recording.

"We're keeping your dad in our prayers. You know, we kept wanting to invite your parents over for dinner, but we have three kids. Two teenagers." He looked at the garbage can. "We just kept pushing it to the next month."

"Yeah," I said. "Everyone's busy."

"We'll definitely make it happen once he's better."

"Sure," I said.

After he left, I walked down the lawn and grabbed the garbage can. As I rolled it next to the recycling bin, I noticed that it was in pristine condition.

Not one dent.

Not one crack.

I picked up the plastic piece of shit and slammed it down on the concrete. I did it over and over, drawing strength from its destruction. The bottom fractured. A wheel broke off. Up and down, up and down, smashing the garbage can against the ground, shards flying. And I was laughing the whole time, reveling in my triumph. My palms were red. I was sweating. My grandfather died yesterday, my dad died today. A luck that defied the odds. I was next in line. I welcomed the train set to hit me tomorrow.

I fell to my knees on the sidewalk before the house that my father had bought, the life that he had built, the place where I could still feel him everywhere, even though he was nowhere.

I shuddered, and my laughs turned into tears. I collapsed, the wind knocked out of me. The pain that overwhelmed me wasn't sharp. It wasn't loud. It was a hollow pain that burned, ached, writhed, as if someone had carved out a piece of my body. Some piece I couldn't live without. *Ni shi wo de xin gan*, I remembered my father saying to me once. *You are my heart and liver.* Now I knew what that meant.

My vision blurred as I saw a figure running toward me.

"Dad?" I said.

"Dad!" I yelled.

Suddenly, I felt arms around me.

"Tammy."

The arms were comforting, strong. The smell—familiar. I reached for his face. "Oliver," I said. A breeze blew strands of my hair into my wet cheeks.

"I'm right here," he said.

I looked up at him. Something within me pulled and unraveled. In the fog of my grief, the only thing clear to me was Oliver. *My Oliver.* He would make it all okay.

I kissed him.

He didn't pull away. He brushed the hair out of my eyes and cradled my face.

"Stay with me," I said.

"Always," he said.

"Oliver, I'm going to kill them," I said.

He kissed me again. "I know."

"I'm going to kill them all," I said, burying myself against his chest.

TWENTY-THREE

Oliver

It was almost 3:00 a.m. when Kip pulled up to The Rosewood. "I'll take care of the car," he said.

"I can go with you," Oliver offered.

"Thanks, son," said Kip. "This will be easier without you."

Oliver hesitated as he got out of the car.

"You're doing the right thing," said Kip, rubbing his shoulder. "Now, wipe it from your mind. Get some sleep."

But sleep never came. Oliver kept sitting up in bed, startled by even the most ordinary of city noises. The high-pitched barks of two yappy dogs. The whining engine of a garbage truck. A helicopter, sounding nearby for a moment before fading away. He closed the windows and lay on the couch. He turned on the TV, searching for a *Friends* rerun, but immediately turned it off when he hit a news channel. He paced the length of the living room, hands clutching at his sides. The jagged comedown from whatever drug that Kip gave him at the club wasn't helping. Mixed with his own adrenaline, he could feel a black electricity in his blood. The more he tried to recall the details of the night, the more slippery they became. The room spun as he tried to rearrange the facts, shave and shape the truth, but it all kept snapping back to the way it actually happened.

The sun cast an orange glow as it rose over the city, heralding a beautiful winter morning. He stepped out onto the balcony. He took some deep breaths, but the tightness in his chest didn't relent. *Was this how his grandfather had felt the whole time he was embezzling from the charity?* No, he couldn't have. This had to pass, otherwise, how could he have lived like a king for over a decade? He must have learned to get used to it or, like Kip had said, wipe it from his mind.

Oliver wondered if he could walk that tightrope, if he could forget that a person had been hit and he might never know if they survived or if he could've done anything to save them. But it didn't matter. Between that stranger and Kip, there was only one choice. *This is what family does*, he told himself. *Protect each other.*

His phone rang. He ignored it.

It rang again.

Then he realized he should check it. It might be Kip.

But then he saw the name of the caller: Tammy.

He scrambled to pick up the call. She was his remedy. Talking to her always made the world feel right again.

"Hey," he said.

"Oliver," she said, between sobs. "Oliver, he's dead."

"Who?" he said. He sat up so fast that he saw stars. And just like that—he already knew. "Coolidge," he whispered. It was the last street Kip had raced past. The street where Tammy's family lived. Where Tony lived. "No, no, no," he said.

"My dad," she said.

"No, it can't be," he said.

"That's what I thought too," she said.

"It's not, it's not," he said, clutching at his throat. He couldn't breathe. "It's not possible," he choked out.

"I don't know what to do," she said.

"I'll come over," he said.

"It's so early. I don't want to ask—"

"You never need to ask. I'm coming," he said.

"Thanks," she said.

He threw on his jacket and was about to grab the car keys when he realized he had to call Kip first. He was going to tell Tammy the truth, but he owed the old man a heads-up.

Kip picked up on the first ring. "What is it?" he said.

"You have to go to the police," said Oliver. "I know what happened. The person you hit—"

"Shut up," growled Kip. "Not over the phone. I'm coming over."

"Wait! I have to go to—"

But Kip had already hung up.

Oliver went to the balcony and looked out at Central Park. He would wait for Kip, and then go straight to Tammy's.

Not even twenty minutes later, Kip knocked on the door. He was dressed in a gray sweatshirt and jeans, just as he had been that night at Harvard when he had ferried Oliver away, protecting him from his grandfather's fraud.

"I'm not surprised," said Kip. "I knew I'd have to come

calm you down at some point, but I didn't know you'd fall apart so quickly."

"You killed Tammy's dad," said Oliver.

"Who's Tammy?"

"Are you fucking serious?" said Oliver.

"The Asian chick at the firm?"

"Did you hear me? The car accident. The person you ran over. It was her father!"

"How do you know?" said Kip.

"She just told me!"

"Told you what? Why would she tell you?" Kip glared at Oliver. *"Told you what?"*

"That—" said Oliver.

"It's too early. If her father only got hit hours ago, why would she call you so soon?"

"Are you fucking interrogating me?" said Oliver. "She called me to tell me she can't make it to work today."

"No," said Kip, walking up to Oliver and poking a finger into his chest. "I asked why she called *you*. Who are you to her?"

"No one," he stammered.

"Liar!" said Kip.

"We *are* liars," said Oliver. "We have to tell the police what happened. It was an accident. Tammy would understand. Maybe she won't even—"

But he lost his words as he stared into the dark pools of Kip's eyes.

"You're going to sacrifice me for your little bitch?" said Kip.

It was always a trade with Kip, thought Oliver. A transaction. That was his relationship to the man all along. And to his parents, his grandfather—to the whole of the cold, calculating strategic world he was born into. But he had learned from Tammy—that wasn't what family was about.

"Tammy is my family too," said Oliver. "I've known her since she was a little girl. Known her dad even before that. He used to work as a doorman. Right here in The Rosewood."

"Wait, wait, wait. You're going to send me to jail over a fucking doorman?" said Kip.

"I love her," said Oliver.

Kip cackled, spit spraying. "That's the funniest thing I've ever heard." His whole face turned red with laughter. "This is what you're going to do. Stay close with her, monitor the police findings, report everything to me, and if we get to this point, you'll smooth over anything that needs smoothing. You knowing this girl—it's our stroke of good luck."

"No, I won't," said Oliver. "I can't do that to her."

"You'll do what you're told," said Kip.

"Or what?" said Oliver.

"Or I take away everything you have."

"You can't take away what I've earned," said Oliver.

"Earned?" said Kip. "You really think you earned anything?" He got up and ripped Oliver's designer coats off their hooks and kicked over the shoe stand full of Hermès loafers. "This? You think you've earned all of this?" He grabbed the Patek Philippe watch off the counter and smashed it on the floor. "Earned? Given. Given! By your grandfather and by me!"

"Stop it," said Oliver.

"I set up the offshore account! If you turn me in, I'll take you and your parents down with me," said Kip.

"You mean the trust? The court gave us that."

"Use your brain!"

"What?"

"There's a secret account, you idiot. Do you think that Soga Trust III was floating all of you?"

"How's that possible?"

"An insider at the SEC tipped us off about the investigation twenty-four hours before they arrested your grandfather. You can do a lot in a day. Like drop millions into an account in the Caymans. Your parents knew. No one told you because we couldn't trust you. Couldn't trust that you wouldn't shit the bed like you're doing right now."

Oliver slumped against the wall. "You're lying," he said. But he knew it was true. He had always known something was off, and he had made the conscious decision to turn a blind eye.

Kip went to the couch and sat down. "Come," he said, patting the leather.

Oliver didn't move.

"You and your grandfather. You're more alike than you think. He had a soft spot too."

"My grandfather doesn't have soft spots."

"Go ask him, if you really want to know what happened, what really brought him down in the end," Kip said.

"It was a whistleblower."

"Keep telling yourself that. It was a soft spot. Just like what that girl is to you. Even the great Matthew Agos couldn't overcome his weakness. He couldn't, but I know you can."

Oliver's mind was sputtering. His thoughts felt tethered and knotted.

"Lighten up," said Kip. "Look around you. Look at everything you have."

In that moment, a ray of sunlight sparkled through the window, illuminating the living room. The high ceilings, the dark wood accents, the marble finishes. The Fendi Casa couch and coffee tables, the Bösendorfer piano that he had flown in from Vienna. The Rothkos on the walls. Oliver marveled at the view of the treetops of Central Park. The branches were bare, but he could've sworn he could hear the rustling of leaves.

"The dead are dead, but this is your life," said Kip.

He was right. Tony was gone, and Oliver giving up his life wouldn't bring him back.

After a moment, Oliver nodded. "This is my life," he said. He walked over and sat next to Kip. "And this is my home."

"You did nothing wrong," said Kip.

"I did nothing wrong."

"Sometimes, things just happen."

"Things just happen," repeated Oliver.

Together, they watched as the sun continued to fill up the room, reaching even the darkest corners.

"Take a shower, son," said Kip. "Clear your head."

Oliver headed to the bathroom. He jerked the shower handle to twelve o'clock—scalding. Then he stepped into the shower, fully clothed, and prayed for the water to wash him clean.

TWENTY-FOUR

Tammy

Three-quarters of a tray of moldy mac and cheese from the Platt family across the street. A Ziploc bag labeled *shrimp + pork dumplings (chives, no garlic)* from my mother's coworker. A completely untouched rotisserie chicken from Costco. I held each item up for a good sniff before throwing it all out. It was five in the morning, the day after my father's funeral.

I was working my way down the fridge door when my mother came into the kitchen. "Keep the ketchup," she said, pointing at the butter compartment, which was filled with a collection of packets from take-out orders. My mother used to roll her eyes at my father's stockpiling—a habit she had cured herself of once we had left Flushing. I had taken her side when she called his behavior "low-class," but now, I touched the shiny red plastic packets with fondness. Rifling through those packets made my father's memory feel three-dimensional. I could feel the rough paper of the fast-food napkins

stashed in the glove compartment of his car. Rub the perma-
nent indent on my middle finger from the hard Paper Mate
pens that he took home from the office. My father—ever the
saver. So busy preparing, so worried about the next challenge
around the corner, that he never actually lived. He couldn't
even allow himself the indulgence of a bottle of Heinz, some
cloth napkins, or a gel-tip pen.

"It's cold," said my mother.

"We can turn the heat up," I said.

"I don't think it'd help."

She was right. I hadn't realized how much energy my father had brought into the home until he left us. There was
a new fragility, an emptiness to the house. It was like the air
had been let out, and the house had become a diorama, a perfectly preserved memento of his absence.

"It was good to see everyone yesterday," said my mother.
"So many people came."

I nodded. More came than I had expected. Almost every
row in the funeral home was filled. Most of the neighborhood turned up, a shuttle bus dropped off a group of my father's colleagues, and my old teachers and friends from high
school came with lilies and white roses.

Even Clara Abadi showed up. Wrapped in a black trench
coat, Clara looked like a ghost of her former self. She slumped
in her wheelchair, chin on her chest. Pockmarks covered her
once-beautiful face and her loud red hair was gray and un-
kempt. Only her emerald eyes remained unchanged. Not as
brilliant now, but they still twinkled with her signature pa-
nache. As the nurse pushed her toward my mother and me, I
wasn't sure if she could even speak.

But she said the only thing that made me feel better that

day. "Tony was a legend. Don't worry about him. He's surf-
ing the clouds."

She then took my mother's hand and gave her a framed
picture of my father's cover of the *New York Post*. "It's been
on display in my home all this time, but I think you should
have it now," she said.

My mother let out a cry and bent down to hug Clara. "He's
still here. I can feel it," my mother sobbed.

"He'll always be with you," said Clara.

My mother moved to the stove to heat up the kettle. "Don't
stand in front of the fridge for too long. You'll catch a cold,"
she said.

"I'm almost done," I said, searching for the expiration date
on a bottle of mayo.

"I still can't believe Oliver paid for the funeral. He's too
generous," said my mother.

"Dad wouldn't have been surprised," I said. "Oliver's always been taking care of us."

"I can tell you what your dad would've been surprised
with."

I rolled my eyes. "It's my decision."

"It's so sudden," said my mother. "Vince is a good man. He
would've made the perfect husband."

"For someone else. He's not the right person for me."

"You live in a fantasy," she said with a sigh. "There is no
'right person.'"

There was. And it was funny to me how she didn't see it.
My father had been her best friend. The person who marveled at every one of her perfections, recognized value in all
of her flaws. He fully saw her—straight to her core. His love
for her was unwavering. Almost religious. He was her soul-
mate in ways I had never felt about Vince.

"It's done. I know it was the right thing to do. Vince will be happier for it eventually," I said.

"I wish your father were here," she said. "He would never let you go through with this."

But my father's absence was exactly what had given me the strength to end my engagement. He, more than anyone else in my life, had beat, pushed, and molded me. For every scar he inflicted, there was something invaluable that he imparted. He had built me up, but I hadn't realized until his death that he had also caged me with his dreams. He had sacrificed for me, and in turn, I had sacrificed parts of myself to make him feel as though it had all been worth it.

But for all his attempts to control me, what he also did was create a person who was capable of making hard decisions, of breaking the cage itself. A person capable of rebelling against him. Someone brave enough to finally shed the roles of Harvard Tammy, Girlfriend Tammy, or American Tammy. Someone who could cross lines, whose life could be messy, who could survive mistakes. Someone who could take a chance on herself.

My mother came up to the fridge next to me and counted the ketchup packets.

"You get it from your dad," she said.

"What?" I said.

"Your stubbornness."

"Thanks."

"You guys were so alike," she said.

"Not really," I said.

My mother dropped a McDonald's packet into her pocket. "We often hate the people who remind us the most of ourselves," she said.

★ ★ ★

The next day, I headed into the city, to another place where I had felt at home: The Rosewood. I had only been nine years old when I first visited, but the majestic imprint of the building in my memory never faded. A bewitching concrete fortress. The tops of its triangular gables looked like they were trying to escape the roof and flee into the sky. Each window resembled the glass pane of an antique lantern. Columns spun from the ground all the way up to the slanted red roofs like steadfast Maypoles. Even as the years rolled on, this building—Oliver—was the one constant I returned to.

We hadn't talked about the kiss, but we didn't have to. It didn't happen the way I thought it would, but in hindsight, it felt inevitable. How long had I suppressed my feelings? When did I grow out of being that little girl at the piano?

I pushed the elevator button—the one I had pressed hundreds of times before. My reflection appeared as the elevator doors closed. I smiled at her. This was exactly where I was supposed to be. It felt like the universe had planned this all along, and now, the dovetails had interlocked.

What Oliver and I shared was palpable, unmistakable. All these years I hadn't seen it, but it had always been there, in a long look, a kiss on the cheek, a wiped-away tear. It took his confiding in me about his grandfather to wake me up. We never said it out loud, but our feelings had a voice of their own. Our actions were our words.

But when Oliver opened the door, I barely recognized him. He had let his stubble grow out—the first time I hadn't seen him clean-shaven. His eyes looked baggy and soulless. He smiled but it looked put-on. I leaned into him as he kissed me on the forehead. He plucked nervously at his sweater.

"It's so good to see you," I said.

I heard a pained hiss as he closed the door. "Jammed my finger," he said.

The usual mint tea and cookies were spread out on the dining room table. As I blew and sipped on the tea, I peered up at him and said, "Are you okay?"

He sat down across from me. I could feel the apprehension coming off him in waves. "What do you mean?" he said, hiding his mouth behind his raised cup.

"You don't look like you've been sleeping," I said.

"Well, your dad."

"You look like *your* dad died."

"You're telling me I look like shit?" he said.

"I'm telling you— Never mind." I had come to tell Oliver that I had broken up with Vince. That I wanted to be with him. I thought we were on the same page, but clearly, he was somewhere else.

"I'm sorry," he said. "It's not you. I've been having a rough week. Like you said—I'm not sleeping. Not that I should complain. Obviously nothing compares to what you're going through."

"We don't have to compare everything to that," I said. "Is it work? Did you and Kip finalize the chemicals merger?"

"Right, that. It's all good. We filed the 10K last night," he said.

"You mean the 8K?" I said.

"Yeah, 8K, sorry, I thought that's what I said."

I reached for his hand. "Oliver, are you okay?"

He looked away. "It's been a hard couple of days," he said.

Then my phone rang.

"Who is it?" he said.

It was the last number I had added to my contacts. The direct line to the detective working on my dad's case.

"It's the police," I said.

I picked up the phone.

TWENTY-FIVE

Oliver

Oliver strained to hear the detective on the other end of the call, but all he could pick up on was that it was a male voice.

"Uh-huh," said Tammy, nodding along to whatever the man was telling her.

Oliver searched her face for a clue.

She frowned.

Good, good, he thought. That meant there hadn't been a breakthrough in the investigation.

"The security camera got something?" she said.

A chill hit the back of his head. Fuck.

"I can come in tomorrow morning," said Tammy. "See you then."

"Sorry about that," she said to Oliver.

"So—they have footage?" he said, bracing for her answer.

"A neighbor's camera," she said. "It caught the car, but they can't make out the plate."

"How about the make? The model?" he asked. Kip wasn't driving a Honda Civic. How many Aston Martin Vantage GTs were there in New York?

"They're showing the images to some specialist on sports cars," she said.

Oliver gripped his thighs so tightly under the table that he could feel the bones. *Pull it together*, he told himself. At least the car wasn't ostentatious. It was sleek, black, and in the dark, could be confused for another convertible.

"It did catch something else though," said Tammy. "Someone came out of the car on the passenger side. They said the footage might be too grainy to run through facial recognition, but they want my mom and me to take a look at it. They hope we might recognize the person, if they're a local. It could be someone we know."

"Tammy," he said quietly.

"I doubt it though. I mean, what kind of person would do something like that?" she said.

This was it. He was trapped. The only way out was to tell her. It was his only chance. She'd recognize him on the tape. He had to get in front of this. If he could just convince her it was an accident and that he would've done the right thing if Kip hadn't stopped him, then she would understand. She would protect him.

"I have to tell you something," he said.

"What? What's wrong?"

"You'll never speak to me again," he said. His eyes pitched an earnest plea.

She tilted her head. "Are you okay?"

"The video. It's me."

"No, it's not. You weren't there yet."

"It was an accident," he said. "Kip was driving. We were dropping off a client in Scarsdale. It was pitch-black out. He couldn't see."

"Couldn't see what?"

"Your dad—he came out of nowhere."

"You saw what happened? You saw the car that hit him?"

"No," said Oliver. "I was *in* the car."

"Wait," she said, standing up. "You killed my dad?"

"Not me. Not me. I wasn't driving. Kip was."

"But you were in the car."

"It was a mistake!" he said.

"You covered it up."

"Kip threatened me. I didn't know it was your father until hours later, and when I found out, I tried to convince Kip to come clean."

"You covered it up," she repeated.

"I didn't want to."

"How could you just sit here? In this fucking apartment, in the fucking Rosewood? Setting out a tray of cookies?" She slapped the cookies to the ground. "You thought about cookies?"

"I'm so sorry," said Oliver.

"Were you ever going to tell me? You saw my dad dying in the street and you just drove away?"

"You don't know Kip," he said. "He's not a good guy. He threatened my—"

"I don't fucking care about Kip!" she said. "When I go to the station, I'm going to see you on the tape. You're the person who got out of the car."

He walked over and knelt in front of her. He tried to rest

his forehead on her legs, but she pushed him away. "Tammy," he said. "Please. You can't say anything. It'd be over for me."

She clutched her elbows and her chin dropped toward her chest. Her rage dissipated and was eclipsed by a desperate sadness. A hopelessness that swallowed Oliver too. It made him wish that she were still yelling at him.

"It's over for my dad," she whispered.

"It doesn't have to be over for us."

"You have to tell the truth," she said.

"You can protect me," he said. "You're the only one who can."

She looked at him as if she'd never seen him before. "No, Oliver. You have to tell the truth."

"The truth is I love you," he said. "That's the truth!"

"Stop it," she said.

"I love you," he said, grabbing at her ankles. "That's the only truth that matters."

She shook him off and went to the door.

At the threshold, she looked back at him, a crumpled mess on the floor. "I love you too."

He held her gaze. "You love me," he said. "Remember that."

Then she left, closing the door behind her.

Two hours later, Oliver was speeding up the I-87 North, a legal folder sitting in the passenger seat. He had already called the warden of Turpin Creek Correctional Facility to confirm that he was still on the preapproved list of visitors. "You better know how to stretch a minute on the road. Last visitation entry's at four," the warden had said.

Oliver swerved into a parking spot with five minutes to

spare. It had been years since he had visited the prison, but the drill hadn't changed. Display identification. Sign the logbook. Pass through the metal detector and then starfish for the magnetic wand. No wallet, wristwatch, or cell phone. Stick a visitor's name tag onto his button-down shirt. Enter a room that looked like a high school cafeteria, complete with chewed-up gum jammed under the tables. The walls, decorated with scenic paintings from the prison's art class—a half-finished sandcastle; a fishing rod arching into a river. Oliver sat in a plastic chair across from a man in beige khakis and a matching shirt. "Hey, Grandpa," he said.

Even in his early nineties, Matthew Agos was handsome. His face easily fell into a smile and he sat tall—his broad shoulders and expansive chest served as reminders of the bull he still was. Though his hair had turned a regal white, Oliver still saw himself when he looked into the old man's sapphire eyes.

"It must be my lucky day," said his grandfather, clocking his name tag. Unlike on his other visits, Oliver had decided to use his given name: Oliver Agos.

A pinging sound made Oliver automatically reach for his phone, before remembering that it was with the rest of his belongings at the security station.

"That's me," said his grandfather, removing a cell phone from his shirt pocket. A gold-colored iPhone—the latest model.

"You can't have that in here," said Oliver.

"I have calls to make."

"Who have you been talking— Wait, Grandpa. A guard is walking over."

His grandfather typed a message and clicked Send. "Who do you think got this for me?"

"Hey, Mr. Agos," said the guard.

An inmate at the other table turned around and pointed at his visitor. "My girl. Set up her 401(k) just like you said to."

"Fantastic," his grandfather replied, veneers gleaming. His bored eyes spelled the truth—zero interest. The inmates all turned back to their visitors, but he retained a sliver of their attention. Oliver could tell his grandfather was the room's center of gravity.

"It's been years," said his grandfather. "Why the sudden visit?"

Oliver slid the legal folder across the table. "I decided to sponsor your compassionate release," he said. "The paperwork's in there for you to sign so that I can officially represent you."

His grandfather didn't touch the folder. The lines in his forehead folded on top of each other, ominously. He nodded at Oliver's name tag. "So—you're an Agos again? Didn't know you still had it in you."

Oliver shifted in his seat. "Grandpa, I'm trying here."

"June," his grandfather said.

"It's February."

"June."

"I don't understand," Oliver said, looking around.

"June 1997."

"Grandpa?"

"That's when I asked for this. June 1997. Nineteen years ago."

"I needed time," said Oliver.

"Time you paid for with my dime?"

"I didn't know that before. I'm sorry. I—"

"I dreamed about St. Bart's last night," said his grandfather.

"St. Bart's?" said Oliver.

"You and me. Wandering the hills before dawn. *Vote Oliver Agos for Action*," said his grandfather. "Do you remember that?"

Oliver ground his teeth to ward off the tears. Of course he remembered. He thought of it all the time. It had been their last family trip together before the scandal broke, the last time his life had felt normal. "You kept saying I could be president one day."

"I believed in you," said his grandfather.

"I know," said Oliver.

"I would've done anything for you."

"I know, I know."

"Where did we end up that morning? That little bakery in Gustavia?"

"The *pain au chocolat*," said Oliver. "You got powdered sugar all over your—"

"Shut the fuck up. It's over," said his grandfather. The old man pushed the folder back to Oliver. "This ship has already sailed."

"Let me do this for you," said Oliver.

"Now? *Now?*" his grandfather said, stabbing the table with a bony finger. "Look at me. My life is gone. And *now* you want to help?"

"I didn't know about the account," Oliver said. "Kip just told me. If I'd known—"

"If you'd known what? That I was paying for you to cool your heels on Central Park West? You still think this is all about the money?"

"The money, your sacrifice, what's the difference?" said Oliver.

"Fuck the money! It was never about that."

"Never about the money? Then why did you steal a hundred million dollars?" said Oliver.

"For the family! For you!" said his grandfather. "So you didn't have to grow up the way I did. Did you have to take a full ride at state college because your family couldn't afford Harvard? What about your summers? Fancy, unpaid internships on Capitol Hill. I lugged a suitcase of used textbooks around campus, selling them to make rent."

"Come on, Grandpa, it wasn't all about the family," said Oliver.

"Money is a tool," said his grandfather. "If you still haven't figured out that life is all about family, about loyalty, then you're dumber than I thought. What are you really here for?"

Oliver didn't know. He had been operating on instinct. After Tammy left, he just knew he had to see his grandfather—the man who had haunted his life as much as he had animated it.

"Something Kip told me."

"Good old Kip," said his grandfather.

"How did you get caught? The news only said that it was a whistleblower."

His grandfather's face grew taut. "Part of my plea deal with the SEC was to keep that part a secret. They didn't want it to garner any public sympathy for me."

"Please," said Oliver.

His grandfather surveyed his face.

"Something happened. It could get really bad for me," said Oliver.

"What did Kip tell you?"

"He said you had a soft spot."

"Kip *would* call it that," his grandfather laughed.

"I need to know," said Oliver.

His grandfather stared hard at him. A flicker of compassion flashed across his face. "A water bottle."

Oliver looked back, blankly.

"It was at one of the billions of galas," said his grandfather. "Everyone was leaving and I saw a water bottle. Just sitting there on a table, completely full, unopened. And a server came up, took it, and just threw it away. Just like that. Like the water bottle was trash, like it was literal garbage. That's when it hit me—people are actually dying for this water. *People can't get water.* And I had actually built something that could help them. By that time, I had everything I wanted. Our family was thriving. I didn't need any more money. I could actually build wells—help people drink clean water. That would be amazing, right?"

"Yeah," said Oliver, "better late than never."

"I found a few companies that could help us over in Uganda, and on a conference call, one of the CEOs realized that I didn't know things that I should've about a project like this. Something about the way I thought his comment about latrines was a joke. He told his SEC buddy about it at a golf game."

"What timing," said Oliver. "Just when you were going to do something good."

"You know what I should've done?"

"What?"

"You tell me," said his grandfather.

"I don't know."

"Nothing!" said his grandfather. "I should've done nothing!"

"You cared," said Oliver.

"Biggest mistake of my life."

"You were trying to help people."

"Fuck them," his grandfather grumbled. "I should've kept doing what I was already doing. That's what you would've done, right?"

Oliver didn't respond. In that moment, he realized that at his core, he was the same as his grandfather. This was what he had come to verify.

"Of course, that's *exactly* what you would've done. Even you know to look out for number one," said his grandfather.

Oliver stood up and, with a lightning strike, punched his grandfather right in the face. The old man's eyes widened with shock as blood began to run from his nose. He raised his hands to defend himself, but not in time. Oliver punched him again, knocking him to the ground. He landed a succession of quick hits before hands were on him, grabbing him, pulling him away.

The guards pinned him down, side of his face against the ground, hands behind his back. But he could still see his grandfather's face, bloodied, on the floor, ten feet away from him. The old man's eyes could barely open. His white hair was stained with blood. Oliver couldn't recognize his grandfather's face anymore. Just like he couldn't recognize his own.

TWENTY-SIX

Tammy

I ran out of The Rosewood and immediately spotted a taxi—an old-school Crown Victoria.

"Where to?" asked the driver.

"Two twenty-four Coolidge Lane. Scarsdale," I said. I didn't know what to think or what to do. I just knew where I wanted to be—home.

It was freezing outside, but I rolled down the window anyway. The wind blew against the sheen of sweat on my forehead. I leaned toward the chill. For a moment, it made me forget. Forget that Kip had killed my father. Forget that Oliver had been there and decided to cover it up. Forget that he had just asked me to do the same.

You can protect me. You're the only one who can.

Oliver had given me a power I wish I didn't have. How much were we supposed to protect the ones we loved?

With every passing street, I grew more nauseous. I closed

my eyes and prayed that the past week had all been one long, lucid dream. All I had to do to fix my world was wake up.

The drive smoothed as we hit the highway.

I poked at the yellow foam shooting out of the splits of the taxi's seat, trying to push it back into its binding. I knew it wouldn't work. Once it had ripped through the leather, there was nothing to do except replace the entire seat.

I fiddled with my phone, but the only person I wanted to call was Oliver. He was the one person I talked to when I wasn't sure what to do. He always seemed to know the answer.

As the driver took the exit for Scarsdale, he asked, "Visiting family?"

"Yeah," I said. The voice barely sounded like my own.

"Good to get out of the city once in a while," he said.

"Right." I wasn't in the mood to engage in any small talk.

"You must have a big job in the city. What do you do?"

"Lawyer," I said.

"Oh really?" He opened the flap of the sun visor and tapped on a picture that was clipped to the side. "My son wants to be a lawyer."

I leaned forward to inspect the photograph. A young boy was dressed in a striped shirt, holding a basketball. Behind him stood the driver and the woman who was probably his wife. None of them were smiling, none of them were touching. It reminded me of old photographs of my family, before we learned to hug each other.

"He's brilliant," said the driver. "Top of his class. Does long division in his head. Memorized the periodic table."

"That's amazing. You must be so proud," I said.

"He's even read half of the books in the Flushing library."

"My family and I used to live in Flushing."

"Really? That gives me hope. My wife hounds me about moving into a town like this," he said, gazing at the row of Colonials on the street. "Where'd you go to college?"

"Boston. Cambridge," I said, but that sounded doubly pretentious. "Sorry, I mean Harvard."

"Harvard? Harvard!" he said. "I would die for my son to go there."

"It's a good school."

"Expensive," he said.

I nodded. What exactly had the tuition been? And the cost of room and board and my food? I knew it was somewhere around two hundred thousand, but I felt ashamed not knowing the exact figure. My parents had given me the privilege of concentrating on *getting in*. There was never a question of whether we'd be able to afford it if I did. They had taken out loans and slowly chipped away at them every month. By the time I received my first paycheck from the law firm, I offered to clear the debt before dealing with my own law school loans. But my parents had outright rejected the idea. "We only have twenty thousand left to go," my father had said. It had become a matter of pride by then. "We need to do this for you as much as for ourselves," my mother had explained.

"I watch courtroom dramas with my son," said the driver. "They're all over the TV." He lowered his voice as he bellowed, "Objection! Hearsay! Overruled!"

I laughed. "It's not really like that in real life."

"That's what I tell my son."

"It's much more boring."

"And there's no justice in real life," said the driver.

"Yeah, that's true," I said. Justice. Wasn't that why I had wanted to become a lawyer in the first place? It was an idea so simple, so pure and powerful, that when the nail salon employee had explained it to me, it had changed the trajectory of my life. America touted itself as a land of equal opportunity—of righteousness—but it had never been that for my parents. They had to work twice as hard and settle for half as much.

"We're here," said the driver, pulling up to my parents' place.

I looked up at the house. This was where we'd found out my family had received citizenship. That night, we grilled hamburgers and finished off a whole bag of Oreos in honor of our new allegiance—our new nation. This was my home. And it was beautiful.

But so was the basement in Flushing, where my father had taught me the piano and my mother had snuck me red bean buns from the bakery. And the old rental at the edge of Scarsdale—the one where my father watched reruns of *Ally McBeal* with me.

It hadn't been Harvard or the law firm or my fancy apartment in the city. It had been these homes that I shared with my parents that had made me who I was.

"Actually, sorry," I said. "I need you to drop me somewhere else."

"Sure. Where do you want to go?"

"The police station," I said.

TWENTY-SEVEN

Tammy

The man next to me gripped the armrests—his knuckles, stark white. With the ding of a bell, the fasten seat belts sign lit up. *Experiencing some turbulence*, said the pilot over the intercom. *A line of thunderstorms ahead.* The flight attendants halted the dinner service. Loose items in the overhead bins rattled. Soft murmurs of worry floated across the cabin.

I made the decision to sink into the blue leather seats on Delta Air Lines three months ago—a day after I had reported Oliver to the police. He had been arrested, but the prosecutor informed me that Oliver had declined to pay the $10,000 bail, choosing instead to wait out his trial in jail.

"I'll never forgive him," I said.

"He's trying to make up for his sins," my mother said.

"He's still a horrible person."

"People are complicated."

"We didn't even know him," I said.

"We can only know another to the extent we know ourselves," she said.

"Confucius?" I said, taken aback.

"It was from one of your dad's Post-its."

Damn, I had thought, how true. I never could see Oliver or my father clearly because I had never fully understood myself. It was like I had been looking through the wrong end of a telescope for my whole life, and now, when I swiveled it around, things were snapping into focus. It made me wonder—what else had I been missing, what else hadn't I seen? That night, I bought my plane ticket to China. At my request, my mother booked her flight to depart a few days after mine. "You'll get lost," my mother had argued. "That's the plan," I said.

Thirteen time zones and seven thousand miles away, Dalian was my birthplace but I barely knew what it looked like. A stock photo on the internet showed that it was a city on the coast. Another, taken at night from an aerial view, was of an eight-legged roundabout, spiraling out into a landscape of sparkling buildings and skyscrapers. From old family albums, I had seen a black-and-white Polaroid of my parents, five years younger than I was now, posing in front of the neon sign of a movie theater. My father's shaggy boy-band hair blended into my mother's waves. There was a picture of me at three years old, sitting on the kitchen table in a red knit sweater. The wallpaper in the background was flowery. My father wrote in his textbook as I dialed my toy telephone. I wondered who I had been trying to call. That had been a month before we moved to this country.

For my parents, the journey to America had been a two-year-long process that almost wiped out all their savings and sanity. For me, it would cost next to nothing: a few clicks of a button, half of my credit card reward points, and seventeen hours on a plane. It was cruel, how easily I could return to China.

When people asked me where I was from, I knew what they meant. They meant *where are your people from? Who are you, really?* I told them I was from Queens or Westchester or New York City. Did I tell them I was born in Dalian? No. But Dalian was where my parents had grown up, wed, and started their lives. A place of which I had no living memory. When my parents decided that Dalian could no longer contain their dreams, they left. That was where I was from.

If I never visited Dalian, I'd never have to see the part of me that wasn't American, the sliver of my history that wasn't pure. I didn't have to accept that it existed. Maybe, if I kept stubbornly at it, people would see me as one of them—shoulder to shoulder with the other students in college, members of a country club, lawyers in a firm. Not set apart with an additional distinction, an extra modifier to our shared nationality. Eventually, they wouldn't designate me as Chinese American anymore and only recognize me as an American.

I had barely slept the night before the flight, waking up every half hour, each time thinking that I had overslept my alarm. As I dragged my suitcase behind me through the lobby of my building, I checked my pocket for my passport for the fifth time. In the cab to JFK, I played around with the emojis on WeChat, messaging my mother a red envelope and a dancing penguin.

The woman at the airport check-in counter weighed my bag. Then a conveyor belt carried it away. In the security line, a dog in a bulletproof vest walked past me. He was here to inspect me. I wondered what he detected from my scent, what odor was *bomb* versus *no bomb*. What else did he know about me that perhaps I didn't know myself.

The TSA officer's eyes flickered at my face and then back down at my passport. His brief hesitation made me hold my breath. A moment later, he slid my ticket back into my passport and handed it to me. "Have a great trip," he said. My pinched shoulders rolled down in relief. The man confirmed that I was legally me.

On my way down a long corridor to the gate, I performed my preflight rituals. I collected two water bottles, a packet of Emergen-C, and a neck pillow from a concession stand. At the second Hudson News, deeper within the terminal, I picked up a magazine that had the latest Hollywood breakup on the cover, the paperback of last year's Pulitzer Prize winner, and a travel-sized bottle of hand sanitizer. As the woman at the counter rang it up, I said, "These too," and plopped down a packet of gum and a Godiva chocolate bar. I wanted more. Everything in the store. I would never have enough things to feel secure. Standing in line to board the plane, I felt the weight of the plastic bag full of airport purchases. All the things that mattered in that moment, but not the next.

I clipped on my seat belt and lifted the window shade. The seat beside me, still untaken. A man stood in the aisle and hoisted his suitcase into the overhead compartment. Then he settled into the empty seat. His eyes were jewellike. A scar on the edge of his palm. No wedding ring. I stopped slouching and ran my hand through my hair. My name was Tammy, I was a lawyer, and I was going to China to visit my parents' hometown, I rehearsed in my head. No, I should say that it was my father's hometown. He had died, and I wanted to see where he came from. The man would see that I was a good daughter, and his sympathy for me would bind us. Maybe he'd lost someone he loved too. I could ask him if he was visiting for business. If he knew anyone there. We could meet up for drinks one night.

A flight attendant went down the aisle and closed the overhead bins with a satisfying double click. Another sealed shut the heavy door of the aircraft. Time for takeoff. The pressure from the plane's acceleration into the clouds pushed me back into my seat. Swaddling me, insisting that I relax. I fell asleep before we even reached cruising altitude.

The shaking startled me awake. It was dark in the cabin, except for the blinking lights near the emergency exit. A soda can rolled down the aisle and a tray table a few seats over unlatched and whipped open. "Daddy's right here," purred a man to his crying toddler. And then the plane skipped like a stone over water.

The hairs on the back of my neck were raised, my throat was dry. An influx of adrenaline left me chilly. *This is the edge*, I thought. Shuttling through the stratosphere in a metal box, batted around by the weather, my life was in the hands of someone I'd never met. Just like it had been for my father on that dark street, someone else was going to determine my fate. The tingles of fear subsided as I leaned back into my seat. I breathed relief—*here, I could rest*.

On the ground, I kept my life harnessed. I controlled how hard I pushed, when I relented, when I reasoned or regretted. I was responsible for who I loved, who I persuaded to love me back, who I couldn't persuade enough. Who I blamed, who I trusted. Who I should have trusted less. All the things I broke and decided not to fix.

But now, in this metal tube, I was only a body. Dispensable and destructible. There was a chance that, soon, none of my choices, none of the labels I had collected, would matter. Chinese immigrant. Raised in Flushing. Ivy League graduate. Lawyer. Fiancée. The Doorman Hero's daughter.

With a quick plummet to the earth, I would be stripped of my decision-making duties. My body, my mind, would vaporize. Floating in the air, swirling through the ocean, landing on soft sand. I would live on in the memories of the living until they died, and then I'd really be gone. There was nothing to really do about that eventuality. No escape. Whether we landed safely or not.

Then, as if we had crossed some invisible border, the plane stabilized. The lights turned back on. The movies on the backs of the seats started up again where they had left off. Three people rushed to beat each other to the toilets. All the little things mattered again.

A flight attendant came around with snacks. His uniform was crisply ironed. His hair, parted the same as my father's— slightly to the side to hide a patch of thinning hair. He carried a small basket.

"Peanuts or pretzels?"

My father would choose pretzels. After all of these years, he had finally come around to the snack. *But was I my father?*

"I don't know," I said.

He nodded knowingly, placed a napkin on my tray table, and handed me a shiny blue packet.

"Peanuts, then," he chuckled. "Everyone loves peanuts."

Did Tammy love peanuts? Was Tammy everyone? Once, when she was younger, she loved cereal. Sweet, frosted corn flakes doused in milk. She loved the cartoon tiger on the box. His biceps bulging with power and might. That was how she came to name her father.

I flattened the napkin and wrote down: *Tony the Tiger.*

Zhang Tianfei, I wrote beneath that.

But those weren't the real letters of my name.

张添飞.

I hadn't written this way in so long that I was surprised how easily it came to me. Muscle memory.

I remembered when I was little, maybe still in Dalian, my father held my hand as we drew my name together. We did it again and again until my fingers knew how to make the strokes on their own. Long line here, short flick there. Then my father underlined the last character of my name, 飞. "*Fei*," he had whispered, "it means *to fly.*"

TWENTY-EIGHT

Tongheng

1989

Dawei bought a refrigerator. Everyone in the university's mechanical engineering faculty room was talking about it, but Tongheng was the first to see it. The two men weren't the best of friends, but they were as close as two colleagues who occasionally competed for the same promotions could be.

Earlier that morning, Tongheng had biked over to Dawei's apartment, his baby girl of one year napping in the front basket, his wife Kuan-yin on a separate bike behind him, expertly weaving through the bustling streets of Dalian. He went in for a handshake when Dawei opened the door, but his friend gracefully slipped past it and turned it into a hug. Tongheng stiffened at the embrace, wishing he could look back at Kuan-yin for a signal of how to react, and then finally patted Dawei on the back as the hug released. He saw someone do that in an American movie.

For a moment, he was worried that Dawei would try to hug Kuan-yin, but relaxed when his colleague simply stepped aside and held the door open for her. Dawei's place was bright, with carpeted floors and plants in every corner. It was lined with the most dangerous color of all—white. White wallpaper, white stove top, white couch. A home that was confident it could fend off the dirt and dust that tarnished most other apartments.

Dawei's wife, Jun, led everyone to their living room. On the table were plates of small treats that Tongheng didn't recognize. Dawei held up a black cookie with white gum inside. "They call this an Oreo," he said and doled them out to the others. Tongheng found the cookie surprisingly hard. He was annoyed that some black crumbs were already rubbing off on his fingers. He watched as Kuan-yin took a wary nibble and tilted her head, gauging whether it was enjoyable. Tongheng took half a bite, but then had to use his other hand to catch the falling pieces of the remaining cookie. His mouth went dry, coated by the crunchy wafer and sugary cream.

"Disgustingly sweet, right?" said Dawei. It really was, but Tongheng still found himself wanting to eat another one. He wondered why his friend still ate them even though they were too cloying for his palate. Answering the unspoken question, Dawei looked off at a blank spot on the wall and sighed. "Memories."

Dawei had recently returned to China from a yearlong research project in America. Other academics at their university had gone before, all coming back with the usual vague but enthusiastic phrases.

"I see the world in a different way."

"Words can't really describe it."

"We named it *Mei Guo* for a reason—it literally is a *beautiful country*."

Last year, after too many drinks at an awards dinner, a flirty professor in her forties had said, in between hiccups, "It was like visiting paradise."

Tongheng was still reminiscing about that night—he had received an innovation prize—when Dawei said, "Actually, Oreos are better with milk." He gave Jun, who had just reached for another cookie, a look and she immediately stood up and said, "I'll need some help with the cups. Should we all go to the kitchen?" Tongheng was grateful for the orchestration, a graceful segue to the main event.

Once the five of them assembled around the refrigerator, Tianfei sleeping in Kuan-yin's arms, Tongheng realized that the buzzing machine was taller than he was. He looked at the white door, which had tiny wrinkles carved into it, and then his hand instinctively went for the plastic handle. Kuan-yin swatted it back down and said, "Wait," but then Dawei said, "No, no, please. Go ahead. Open it."

Tongheng grabbed hold of the door handle and pulled so hard that the door almost hit Jun.

"Easy," said Dawei, laughing, "it's not made of steel."

Normally, Tongheng would step back, embarrassed, and profusely apologize, but what he felt was anything but normal. A cold breeze was gently wrapping itself around his body. *It was coming from the refrigerator.* He could stand in front of it forever. Was this also what air-conditioning felt like?

Then his eyes sharpened their focus on the filled shelves and drawers—tomatoes, a head of white cabbage, two pears, and a plum. Dishes of leftovers—shrimp-and-chive dumplings, *jing jiang* pork shreds. There was even food on the inside of the door—a stick of butter, a bottle of Coca-Cola, and half a dozen eggs. Tongheng's apartment would've stunk like a landfill within days, but Dawei's smelled of clean.

As Jun grabbed the gallon of milk from the bottom shelf, she said, "Might need to go back to the market soon. We're low on fruits."

"When's the last time we went? A week ago?" said Dawei. He sounded casual, but Tongheng knew it was his way of "accidentally" showing off. Everyone else had to go to the market every day or risk the food spoiling.

Kuan-yin and Jun went to the counter to pour the milk, and he heard snippets of their conversation. "A lifesaver," said Jun. "Your family should really consider getting one. Worth every penny." He saw the tension on Kuan-yin's face as she nodded, and he felt an urge that he hadn't experienced since he was a boy.

He and his three siblings had shared a single toy—a train. They would each take turns crouched over on the floor, pretending to move it along an invisible track, calling out destinations.

"Hong Kong!"

"Shanghai!"

"The moon!"

When he was seven years old, he went to a friend's house and saw a much bigger train. This train had one very special thing that made him know that he *had* to have it—*wheels that actually rolled*. An animalistic part of him overruled everything he had learned about right and wrong. When his friend went to the outhouse to relieve himself, Tongheng ran home with the train under his shirt. He felt like a hero when he set it down in front of his siblings.

A few days later, his friend's mom came over. After hearing what she had to say, Tongheng's father grabbed him by the back of the neck like a dog and threw him against the ground. He carried around bruises on his elbows and knees for a month, but it was worth it. He had learned the importance of money. Money meant never having to steal. Money would give him the power to buy whatever he wanted. Whatever his future wife and child wished for.

Kuan-yin was in disbelief when he had shared that story with her. "All that over a train?" she said. She had played with a whole set of trains as a child—and on a track that lit up. She grew up in a modern apartment building with her architect parents near the center of Dalian. Upper middle class. Once they wed, Tongheng and Kuan-yin never spoke about the gap between their upbringings. After a while, he forgot they even came from different levels. He wondered if she did too.

Tongheng closed the refrigerator door, but his hand lingered on the handle. With his salary, it'd be a stretch to purchase a refrigerator. But it was easily manageable for people who'd returned from working in America, the exchange rate of a dollar for a renminbi being what it was. He stepped back from the fridge as he felt his friend's eyes on him and said, "How's it being back here? Do you miss *Mei Guo*?"

Dawei said, "Home is always home. It's nice to know what everyone here is saying, what they mean with their words."

"Americans are full of shit, huh?" said Tongheng, chuckling. The local government-owned newspapers often ran articles about how Americans were liars and manipulators, not at all like the noble, hardworking Chinese.

Dawei glanced at his wife, who was back on the couch with Kuan-yin, and then said, "Not really. They're strangely honest, but that made it really confusing for me."

Tongheng nodded, but he didn't know what to make of his friend's remark. Did Dawei think that he wasn't honest? That he was hiding something?

"I'm not talking about you or our good friends," Dawei said, clarifying his statement. "But you remember when Professor Li volunteered to drive us home when it was raining last week? It was an empty offer. Of course, we had to decline. We didn't have cars—which he was very well aware of—so we couldn't repay the favor another time. He got to act all generous and considerate, but we still got completely soaked on our bike rides home. What was with all that theater?"

Dawei was right, but Tongheng had never thought of it that way. He just accepted that it was what people did. He didn't think about why. As a child, he watched adults only scratch the backs of others who could scratch theirs. When he told his dad that a friend from school wanted to help him with his math homework, his dad told him not to shame the whole family by inviting the kid over. "No one except your own family cares about you. Everyone else just wants something from you," he said. And that was how it was. That was the way people operated.

"In America," said Dawei, "people ask you if you need help with something and they actually want to help you. For free sometimes."

Tongheng looked up at the ceiling in thought. "That's something."

Dawei wagged his finger and said, "*Direct*. That's a more appropriate word than *honest*. They just mean what they say over there." He let out a booming laugh, his chest stretching wide. Tongheng noticed that he had gained weight in America—all muscle. Dawei looked like a mountain. He looked like a man who owned a fridge.

They joined their wives on the couch and used their chopsticks to dunk the Oreos in the milk. "I can't imagine using my fingers for this like they do over there," said Kuan-yin, a smirk on her face. "How uncivilized."

Kuan-yin did this every now and then, ridiculing America the way his own father had. Whenever people brought up going to the United States, his father would mutter, "Guns, gangs, homeless people on the streets." If people extolled the virtues of free speech and capitalism, he would say, "Too much freedom is bad for the people, bad for order." His father consistently criticized America, but Tongheng had deduced that it was a decades-old defense mechanism. His father never got the chance to go to America—it wasn't an option until recent years—and he had to convince himself that it wouldn't have been worth the trip anyway. Once, Tongheng had said, "If I go, I'll bring you over too." His father had scoffed and said nothing.

"Did David tell you?" Jun began.

At the confused looks on his friends' faces, Dawei quickly said, "David—that's what they called me in America. I asked Jun to keep using it." Tongheng wondered what he would be renamed. The only English names he knew were George and Ronald, America's first and current presidents.

Jun went on to tell them that Dawei got a promotion at work. "A full-fledged professor at the ripe old age of twenty-six," she said. When Dawei turned red, she lovingly rubbed his shoulder and said, "Let a proud wife brag about her husband."

Kuan-yin touched Tongheng's shoulder too, but it was to keep him calm. He had just learned that a man who was a year younger than he was and with fewer published papers to his name now outranked him. Dawei was getting his own lab and a larger team of dedicated graduate students. In America, Dawei had figured out the solution to his electromagnetic braking system. "Well," he said, "to be fair, the Americans had figured it out a few years ago. I got lucky that they showed me how to do it."

Tongheng didn't say much for the rest of the visit, but he made sure to keep a smile on his face. He almost let out an audible sigh when it was time to leave. At the door, Dawei went for a hug again, and this time, spurred by a small urge to attack him, Tongheng hugged him back. The warmth of his friend surprised him—immediately defusing his animosity. He sensed a real affection in the embrace; something that whispered, "It was good to see you. I've missed you." Maybe Dawei was a better person than he had originally thought.

"Dawei looks great, doesn't he?" said Kuan-yin, as they walked down the hallway.

"Sure," he said. He didn't want to make a fuss out of her comment. He didn't want his wife to catch on that he was jealous of another man. During the entire bike ride home though, he kept looking up at the sky. He barely noticed his baby girl giggling in her basket.

A little later, the family of three entered their four-hundred-square-foot apartment. It wasn't much—graying walls, wooden furniture, cold concrete floors—but it was free. Along with his salary and tenure, the university provided housing. Kuan-yin had warmed up the place with a citrus palette: peach couch, coral curtains, apricot rugs.

After Kuan-yin placed Tianfei in her crib, Tongheng said, "I think we should consider the possibility of going to America."

"I thought we decided that we're happy here," she said. "Aren't we?"

That was true. They did say that this was enough. Their life was comfortable, definitely above average. Going to America would mean starting from the bottom again, but Tongheng worried that they'd almost hit their ceiling in China. This was about as good as their lives were going to get. Maybe they'd upgrade to a two-bedroom apartment. Move ten floors up to get an even better view of the water. Buy a television in a few years. But then what? Could he live like this forever with no hope of more?

"Dawei landed in New York City with five hundred dollars in his pocket. Look where he is now," he said.

Kuan-yin snapped back, "The top surgeon in my hospital went there for two years. She had to rent a place—someone else's disgusting basement—and ate peanut butter sandwiches for lunch." She wrinkled her nose and raised her upper lip. Tongheng couldn't argue with that. Their future in America would look the same. Maybe worse.

"It would be temporary, but even blue-collar jobs there pay well," he said. It would only take them two days working as cashiers in America to match their monthly salaries in China. The work wasn't ideal, but the money was there.

Tongheng knew that there was only one argument that could persuade her. "It would be hard, but we would be setting up Tianfei for a better life," he said. "She could go to Harvard." He walked by the crib and rubbed his daughter's belly. She reached up to grab his face.

"She's not the reason you want to go," said Kuan-yin, hands

on her hips. "You're willing to uproot our entire lives just because you lost out on a promotion to Dawei?"

He didn't know how to reply. She was right, but not completely. He just wanted *something more*, something that he couldn't quite articulate, and it wasn't for one reason, but it was for every reason. For his daughter, for his wife. For a better job, for money. For himself, for his pride, for the chance to become a better man. For the adventure. For a refrigerator.

This journey would take years. Two or three just to receive permission to land on American soil. He could think of a few routes. One would be to get hired by a Chinese company that had operations in America, and then request an intracompany transfer. Another was to attend an American university, which required studying English to pass the TOEFL. He could also lobby the department dean to sponsor a J-1 visa exchange. Whichever way he chose, it'd be a hurdle, but he knew he could clear it. The real challenges were in America.

Who was he to try? What made him worthy? He felt his resolve—his nerve—faltering. A good life in America seemed impossible to achieve. He squeezed his hands together and closed his eyes. It would be hard, but wasn't that what made the journey worthwhile?

Over the course of the month, he finally got Kuan-yin on board. He could have played the husband card, and she would've acquiesced, but he didn't want to. He needed her to be as dedicated to going as he was. After all, she would probably have to change her entire career. Her medical certifications wouldn't be recognized in America, and it was unthinkable for her to get a handle on medical terminology in English. She wouldn't even be able to properly converse with her patients.

One night, as she served him dinner, she finally said, "I can do this. For Tianfei. For her future." She then looked at him and added with cold sincerity, "But it's on you if this doesn't work out."

He felt a sharp jolt in his chest and rubbed his hand over his heart. "I know," he said.

After he finished eating, he called his parents to tell them the plan. His mother reacted like he'd thought she would. "This is a difficult endeavor, but I know you can do it! We'll do anything we can to help."

His father stayed quiet. Usually, Tongheng preferred this. Even though they had grown closer over the last few years, he still never forgot the kind of man his father had been. When he was young, the only time his father had anything to say was when he was shouting at him before the fists hit, before he whipped his belt out from his pant loops. Once, in the middle of a beating, his mother pleaded with his father to stop. "A soft hand never molded steel," he said calmly, as if he were in the middle of reading a newspaper.

The day that Tianfei was born, he swore to himself that he would never lay a hand on her. Whatever his father's reasons for hitting him, the cycle was stopping with him.

Still on the phone, Tongheng held his breath as he said, "Dad?" He wasn't sure if he had the courage to go if his father said no, but on the other hand, his dissent might be even better. It would fuel his tenacity. *Make him have to succeed.* He spent his whole life going after things just to prove his father wrong—being top of his engineering classes, already making more money than his parents' salaries combined, marrying a woman from a much wealthier family than his own—but this mission was for himself. America was his final frontier. Still, he could imagine the smug look on his father's face if he returned to China, tail between his legs.

"Dad?" he said again, louder this time, needing his answer.

His father cleared his throat before saying, "It is very hard to make it there. I hope I've prepared you enough."

Kuan-yin went to bed early that night and Tongheng stayed out in the living room, rocking Tianfei's crib. He switched on the radio to a low volume. It was tuned to the *Learn English Now* program. He listened intently, memorizing and repeating out loud the words that the host was teaching that day. *Green. Breakfast. Star.*

Then a toy commercial came on. A little girl begged her father to buy her a set of ponies. "Daddy, please!" she said, her voice full of eagerness and excitement. "Daddy!" she squealed. How could anyone deny her?

He poked Tianfei's nose. Her hand curled around his finger but her eyes stayed closed. *Daddy*, he thought, as if it were the only name he'd ever had.

★ ★ ★ ★ ★

ACKNOWLEDGMENTS

My deepest gratitude to Stephanie Kip Rostan, my dream (and real-life) agent. Thank you for always keeping the faith. I would not have wanted to go through this process with anyone else.

Paper Names grew up in the wonderful home of Hanover Square Press. A million thank-yous to my editor, John Glynn, who was a true champion of this book. And to Eden Railsback and the rest of the team for all of the behind-the-scenes work I didn't see but truly appreciate.

Warmest thanks to my publicist, Laura Gianino, whose creative pitches and earnest advocacy turned people's heads toward this book. Thank you to my marketing team, Rachel Haller and Dayna Boyer, for shining a spotlight on *Paper Names*; to Bill Rowcliffe and Janet Chow and the Typesetting team for their patience and for giving me the room to see through my vision; and to everyone else at Harlequin and HarperCollins who supported the book. It truly takes a village.

Thank you to Piper Weiss for helping me breathe life into these characters and for believing a very tired banker could actually become an author.

To the unparalleled Jack Livings, who helped me pull the manuscript across the finish line. I hope that your critical eye, patience and self-deprecating humor follow me throughout the rest of my career.

Stephen Sainato—thank you for believing I always had wings. Whenever I think the universe has turned its back on me, all I need to remember is how lucky I have been to meet you. Our friendship is a treasure.

My sister, Linda, who has heard me read out loud every single word of every single chapter in this book, as well as all those in the dozens of drafts before—you are the best person I know.

To my parents—I have scoured the English language and have not yet found any words that could capture your love for me. It is beyond. Thank you for pouring every dollar you could make and every penny you could borrow into raising me.

Lastly, I could not leave out Delta. Chief cuddling officer. A most loyal hound. You deserve all the bones.

DISCUSSION QUESTIONS

Paper Names is a poignant commentary on the American experience through a multicultural lens. Utilize the questions below to help facilitate your next book club through a guided discussion surrounding the novel.

1. Which moment in this novel had you hooked?

2. How does the immigrant experience affect the Zhang family's interpersonal dynamics with other people in America, particularly in workplaces and social settings?

3. At one point in the novel, Tammy says she feels like "speculative stock" in which her father has invested. Do you think this is a fair description of how her father views her?

4. What is it that makes Tony and Tammy's relationship so complicated? Why do you think so much of Tony's anger was directed at Tammy over the years rather than at his wife or his job? Where do you think his rage stems from?

5. How do you feel about Tammy and Oliver's relationship? Do you think they have chemistry? Why do they become such important figures for each other?

6. What do you think of Oliver's moral stance on his grandfather's crimes? He vocally condemns his grandfather, but is this condemnation reflected in his behavior?

7. What do you think of the time jumps in this novel? Did they make the storytelling more effective?

8. How did this book make you feel about the immigrant experience in the West and, in particular, the notion of the American Dream? How do you think Tony's idea of the American Dream evolves between his time in China and his later years in the US? Do you think he fulfills the goals he had for himself and his family before he left China?

9. There are frequent references to product brands, particularly Western brands and designer clothing brands, throughout the novel. Why do you think this might be? How are brands and products connected to the American Dream?

10. Why do you think Tammy feels so disconnected from her Chinese background? Do you think visiting China will change her in any way?